THE
KING
IS
DEAD

BY BENJAMIN DEAN

The Secret Sunshine Project
Me, My Dad and the End of the Rainbow

THE KING IS DEAD

Benjamin Dean

LITTLE, BROWN AND COMPANY
New York   Boston

Little, Brown and Company
Hachette Book Group
1290 Avenue of the Americas, New York, NY 10104
Visit us at LBYR.com

Originally published in 2022 by Simon & Schuster UK in the United Kingdom.
First U.S. Edition: July 2023

Little, Brown and Company is a division of Hachette Book Group, Inc. The Little, Brown name and logo are trademarks of Hachette Book Group, Inc.

The publisher is not responsible for websites (or their content) that are not owned by the publisher.

Library of Congress Cataloging-in-Publication Data
Names: Dean, Benjamin (Children's author), author.
Title: The king is dead / Benjamin Dean.
Description: First U.S. edition. | New York : Little, Brown and Company, 2023. | Originally published in year 2022 by Simon & Schuster UK in the United Kingdom. | Audience: Ages 14+. | Summary: As the newly crowned first Black king of England, seventeen-year-old James faces intense media scrutiny and a blackmailer intent on disclosing his deepest secrets, including his sexuality and hidden relationship.
Identifiers: LCCN 2022037382 | ISBN 9780316519144 (hardcover) | ISBN 9780316519403 (ebook)
Subjects: CYAC: Kings, queens, rulers, etc.—Fiction. | Black people—England—Fiction. | Gay men—Fiction. | Secrets—Fiction. | Interpersonal relations—Fiction. | Racism—Fiction. | LCGFT: Romance fiction. | Novels.
Classification: LCC PZ7.1.D39844 Ki 2023 | DDC [Fic]—dc23
LC record available at https://lccn.loc.gov/2022037382

ISBNs: 978-0-316-51914-4 (hardcover), 978-0-316-51940-3 (ebook)

Printed in the United States of America

LSC-C

Printing 1, 2023

For Mum, as always, and for
Amina and Chloe—we did it!

Part I

A
WHISPERING
PALACE

CHAPTER ONE

LONG LIVE
THE KING

*T*HE *KING IS DEAD*.
  The words were printed at the top of the *Daily Eye* newspaper in ugly block print—a slash of black that made my stomach lurch with every word. The other headlines had been kinder, but this one got right to the point, as if it were simply reporting that the sun would rise in the east come morning. I'd thought I'd be prepared for this day, but no matter which way I looked at the words, they didn't make sense. My eyes could see them, my brain could spell them out, my ears could even hear a voice in my head reading them back to me. But I'd read those four words a million times this morning and they still refused to sink in.

  The palace halls were thick with silence, only broken by hurried footsteps beyond the door that Gayle had pulled tightly shut. A flimsy slab of wood was all that was protecting us from the world right now. The gentle patter was frantic, the footsteps of people in a hurry to deliver bad news, or maybe running away from it. No doubt there was chaos unfurling in other rooms as the palace tried to keep more secrets from breaking free of our clutches. We usually had a way of keeping secrets hidden, but this one had already seeped through the cracks.

I'd been woken by Gayle just as the eleventh day of August ticked into the twelfth, and as soon as I saw her face, I knew. Dad had been sick for a while. We were meant to have more time—another year, or maybe two if we were lucky. But instead, while away on a public engagement, he'd slipped away in his sleep, one small mercy buried within tragedy. Somehow, the media had found out almost as soon as we had, which posed a frightening question: *How?*

"His body's not even cold. How do they know already?" my brother Eddie said, his jaw clenched so tight that I thought his teeth might shatter. While I stood in a shadowy corner, as far from the offending headline as I could get, he paced through the middle of the room, stopping every few seconds to look down in disgust at the newspapers splayed out on the table.

Gayle and Jonathan stood like statues by the door, hands clasped behind their backs and heads slightly bowed. I'd seen Gayle's face every day of my life and knew every line and crease by memory, as if she were my second mother—as my mum's private secretary, she basically was. She was white, like nearly everybody else in the palace, with metal-grey hair that was always gathered in a low bun, revealing a

4

stern mask that only softened when others weren't around. In the early hours of the morning, she'd ushered us all into this room and ordered everyone else away, except Jonathan, who jumped at the sound of his name and nearly dropped the stack of newspapers he'd been holding under one arm. He'd only been her intern for a few months. He hadn't been prepared for this. None of us had.

Except that was a lie. We'd all known that this day was coming. And yet, even with the knowledge that the sand in the hourglass was trickling away, and after months of telling ourselves that we'd be prepared, I could feel myself sinking.

Mum was the only one who was sat down. Her entire body was rigid, her face blank but for a vague cloud of some emotion that I couldn't pinpoint hovering around her eyes. Was it grief? Despair? Fear? All of them weaved together into some ugly knot that couldn't be untangled? Despite the early hour—the sun had yet to break over the palace walls—a string of pearls clutched her neck, and her hair, naturally thick, was pinned back into a complex bun, just like it always was, that sat at the nape of her neck. Mum never let her guard, or her hair, down, even when we were in the palace that we were supposed to call home. But the perfect smile she'd refined over decades to protect herself from those waiting for her downfall was gone like it had never existed in the first place.

"How can they know?" Eddie said again, his voice laced with dark rage.

Jonathan cleared his throat, refusing to look anybody in the eye. At eighteen, he was younger than most who worked

5

in the palace. He was tall and thin, with brown skin a few shades darker than mine. He always wore a slight frown, his forehead creasing as if he'd thought of a question but couldn't find the answer. But in those fleeting moments when he dared to look up, his dark and watchful eyes promised warmth, inviting you in and urging you closer.

"We don't know, sir," Jonathan said. "The news broke a few hours ago, and from what I can understand, the papers were able to change their front pages in time for print."

"Yes, that's pretty obvious," Eddie muttered, and Jonathan blushed furiously. I knew he was kicking himself inside, even though he'd only answered the question Eddie had asked in the first place. I tried to catch his eye, but he wouldn't look up from the floor. Not until Gayle gave him a firm nudge, when he raised his eyes to stare at the top of the table leg instead.

Jonathan had joined the palace just as fresh hell threatened to erupt in our faces. The spotlight created by poisonous pens always had its glare trained on Mum. The media clung to its hatred of a Black woman "infiltrating the Royal Family" and "destroying the monarchy" and it was committed to taking her down. But as news of my father's poor health spread, the glare had turned on me instead, planting rumors and lies. Except those "lies" were closer to the truth than anybody knew. I would never admit it, though, even to my own family. There was too much at stake if I did. The world could barely cope with the idea of a Black king—they'd lose their heads if they knew he was gay too.

"We are, of course, refusing to give comment to the press

for now, but we can't hold them off forever." Gayle took over, addressing nobody in particular. Her voice was measured, calm and clear. She'd weathered many storms with our family. This might be the biggest one yet, but she wasn't going to be unmoored by it. If anything, she looked more determined than ever to keep the boat steady. Protecting the crown was her duty, and one she took seriously. "They've already run the stories and are sniffing about anywhere they can. The phones haven't stopped ringing since just past midnight, and I doubt they'll stop any time soon. But we've been preparing for this day. It might've come sooner than we hoped, but everything is in place. We just have to follow the script."

She paused, glancing at the curtained window. Through a slit at the top, I could see that the pure black of the night sky was quickly fading, strokes of purple and dark blue painting a bruise above us. Gayle had been doing this job since before Mum had even walked through the palace gates for the first time. She'd held her hand through those first few years as she adjusted to life as queen, held our hands as we grew into a world that wanted more from us—or less from us—than we could understand. It was only right that she guided us now, when we needed it most. Dad would want to see us sticking together.

Finally, Gayle took a deep breath, her eyes moving over the room until they'd found the person her words were meant for. "So, what do you want to do, Your Majesty?"

Mum looked up from the table. Eddie stopped his pacing. Jonathan seemed to be holding his breath. But she wasn't talking to any of them. She was talking to me.

"What do you mean?" I said with a croak. I glanced at Eddie, as I usually did when I needed him, but his mouth was folded into a grim line and he quickly looked away. We used to be an island together, brothers who had each other's backs. Eddie had always been more extroverted, and that charisma protected me in some way. In school, I had hidden behind it, letting Eddie's natural ability to make friends gift me friendships by association—Ophelia, for example. In school, we were rarely apart. But with every passing year, the crown had made sure to remind us that our bond as twins couldn't protect us from fate. And now, hiding behind him was no longer an option.

Gayle shifted uncomfortably before regaining her poise. She stood up a little straighter, the way she did when delivering formal news, and in that moment, I felt the blood rush through my body, whooshing like an alarm in my ears.

"Your father has died. As his oldest son, you're the heir apparent—the first in line to the throne." Gayle paused and Mum let out a gentle sob that flitted around the room, echoing in every dawn-stained corner. Before continuing, Gayle bowed her head low. But she wasn't hiding her face— she was curtsying as I'd seen her do to Dad so many times before, even though he insisted she only need do it in formal company. My throat went dry as she rose from the floor. I couldn't breathe. The room was closing in from every side, trapping me in the shadows. But the words still came.

"As the heir to the throne, Your Majesty...you are now king."

I'd known it was coming. With my father's deteriorating

health, conversations had already been had about what would happen next, plans gently put in place to secure the monarchy when the time eventually came. But I'd pushed the thought away, refusing to succumb to the panic I now felt tormenting me. I had no choice but to face what had always been my biggest fear. Every sound ceased until I could only hear my own frantic breathing. Secrets and lies reared their heads within me, begging to be let out into the open one by one.

And in that moment, I thought of his face: the one I'd been studying up close for four months, under bedcovers and secrecy; the one I'd cradled delicately in my hands like it could break; the one I'd dreamed and yearned of in its absence. I needed his eyes to tell me that everything would be okay. That *I* would be okay. Maybe my secrets could've saved me from my duty if they'd all spilled out into the room. But I knew that wasn't an option. If the monarchy crumbled, it would send the country, and my family, into free fall. We were the symbol of unity that resided over the nation, our stability offering hope. People were supposed to look at the crown and have faith in those who wore it. The need for royalty to prosper was a tradition handed down from one monarch to another, nobody wanting to let down what their own mother or father had fought so hard to preserve. We couldn't fail. So, for the first time, I pushed the thought of him away until the room faded back into my sight. I needed to focus, at least for now.

"He can't be king," Mum said, her voice small but strong. Its strength was only belied by a faint tremor, a quiet pleading as she raked her eyes over me. "He's just a boy.

He's not even eighteen yet." Every eye in the room rested on me in pity, and I felt myself shrinking back once more.

"It's the only way," Gayle murmured. "I'm sorry." She collected herself and tried again, talking to the room but still only looking in my direction. "Of course, abdication is an option, but not one I would advise. Many see it as a betrayal to your country. Such a move would send the monarchy into a spiral. And if you choose to abdicate the throne, the problem won't be solved," she added gravely.

Eddie stared straight ahead at the wall. He'd be next in line, left to clear up my mess if I stepped down. Even though the responsibility scared me, I couldn't let my duty fall to him. I was his older brother, even if only by eight cruel minutes. I had to protect him, and my family too. I couldn't let this be the end of us.

"The coronation will formally mark the ascension to the throne, but that could be weeks away, months even," continued Gayle. "We'll have time."

"Time for what?" I stuttered, finally finding my voice. "Weeks, months, it doesn't matter—it's still going to happen. I'll be thrown out there to be king for people who don't want me on the throne. They'll never want me to be king. Look at the way they've treated us! These rags"— I thrust a finger at the newspapers on the table—"have stoked the fire since Mum walked through those gates for the first time, since the day we were born. They've never wanted a Black woman on the throne, and they'll sure as hell not want a Black teenager sitting on it either."

I was shaking, but nobody tried to calm me. And then

10

it hit me that they wouldn't. Couldn't, even. Mum's deep brown eyes were shimmering with tears. She blinked and a trail leaked from each one, brimming from the corners and slipping down her cheeks. I couldn't bear to see it. Then I realized I was crying too.

In flashes, as if I were dying, pictures of me at different ages popped into my head: as a child, gripping Eddie hard before our first day of school; as a young boy who learned that being born first, even if just by a few minutes, set our paths apart; as a wide-eyed teenager who was told that his path would be rockier than his father's because of the way he looked; as a young man who knew that being a Black prince was cause for celebration for some around the country, but a cause for disdain in others; and now as a seventeen-year-old, suddenly fatherless. Suddenly king.

"Mum...," I said into the silence between us. Her lip quivered as she tried to fight back the tears, but more came until she was sobbing in earnest. Immeasurable, wretched cries—for my dad and for my brother, but most of all for me. My mouth was open, words clawing up from within to be spoken aloud. But there were too many lodged in my throat, so many that I thought I might drown in them.

"Mum," I tried again. She took a breath and raised her head to me, but nothing else came and nobody said a word. My own just hung over us, soaked in desperation.

"I need to be alone," I spluttered by accident.

I didn't mean it—not really. I didn't want to be alone for fear of being in the company of my own thoughts. But Gayle and Jonathan both nodded, one curtsying, the other bowing, before slipping out into the hall. Mum rose from the table, regal even in despair. She swept across the room and enveloped me in a hug, like the ones she'd given me as a boy.

"I love you," she whispered in my ear. She lowered her voice, as if afraid the palace walls were listening. The newspapers on the table suggested she was right. "We will protect you. I promise."

She pulled away, giving my arm a squeeze. Then, drawing her shoulders back and blinking quickly, she turned on her heel and made to follow after Gayle and Jonathan. At the door, however, she hesitated, her back still to the room. Her slender shoulders rose and fell steadily. Then she turned, looked me in the eye and bent her knee. The hem of her cloak pooled below her as she dipped, bowing her head once. I held my breath, heard my brother hold his. With one final nod to us both, our mother stepped out of the room.

Eddie didn't move and I didn't want him to. My reflection stared back: black eyes morphing into shades of brown as morning light found us, hair shaved short with immaculate precision, a soft-edged face slightly tilted to one side. We took each other in from opposite ends of the table, the distance between us farther than it seemed.

"Eddie...," I started. But the weight of this moment, still dawning within me, crushed my words. With the death of my father came the death of me. I was no longer Prince James, a son and brother. I was the king.

I'd known since I was eight or nine that it would happen someday. My dad sat me down, telling Eddie to leave

12

us alone while he prepared me for a job I could barely understand. That was the first time I'd felt torn away from my twin, when I realized that we were destined to go down different paths. All I knew was that being king was important and that only one of us could do it. Whether I liked it or not, it was my duty to wear the crown. In some cruel twist of fate, Eddie would've made a better king—everybody knew it—but centuries of tradition couldn't be torn down just because I favored the shadows.

"I guess this is it then," Eddie said.

"Don't." I knew what he meant. This was where our paths splintered, one becoming two. "It's just a crown. You're still my brother."

"You know that's not true," Eddie countered. "That crown means something. It means *everything*. It all changes now."

"Nothing has to change. Why should it?" I was trying to convince myself as much as him, but we both knew I was lying. "Please, Eddie. I can't do this alone."

"Every soul in this palace is now tethered to yours. *You* will never be alone." Eddie sighed, shaking his head. When he spoke again, his voice was breaking. "I lost my father last night. But I'm losing my brother too."

It was true. How could I tell him that it wasn't? Just because I didn't want the crown to change things didn't mean it wouldn't.

I rounded the table without another thought and crashed into my brother, like I could keep us together if I just held on tight enough.

"I won't let it come between us," I uttered into his shoulder. "I promise."

When we broke apart, Eddie's eyes had softened slightly. He studied me carefully, then with a wry smile said, "Long live the king." I tried to smile back, but I couldn't. It was like I'd forgotten how.

With a swift bow, Eddie left the room. And then it was just me, the silence and the frenzied flutter of a thousand thoughts winging around my head. I closed my eyes and took a long, steady breath. When I opened them, piercing green eyes looked up at me, frozen in time on the front of every newspaper. The biggest picture, under a caption that claimed the death of the king was the end of the monarchy as we knew it, was an official portrait. The crown towered proudly over him, catching the light as it always did and winking back at the camera with a smug glint. Dad never smiled when he wore it. He always complained it was too heavy.

Day was breaking in earnest outside the window, rays of early morning sunlight creeping inside the room like a thief. It caught the diamonds in the chandelier, sending shimmers of rainbow light dancing along the walls. I warily stepped around the table and up to the curtains, pulling one back slowly. The front of the palace was half-bathed in shade, the sun stretching its fingers farther into the shadows with every passing second. The gates stood tall and proud, their tips spiked with gold. Beyond them, the city was starting to wake up too.

Small crowds were gathering already, a sea of flowers piling up by the railings. I watched as an older couple approached, holding hands. They bowed their heads, kneeling for a moment in prayer. When they were done, they made the sign of the cross, gazed at the palace and retreated. I watched them go and wished I could do the same.

My phone buzzed in my pocket, drawing my attention away from the window. I knew who it'd be before I'd even looked. Of course it was him. My heart leaped as I read his name—or his code name, rather, just in case—and it leaped again, like it always did, when I opened the text.

> I'm sorry. If you want to be alone,
> I understand. But I'll be in our
> usual place tonight. 8:30? x

I read the words over and over, drinking them in, every letter a life jacket keeping me afloat in stormy waters. But at the back of my mind a new thought was blooming: I was king now. This had to stop.

My thumb hovered over the phone, but in the hesitation, another thought simmered, sparking a fire that'd burn me if I gave it the chance. The flames grew inside my head, singeing every other thought until I could think of nothing else: *I needed him.*

And so I typed a reply and pressed send, praying that my greatest secret wouldn't become my greatest undoing.

CHAPTER TWO

THE GRIEF PARADE

There was a hushed mayhem unfolding within the palace, the kind that comes with bad news. It was there in every private corner, behind every closed door, whispers chasing one another through the halls.

I was used to people becoming mute in my presence, but as I walked back to my quarters in a trance, people ducked behind pillars or melted into walls, almost begging for the brick to give way and hide them. Others bowed so low I feared they might not get back up. I might not have noticed, being in such a daze and so bothered by my own thoughts, but every time I passed someone scurrying by, they'd hastily murmur, "Your Majesty" in the same tight voice, the words stiff and squashed together. As a prince, I'd always been *Your Royal Highness*. There was only one person who was ever called *Your Majesty*, and it sent a shiver down my spine hearing it tossed in my direction now.

The staff who didn't turn and flee instead bowed and rushed to open doors before I could come within a meter of opening them myself. It was ludicrous to never open a door, to never step out of a car unaided, to never pour a drink of your own or to make your own damn bed. The one time I did that, the maid looked as if I'd slapped her across the face, so I never tried again.

I understood how strange the whole situation was. Being in this family meant our name alone was enough to send armies to war. And yet, I didn't understand it at all. I never had. How could one person be born with so much power having done so little to earn it? I hadn't achieved anything great. I hadn't worked harder than anybody else. I hadn't worked *at all*. I'd been gifted this life at birth, but who was to say I couldn't have been born to a hairdresser and a baker, or an accountant and a teacher? Why had the stars aligned so as to put me in this position? Why not someone else?

I crashed through the door of my quarters, the room tilting dangerously one way and then the other. The floor seemed to turn to water as I scrambled, fell, then crawled to the bathroom, the cool, unforgiving tiles burning through my clothes and branding my knees. I'd barely made it to the toilet, which was a ghastly creation of white and gold, when I retched. My entire body heaved with the sheer force of it. Again and again it came, the nauseous wave pausing with a wicked threat before rolling up through me once more. I hugged the toilet, squeezing the porcelain hard with each violent lurch of my stomach. When I was done, all I could do was lie on the bathroom floor in defeat.

"The king, ladies and gentlemen," I muttered.

A knock at the door of my quarters interrupted my self-pity. I didn't answer, praying they might go away until I got myself together.

"James?" It was Gayle, of course, the only person who wouldn't just turn on her heel and leave if not immediately invited inside.

"Give me a minute," I said through gritted teeth, using the last of my energy to drag myself up off the floor. I leaned over the sink and swilled my mouth with water, wiping my hand across my face instead of bothering to find a towel.

I looked at myself and the king looked back. The mirror wasn't kind. My face had somehow sucked itself in, sharp and hollow, and my bottom lip was littered with puncture marks where I'd bitten down hard in an attempt to stop myself from falling apart. My eyes were swollen and puffy, red lines shooting off in every direction like shattered glass. I couldn't bear to look at myself much longer, so I took a deep breath and made for the door. When I opened it, Gayle and Jonathan stared back with ill-hidden concern.

"James," she said again, her voice close to breaking. But, of course, she held it together because there was a job to be done. "When you're ready, it's time."

18

"Ah, the Grief Parade," I muttered, trying to keep my nausea at bay. I made for my bedroom, a large and perfect square with a too-big, solid-oak, four-poster bed that had been hand-carved. Velvet drapes hung open on all sides, revealing the perfectly fitted and ironed sheets that were changed every day. Ridiculous, I know.

The Grief Parade was what we called the little stage performance we were forced to put on to show the public that, despite the fact it was us in mourning, we were still putting them first. We would have to fix our mouths into a grim line, step outside the palace gates to marvel at the flowers and gifts laid against the railings, shake hands and thank people for their well-wishes. It was just another thing that we were expected to do—something to make *them* happy.

"I know it's absurd, and I'd rather we do anything else, but the sooner we get it over with, the better," Gayle said matter-of-factly. I sighed and reached for the crisp white shirt that had been left out for me alongside a simple black suit. Gayle and Jonathan took their cue and stepped back out into the living room while I changed.

"Let's get this out of the way," I mumbled when I reappeared, still fighting with the tie I'd slung around my neck.

"Let me," Jonathan said, stepping forward as Gayle continued her mutterings about what awaited us outside.

Jonathan took hold of the tie, gently pushing the knot up to my throat. He nodded when it was perfect, folding the collar back down and resting his hands on my shoulders for a moment before stepping back and glancing down to the floor.

"Cassandra will also be in attendance," Gayle said, pursing her lips. "There'll be a hundred cameras out there, so it shouldn't come as much of a surprise."

I fought the urge to groan. My cousin was now second in line to the throne and by far the most popular member of our family. As heirs to the crown, we'd grown up together in the confines of Buckingham Palace. She'd never quite got over the fact that she was a couple of years older than me but still inferior according to rank, and as a result, she'd made my life miserable whenever she got the chance. It was all petty stuff that didn't really matter, but she'd only gotten worse, more bitter, as we grew up in the royal circus together. She had plenty of faces, a million different masks that she wore so it was impossible to tell who the real Princess Cassandra was. All I knew was that the public who adored her saw only one of those masks, carefully chosen to show her off in the best light. The fact that she was white no doubt helped her popularity, especially when she stood next to the rest of us like some delicate angel who just wanted to do her best for everybody else. If only they knew.

"And I've asked Ophelia to come too," Gayle said, her voice now a notch above a mumble, like she was hoping I wouldn't hear.

"You're kidding, right? I'm not pretending to be in love with Phee, today of all days, just so the cameras have a shot of their grieving king and his *supposed* girlfriend."

Jonathan was shuffling uncomfortably by the door, and my cheeks were getting hotter by the second—whether with rage, shame, or a mixture of both I couldn't be sure. Gayle sighed, hands up in surrender.

"We're not asking you to get down on one knee and propose marriage," she said as we left my quarters, heading in the direction of the majestic doors that separated my rooms from the rest of the palace. "We're just trying to give people something else to focus on. It'll take the pressure off you."

Ophelia had been a ploy for a couple of months now. She'd been Eddie's friend, naturally, and his first real crush after they'd paired up for a history assignment in our second year of school when we were thirteen. I'd always liked Ophelia because she preferred to sit on the outside of a circle rather than bask in its center, which was probably why we got on so well. "Everyone's so desperate to dance in the spotlight," she murmured to me at a birthday party once. "I don't know how people can enjoy so much attention."

Then, when we were fifteen, we'd been thrown into a closet together for a game of seven minutes in heaven. All we did was awkwardly laugh about the ludicrousness of the situation and talk about *EastEnders* until the time was up. We'd been good friends ever since. As the heir to the throne, I'd never entrusted my secrets to anybody, but Ophelia was someone whose company I enjoyed more than most, particularly since I had no other close companions to speak of.

However, when rumors about my sexuality started being spread with insidious glee, we had to prove them wrong. The newspapers pointed out that I'd never had a girlfriend, nor had I ever shown even a slight interest in having one. A video resurfaced from the year before, where I'd been asked for my thoughts on a potential future queen. I'd stuttered and stammered my way through an answer, the whole while looking like I was seconds away from throwing up. People said it all but confirmed that the rumor must be true—the future king of the country might be gay.

Gayle rubbished the mere question of my sexuality immediately, as if it were simply impossible that I could be anything other than straight. She said it was just the newspapers looking for any reason to drag me through the mud, and the rest of my family agreed before I even had to lie for myself. It was Gayle who suggested that Ophelia stand by my side, and I quickly accepted. I hated the idea, but it helped to push my own secrets further into the dark.

I'd known I was gay for a while by then. For years I'd felt *different*, like I was tracing a life I was meant to lead but couldn't quite follow the lines. When I finally admitted it to myself after my fourteenth birthday, I pushed it away for as long as I could, reluctant to face what would only make my life in the royal bubble more difficult. But it was who I was, and there was no point denying it to myself, even if I wasn't prepared to confess it to my family or my friends. And so I'd kept it a secret from them. From almost everybody, except one person.

As I descended the sweeping Grand Staircase, I heard my family before I saw them, gathered on the scarlet carpets of the Grand Hall at the bottom. Golden alcoves housed marble statues on plinths, while marble pillars with gilded tips appeared to hold the ceiling up. The doors of the Grand Entrance were flanked by guards who stood poker straight, staring at the wall opposite. Peter—an imposing man with fair skin, a shaved head and a no-nonsense demeanor—slinked out of the shadows to stand beside me. He'd been my personal protection officer since I was fifteen. I saw him more than I saw anybody else.

"Morning, Your Majesty," he said with a nod stiffer than usual. I wasn't the only one nervous about heading out into the lion's den.

Ophelia sidled up next to me, linking her arm through mine. She was better at this acting stuff than I was, always knowing what to do and when for the best effect. She clutched me tighter than she might've on a regular day, looking up to find my eyes.

"You okay?" she murmured, low enough that only me and Peter would hear it. I shrugged, not trusting myself to speak.

"It'll just be ten minutes—less, if I have anything to do with it," Mum was telling Eddie. He wore a sour look on his face, but I knew he'd been crying. Mum, of course, looked as regal as ever, although a shadow of mourning had fallen over her. She wore a black dress with a matching hat and a short mesh veil, which would hide at least

23

part of her face from the hounds with cameras. She'd been burned by unfortunate shots before, a million times on a million front pages. She wouldn't let them do it today.

"Can we just get this over with?" Cassandra said loftily, her voice cutting through the rest. She floated down the stairs, her own protection officer on her heels, looking like she'd rather be anywhere else. "I've got a massage at eleven and I've already had to reschedule it once because of this."

I wheeled around, ready to explode. Asking Cassandra to have a heart was too big an order, but she'd crossed the line. Trust her to think of nobody but herself. However, Mum beat me to the punch.

"Nice of you to make time in your schedule for us, Cassandra. I'm sure George would wish to extend his thanks if he were here now." Mum met Cassandra's glare with one just as icy.

Gayle jumped in as Cassandra went to open her mouth. "We walk out, look at the flowers, shake a few hands, and then get back inside like wild dogs are on our tail." She eyed the grand doors and their golden handles with a steely glare. "Of course, we have control of the crowds in a physical sense, but we do not have control over their mouths. I suggest we use our selective hearing should anything . . . unfortunate arise."

"You mean if people wish to celebrate another royal death," Eddie spat. Cassandra's untroubled mask flickered for a moment. Her dad, the brother of the king, had been the last of us to pass. Well, until today.

"Edward," Mum said warningly. He sighed with disdain and started for the door. Someone quickly snatched it open before he came close, letting the light spill in onto the carpets.

"Edward," Mum said again, this time more gently. He paused, then barked a sharp laugh.

"Of course," he said, stepping aside. Everybody looked at me and waited. The king always went first. Cassandra tutted. Gayle nodded her encouragement, but warily, as if she was worried for what might happen next.

With my entire body wound tighter than a spring, I began the walk as if I were on death row. This would be my first time stepping outside as the monarch. My first time facing the people—my people—as king. It took every bit of willpower to put one foot in front of the other, each step bringing me closer to a responsibility I'd been trying to avoid my whole life.

Ophelia wasn't so much holding on to me as she was keeping me upright. For a moment, I felt glad that she was there after all. I straightened up, my mind wiping itself of any emotional trace. Somewhere deep inside me, a trapdoor opened, swallowing the person I knew and replacing him with one I hated. The one who knew there was a job to do. The one Dad would be proud to see. The one Mum feared.

The hush was immediate the second we stepped outside, the morning air holding its breath. The crowds hadn't seen us yet as we crossed the courtyard and made our way under the arch, but they knew I was coming. The guards and metal fences that had been put up had probably given us away. We strode on toward the edge of the palace, the spiked railings ahead. My breath caught in my throat, but there was no turning back now. Just like Gayle had said: a few minutes of torture and we'd be out of there.

A gasp sounded from somewhere, followed by a murmur that began to ripple through the crowd as we walked out of the open palace gates. The crowd was a singular mass, moving, breathing and analyzing my every move. I lifted my chin, willing my body to ignore the fear coursing through it, and eyed the member of the public closest to me.

She was older, in her sixties maybe, white, with wispy grey hair and a buttoned-up cardigan. She bowed her head, extending a hand, which I grasped in my own. It was clammy and slick with sweat, but I fought the urge to recoil from her touch.

"Your Majesty," the woman said with a deep, gravelly voice. "My condolences to you and your family."

I wore the well-wishes like a cloak that I desperately wanted to shrug off but clung to all the same. I was running on autopilot, doing the job I'd seen done countless times before. But the thoughts of my father that I'd tried so hard to rid my mind of—at least for now—suddenly returned in an unforgiving whirl, and I felt a searing pain behind my eyes.

It was as if the crowd was pressing in from all sides. A dozen hands flew out to greet me and grab me as I worked down the line with a plastic smile on my face that they could surely see was fake. Whether friend or foe, I couldn't be sure, but I shook the hands anyway, fighting the anxious shiver raising the hairs on my arms and the back of my neck. Peter, our shadow, stayed with us the whole way, ready to intercept at less than a moment's notice.

"Thank you," I murmured to as many people as I could, my voice as lifeless as a graveyard in the dead of night. The only thing alive within me was the ghost of who I'd been yesterday, cowering in the corners of my head.

I was halfway down the line when I noticed a mother and son standing together, her hand gently placed on his shoulder. They were both dark-skinned with identical, easy smiles and dimples in their cheeks. The boy couldn't have been older than eight years old, with a short afro and a bunch of flowers in his hand. He peered up at his mum, who nodded her encouragement. When he turned his attention back to me, his smile was bright. Taking a leaf out of my mother's book, I crouched slightly so we were at the same height.

"Hi," I said quietly, tuning out the noise and stares surrounding us. I focused on his face, letting everything else fall away so that it might've just been the two of us standing outside the palace gates.

"Are you *really* the king now?!" the boy asked, half-breathless with excitement. "Do you have a crown and a throne?" I couldn't even answer before the boy rushed ahead. "That's *so* cool! I wish I had a crown. Then I could be in charge just like you!"

There was a ripple of laughter from the people close enough to overhear us. Despite myself, and the fears I held over the title I now claimed, I breathed a laugh too.

"You'd like to be the king one day?" I asked gently.

The boy didn't hesitate, nodding his head vigorously. "If you can be a king, then I can be a king too, right? My mum says I can be anything I want to be if I put my mind to it, and I want to be just like you."

I glanced up at the boy's mother, who offered me a warm smile of her own. "Your Majesty," she said in a delicate tone. She bowed her head, then nudged her son. "You have something for the king, Michael?"

Michael, realizing he'd forgotten the duty he'd been bestowed, looked serious for a moment, then thrust the bouquet of flowers into the space between us. "These are for you," he said.

"Thank you, Michael," I said, taking the flowers and trying to pull back on the emotion that was attempting to crawl past my defenses. "Thank you."

We'd surely been outside for hours now, or maybe it had just been seconds, but I felt Gayle's eyes on me and knew it was almost over. Somewhere up the line, Eddie shook hands and listened intently to the grief he was being pummeled with. Mum stayed a little farther back, only reaching out to accept the hands of a few with a gloved one of her own, before choosing the safer option and inspecting the sea of flowers with a mournful eye. Cassandra had perfected her look, one of emotional turmoil at the death of her uncle, one that was close to tears and only just holding it together. People reached for her with consoling hands. She rarely let them touch her, but one caught her off guard, brushing her wrist. Jonathan stood well back, watching with glum amazement as his first Grief Parade came to a close.

But it wasn't over yet.

Assured that it had gone well, and buoyed by the young boy's infectious joy, I chose one last person. He was tanned, like he followed the sun all year round, with impossibly white teeth, cold grey eyes and a confidence that he brandished like a weapon. He wasn't the one I'd meant to choose, but he forced his hand out, fencing me off from the rest of the crowd. I went to shake it, but realized, too late, that I'd made a mistake.

"How does it feel to be the first Black monarch of the United Kingdom, Your Majesty?" the man said, loud and clear, thrusting his microphone up into my face. A camera popped up behind his shoulder, a red light blinking its warning. When I didn't immediately answer, too consumed by terror, he went on: "How do you think people will react to having a Black king on the throne for the first time, considering the, shall we say, mixed reaction your family has received in the past, and the criticism your father has faced over the years for his decision to marry after Princess Catherine? To marry someone like your mother?"

Fear turned to white-hot rage, burning me from the inside out. It scorched through me, and before I could stop it, my mouth opened in answer. "You mean his decision to marry a Black woman? A woman you will not accept as queen because of the color of her skin, despite my father loving her more than anything or anyone?"

The reporter looked blank for a moment. Then a smile,

more terrible than anything I'd seen before, spread across his face. Peter's firm hand was suddenly on my elbow, but it was too late. The damage had been done.

"Thank you, Your Majesty," the reporter said, a smug taunt hiding behind each word.

Peter steered me back toward the gates, toward safety. Out of the corner of my eye, I saw Eddie and Mum start after us, a trot in their step. We were almost over the boundary, behind the shield that would protect us from the eyes drinking us in. And then it happened.

"YOU WILL NEVER BE HER! YOU'RE NOTH-ING BUT A WHORE!"

The words rang out, amplified by the mournful silence. Eddie whipped round, searching the faces for the source. I froze on the spot too, even though, of course, they were not meant for either of us. Mum didn't break her stride, though, keeping her head high as if she hadn't heard a thing. But, with her back to the crowd, her mask slipped slightly, the corner of her mouth shaking.

All hell broke loose behind us as the crowd erupted. The palace security swooped in and enveloped us, herding us swiftly through the arches, away from the chaos unfold-ing like a rumble of thunder. Jonathan was the last inside, slamming the door and immediately cutting off the sound.

"That went well," Cassandra said brightly, fake tears still glistening on her cheeks. She cast a sneer in Mum's direction. "Now if you don't mind, I must wash my hands. God knows what disease I might've picked up taking part in that little game." And with one last smile, she was gone.

CHAPTER THREE

A Chip in
the Crown

I'd often imagined what my first day as king would be like. It wasn't ever a happy thought—more something morbid that I couldn't shake, because I knew with dreadful certainty that unless I were to die first, the day would definitely come. It was just a matter of when. And those thoughts weren't only terrifying, they were filled with absolute misery too. Because to be king, my father would have to die. I was nothing but an understudy, my own life stripped of meaning until my fears came true. Now they had, and things were already getting worse.

"Who was that reporter?" I asked, blustering into my quarters, Jonathan and Gayle on my heels. I clawed at the tie around my neck, tearing it off with trembling hands.

"Quinn Buckley, sir. Works as royal correspondent for

the *Daily Eye*." Jonathan bit his lower lip, his head leaning to one side as he pondered something.

"What is it?" I said, although I knew I wouldn't want to hear the answer.

Gayle raised her eyebrows and pursed her lips, irritation carved deep into her face. Jonathan sighed. "To put it bluntly, Buckley's something of a nuisance."

Gayle cleared her throat. "That's an understatement."

"He's been on a mission to . . . well, expose the Royal Family for a while now. He's been sniffing around, speaking to anybody he can get his hands on. We've managed to keep him mostly at bay with the threat of lawyers, but he's not like the others. He has the full support of the *Eye* behind him, and they've never been afraid of their stories landing them in court. If anything, our threats have only emboldened Buckley. He thinks there's something we're hiding, and he wants to know what."

"And you didn't think to tell me any of this?" I said accusingly, hurt rising in me. I fell back on my bed, groaning like a petulant toddler.

Jonathan squirmed, but Gayle took over. "It's our job to keep these *lies* away from you. If we ran to you every time a story was printed, we'd need to clone you three times over to read them all. Your father knew of Buckley and his stories, but he had a similar attitude—if he didn't need to know about it, he didn't want to be informed."

"He didn't want to know what was going on?" I said in disbelief.

"Well, he had good reason. Buckley has been leading

the charge when it comes to stories about the queen. The Queen Mother." Gayle quickly corrected herself and I shuddered. "At first, it was just snide remarks dressed up as observations, about how she was the first Black royal and how it was an 'interesting choice' for a wife after Catherine."

I flinched at the name, one that was rarely uttered inside the palace. Dad's first love had always been seen as the perfect choice—a lady of royal blood. While he was away on a tour of Africa, it was suggested by my grandmother that he shouldn't waste any time; Catherine's hand in marriage was sought after by many. And so, worried he'd miss his chance if he didn't act, he courted her through letters instead. They finally met when he returned and were engaged within weeks. They'd fallen madly for each other, and the whole world had fallen with them.

And then she died.

Four days before the wedding, a spectacle that the world had been waiting for, Catherine was gunned down as she left the bridal shop in charge of designing her dress. The location had been top secret, until the *Eye* found out and splashed it across their front page. A man who claimed Catherine was the love of his life and couldn't bear to see her marry someone else had waited outside, enfolded in the crowds gathering to catch a glimpse of their princess. There were three steps between the door and the car. Catherine only took one and it was her last.

Dad was devastated and swore he'd never love again.

But then he met Mum a year and some change later. He fell head over heels and proposed after eight weeks. They were happy. In love. The country, however, was not. The grief had yet to dissolve in the hearts of a nation that had loved Catherine without really knowing her at all. They enjoyed feeling sympathy and pity for the "Lonely King," but when happiness came along and gave Dad a second chance, the tide quickly turned.

The ironic thing was that Mum and Catherine weren't too different from each other, or so I'd read. They were both wrapped in elegance and grace, with pure hearts to help those in need. They were regal, but also soft and gentle, with the power to make you feel seen in a room of thousands. There was only one clear difference.

"We'll deal with Buckley as and when we have to," Gayle said. "You've got enough on your plate right now, so let us handle whatever he tries to throw our way."

I nodded because that's all I could do. Gayle was right—the small matter of being king was taking up enough of my headspace, and the grief I'd been suppressing was starting to trickle into the crevices of my body. Quinn Buckley wasn't my problem. And what trouble could he really cause anyway?

⊙⫘⫘⊙

It felt like hands had been reaching for me all day, pulling me in every direction as morning slipped into afternoon, then merged into evening. They were like relentless waves turning me over and around until I didn't know how I

34

would ever find my way back to the surface for my next breath.

I stood still, eyes closed, yet more hands grabbing at me. There was a tap on my calf, and I automatically raised my right leg, then my left, stepping into crisp trousers I'd only ever see once. A tap on my arms and I lifted them, felt the brush of a new shirt until it covered my body. Fast and careful fingers moved over me, fastening buttons, securing a belt, folding down my collar and positioning my tie.

Then a pause. "Your Majesty?"

I opened my eyes, finding myself back in my quarters. The others had stepped away, their jobs now done, but one man remained, crouched at my feet, socks in one hand and polished shoes in the other. I fought the urge to suggest I do this bit myself. If I was capable of leading a country, I was capable of tying my own laces. But instead, I sat on the edge of the bed, my fight long dissolved.

"Everything you need to say, you've already said a hundred times." Gayle swept over to get a better look at me. She held my gaze, raising her eyebrows slightly in encouragement. "You can do this."

The clock read eight minutes to six, taunting me with every tick. Fear had entwined with my adrenaline, leaving me jittery and sick. There was nothing more important than this speech. I knew there'd be doubters—too many of them to comprehend—who'd delight in my downfall. They were circling like vultures, waiting to swoop down and take a chunk out of me. This would set the tone for

35

everything. It didn't matter that I was now a son without a father, that my insidious grief was attempting to cut me open. All that mattered was that people still believed in the crown. That they now believed in me.

As Gayle and I strode out into the hall and began making our way through the palace, I tried to go over what we'd rehearsed. It was simple. A short speech, to the point, marking the country's grief, as well as my own. I'd read it over a dozen times without a hitch. But now it was time to read it again—this time in front of the world.

Ophelia waited ahead, her hair pulled back into a sleek knot so every flicker of her face could be seen. It was showboating to have her here again, standing with me while I made this speech, but it would be the distraction we needed.

"It'll draw their focus away from you," Mum had said, echoing Gayle. "They want to see their king stand next to a potential queen. It's ridiculous, yes, but we wave with one hand so they don't see what's in the other."

"Your Majesty," Ophelia uttered, more for Gayle's benefit than mine. She curtsied, then reached for my hand. I fought a flinch, one that didn't escape Gayle's attention. Ophelia's hand was warm, comforting even, but it wasn't the hand I wanted to hold.

"You can do this," Ophelia continued quietly, her voice as soft as a breath of wind on a starlit night. "Just imagine them all naked."

Despite my fears, I snorted. "I'm trying *not* to be sick, thank you very much. And who said I was nervous

36

anyway?" I forced my mouth up into a half smile. "It's only a speech that'll be watched and then dissected by a few million people. Are you telling me I should've been nervous this whole time?"

Ophelia giggled. "I'm glad to see being king hasn't changed you one bit."

"Don't tell them that," I murmured. "They'd be so disappointed."

Mum and Eddie joined us, their own cohort of aides on their tail. Mum didn't break step as she crossed the space between us and folded me into a hug. "Give them hell," she whispered in my ear.

"Break a leg," Eddie said with a wink over her shoulder, nudging me with his elbow as he passed to take his place.

"No Cassandra?" I peered around for sight of the Heir from Hell. As second in line to the throne, she had her own formal quarters in the palace, which she used to escape the watch of her mother, Cecily—a nosy gossip who the rest of my family despised, and who rarely left the gilded confines of Kensington.

To my relief, Gayle shook her head. "The princess says she has other matters to attend to."

"Try not to take it personally," Eddie quipped. "Those massages are *really* important."

We moved as one, me ahead of the pack, the others following in my wake. As I walked through the tall doors of a reception room that'd been completely redone for this moment, the murmurings of a crowd ceased. All around, people wilted into bows and curtsies, some almost afraid to look me in the eye. They all stood behind hulking cameras mounted on tripods aimed at a lone podium and the stage it stood on.

I found Jonathan at the back of the crowd as I took my place, apprehension tracing lines into his face. Afraid of those watching, I tore my eyes away before he could give me any encouragement. There was a wave of clicks from the cameras when Ophelia reached up to kiss my cheek—except she positioned herself just right, away from their lenses, so they couldn't see that her lips hadn't even brushed my skin.

"They're all naked, remember," she whispered, and stepped back behind Eddie.

The small crowd focused in on me, and this time, me alone. This was how it'd be from now on. I could have all the help and advisors the world had to offer, but the crown rested on *my* head. Now, the world was watching how I would bear its weight. I cleared my throat, lifted my chin and opened my mouth to begin.

But when I looked down at my speech, one that had been carefully scripted to cover all bases, panic threatened to engulf me. The speech jumped straight in with its first line. It felt abrupt. Too abrupt. And so, I made my first mistake and said: "Hello."

A ripple of laughter flitted among the crowd. I shuffled uncomfortably, wishing I had water to soothe my dry throat. Out of the corner of my eye, I saw the monitor reflecting what was being broadcast live on TVs around the globe. I couldn't mess this up.

"It's often with immeasurable sadness that we contemplate the end of a life. How do we begin to honor that life? To give it the same color and vivacity it had? When a light once shone so bright, it can feel impossible to continue in the darkness it leaves behind. But I stand before you today, sharing in your grief—*our* grief—for when we stand together, we do so taller, stronger and with hope in our hearts."

I made sure to glance up, to show them that I wasn't afraid, even if I was. I couldn't afford to let them close enough to see the truth.

"So, I hope it's not just with immeasurable sadness that we contemplate the life of a king as great as my father, but that it's also with immeasurable fondness, and the hope of a future as great as the one my father once created."

I was almost there. The speech was short on purpose, so I didn't have the chance to break. But the memory of my dad, so strong he could've been next to me, tugged at my conscience. My father wasn't a faceless crown. He deserved more than a carefully scripted speech written by advisors. He deserved more than this.

"My dad was a great man," I said, and Gayle's head whipped round like she'd been slapped. At the back of the room, behind the world's cameras, it dawned on her that I was going off script. But at that moment I didn't care. "You knew him as the king of this country. But before anything else, he was a father, a husband, a brother, a friend. I can't put into words how I feel right now. My family is broken. There is an empty space where my father should be, and I fear it will never be filled."

Gayle had sprinted behind the cameras and was now waving her arms in utter panic to get my attention. Every head in the room was turned to me, some sharing in the tears I was now shedding, others smirking and readjusting the focus on their cameras. I recognized one face, and the ghoulish sneer plastered on it. Quinn Buckley was enjoying every moment of this.

Seeing him knocked me back into reality, the safety of which I should've never stepped out of in the first place. I quickly glanced back down at my speech, the lines now blurred by the tears still hot on my cheeks. This was a disaster. A king didn't wallow in weakness. A king didn't flinch—not in public, not even for a moment. I'd cracked, and what was worse, I'd let everybody else see it too. What had I done?

"I stand before you today as king, in the place my father stood before me, and in the place my grandmother stood before that." I forced myself to keep going, despite my shaky voice. "I pledge to continue my father's legacy. I pledge my life, no matter its length, to continue leading our nation into greatness. And I pledge to do what I can to carry out my duty to this country. My duty as king."

I kept my face dipped, away from the cameras, unwilling to let the world see me as a broken teenager. Before they'd even stopped recording, I was bundled away from the reporters, enclosed within a human shield that pushed me toward safety.

"No need to panic, Your Majesty. We've got you,"

Peter said calmly in my ear, having appeared out of thin air with a swarm of security.

I vaguely heard Gayle give orders to have Ophelia taken home, but I couldn't see her through the bodies now surrounding me. All I could hear was a rumble of whispers chasing after me as I was herded into a side room. My heart sank as I saw the muted TV in the corner and my own tear-stained face looking back.

"How bad was it?" I murmured, head bowed in shame. But a king needed to face his decisions and the consequences they bore, so I lifted my eyes to find my family staring back.

"Do you want the bad news, or the really bad news?" Gayle said, her words pinched and clipped. I shrugged. Did it really matter? "Well, let's start with the bad. The speech was specifically written to avoid saying the *wrong* thing, to avoid saying something that could rock the boat. You as good as told the world that being king comes second—that your father put his personal life before his duty."

"And where's the lie in that?!" I spluttered. "You *know* Dad always put us first."

"*We* know that. But the people out there? The people who looked to your father—who now look to *you*—as king? They can *never* know that. They must think that your life is ruled by the crown, and that every decision you make is in the interest of it. Because if they think otherwise, it will be the end of this family and the end of the monarchy."

Each word punched through me, settling in my gut like poison. Gayle's face softened slightly as her hands came to rest on my shoulders. "The throne sits on unstable ground. Each day, faith in us dwindles. If we blink, if we make one wrong move, then it will destroy us. That crown is nothing more than a smoke screen. We hide behind these walls, because if people come too close, they'll see the cracks we've worked so hard to hide. And then they'll discover our greatest secret of all—that they don't need us. That they've *never* needed us."

I already knew this. We all did. We didn't show emotion. We couldn't let others see us as weak. To humanize the crown was to invite others to inspect it closer, to make them realize that we were people like them and that this establishment rested on nothing more than the belief they instilled in us. We provided the image of unity and stability that a government, who were voted for, could not. It wasn't like I *wanted* to sit on the throne. But if I stepped aside, I'd be leaving Eddie to deal with the mess I left behind. I wanted to protect him, like an older brother should. And if I stepped aside and Eddie chose to abdicate too, then we would be at the mercy of Cassandra. She could banish us entirely, strip us of our titles, leave us penniless and without protection. I would journey to hell before I let that happen.

Mum stepped toward me before Gayle could continue, freezing the thoughts that were palpable between us all. "You did nothing wrong." Gayle opened her mouth and quickly closed it again like a goldfish. "To show emotion is not to show weakness. It's to show strength. And if they can't see that, then to hell with them all."

"What's the problem with a couple of tears anyway?" Eddie said. "At least he doesn't look ugly when he cries."

I ignored Eddie and addressed Gayle. "If that's the bad news, then what's the *really* bad news?"

Gayle hesitated. "It's Quinn Buckley," she said. Panic began to swell within me. *What now?* "He's apparently bragging about some story he's writing. Jonathan overheard him just before your speech began."

Every eye in the room turned to Jonathan, who all but shrank back into the door. He cleared his throat. "I didn't hear much, but he said he has a source—someone who knows everything. He said it could be his biggest scoop yet." Jonathan's eyes lingered on mine for a second longer, the same fear I felt reflecting back at me.

"We're already investigating a possible leak," Gayle said, oblivious. "It seems not everybody who wanders these halls is on our side, whether they pledge allegiance to us or not. We need to lie low, at least until Quinn reveals his hand."

"He's on the news," Peter said, pointing at the TV. Sure enough, Quinn had appeared on the screen next to an interviewer, his head thrown back in laughter. Unable to resist, I reached for the remote and turned up the volume.

"It's not what you want to see in a *king*, is it? A weeping, fragile *boy* who can't pull it together when the country needs it most." Quinn Buckley was standing outside the palace, milking every second of the spotlight. "I've said it before, and I'll say it again—this country needs more than a family who parade up and down in fancy dress, balancing crowns and tiaras on their heads for show. And it certainly needs more than a teenage boy. No wonder there's never been another king like *him*."

43

The room had gone cold, or maybe it was just my body freezing from the inside. All I could see was Quinn, his glinting grey eyes taunting me through the screen.

"As the first Black monarch, James has a lot to prove. I fear he's not off to the best start." He gestured to the palace behind him. "His father comes from a long line of respected kings and queens. Things only soured after he chose to marry Alexandra, which added a . . . let's say, different flavor to the palace."

I didn't want to hear any more, but I couldn't turn it off.

"I have eyes and ears everywhere, and whisperings tell me that the king may be hiding something," Quinn was saying. "The question is . . . what?"

Everything around me fell away. Quinn was gloating right outside the place that was meant to keep me safe, like he knew *exactly* what I was hiding. Part of me had known that my secrets would catch up with me sooner or later. Quinn might not know anything yet, but it could only be a matter of time.

"The palace is built on greed and lies, and I won't rest until I expose it for the mockery it is," he carried on, letting his threat marinate in the air. "Let's just say you'll want to be reading my column in the *Eye* over the next few weeks. There are secrets lurking in the shadows of Buckingham Palace, but they'll soon emerge into the light. Mark my words."

Gayle grabbed the remote from me and shut off the TV, but Quinn's malicious grin stayed burned into my mind long after the screen had faded to black. I wasn't going to forget about Quinn Buckley, or his threats, any time soon.

CHAPTER FOUR

THE SAFETY IN A STORM

I t was a few hours later, past eight p.m., and I wore the day around my shoulders like a straitjacket. The exhaustion was deep in my bones, rooted so far inside me that it felt impossible to imagine I would ever be free of it. I hadn't been alone all day. Instead, I'd been bunkered down in various rooms of the palace as plans for my father's funeral began to take shape and I was briefed on my first duties as king.

My father would be buried on a Saturday, eight days from now, meaning we had to move fast to make sure everything was perfect. But we'd also have our own private vigil tomorrow while my father lay in rest. I'd have to face my grief head-on, whether I was prepared to or not.

But it was all too calculated, too robotic and void of any emotion. The conversations about the funeral were matter-of-fact, remarks made in the kind of tone that was used to report the news. Eddie sat in the corner of the King's Conference Room, staring out of the window in silence, away from the utterances of Gayle and the small group of senior aides tasked with making everything perfect. Mum did her best to pull us all together, to keep what was important in our sights—that we give Dad the send-off he'd have wanted, not the send-off expected by others.

There were lists of upcoming public engagements I would need to undertake over the coming months too, as well as state visits that were being planned in order to introduce me to the world. Audiences with the king would be put on hold to allow me a small sliver of privacy, but it wouldn't be long until they'd resume and I'd be expected to host politicians and heads of state, throw parties and dinners, find causes and charities to invest in and support. It didn't matter that grief curdled in the pit of my stomach. The monarchy had to go on. So, I sat at the head of the table in silence, giving a nod here, a shake of the head there. Gripping the arms of my chair, I refused to let thoughts of my dad's death, or Quinn Buckley's threats, consume me.

When I saw the time, my heart began to beat like it was coming back to life. The warmth that filled the wounds was a cruel cocktail of selfish yearning matched by a bitter guilt. It was like I could feel him close, my body so attuned to his and instinctively understanding that it wouldn't be lonely for much longer. I excused myself from the table and requested I not be disturbed for the evening. For once, I didn't have to come up with some intricate lie—everybody could understand why I'd want to be alone after the day we'd had.

I all but ran along the corridors, head low and heart racing, through the Picture Gallery and then into the White Drawing Room, breathing a sigh of relief when I saw it was empty. Nobody had any reason to be here so late, which was part of our usual plan. I leaned against a wall, trying to catch my breath, but as the seconds ticked by, a rush of anticipation welled up within me, every sound putting me on edge.

He was late. Maybe he wasn't coming after all. Maybe he'd been caught trying to slip away. Had our secret finally been rumbled, our luck snatched away from us? We'd had too many stolen moments already, aware that each moon-lit tryst could be our last. We knew that everything was on the line for us, that our lives could be ripped apart if we were caught, but still, we couldn't resist each other.

There was a creak outside and suddenly the door was opening, slowly at first and then whipped aside. I let go of a breath I'd been holding as I saw him walk through, quickly closing the door and rushing across the room in desperate strides to get to me.

Our bodies collided like burning stars, his warm against mine as he wrapped himself around me, my own melting under his scorching touch. He whispered my name as I clung to him with everything I had, tears suddenly hot on my face as the grief I'd built a dam around began to burst. His hands held me as I sobbed, and it was like they'd never let me go again.

"I've got you," Jonathan whispered. "I've got you."

We stayed that way for longer than we should have. Anybody could've walked into the Drawing Room and found us, but at that moment, I didn't care. I'd been drowning all day and now I finally had something to hold on to.

"I needed that," I said, pulling away at last and fighting the creeping shame that I'd burst into audible tears in front of him. I quickly ducked my head and tried to wipe my eyes with my sleeve, but Jonathan stepped in and raised my face to his, wiping my tears with his thumb.

"I'm so sorry," he uttered, leaning his forehead against mine so there was nothing but a breath between us. "Your dad . . . everything . . . I'm sorry."

I shook my head and held him tighter. I couldn't find the words I wanted to say so I didn't say a thing. Only when footsteps hurried past the Drawing Room door did we jump apart, breathing quickly.

"Let's go," I said quietly.

I took his hand and led him across the room toward the giant mirror on the opposite wall. It was gilded with gold, heavy and ornate, with intricate swirls at its corners. It looked solid, and it was, but it hid a secret. Grasping the edge with two hands, I pulled, and slowly the mirrored door opened. It led into the Royal Closet, a small room that was hidden away and linked to my private quarters. We all had shortcuts to our rooms, secret passageways to get each member of our family from one place to another without the need to cross paths with anybody else. This

48

one was mine and I'd never cherished it more than when Jonathan had entered the picture....

⟨✺⟩

It was March and my father's life had just been set against a timer, the news of his ill health turning him from a king into a human, when Jonathan arrived at the palace. He'd been hired at my father's request, something that confused just about everybody since he was so young and unqualified. But Jonathan hadn't been hired because he was the perfect fit for the job. He'd been hired because my father knew his time was running out, and that, when I was king, I might need somebody I could rely on, somebody my own age whom I could trust, who could relate to me on a level that Gayle and the rest of the staff couldn't.

"Your Highness," Jonathan said, snapping into a bow as Gayle introduced him to the family on his first day in the palace. When he raised his head, we locked eyes for a brief second and it felt like daylight pouring into the night.

"It's a pleasure to meet you," I said, offering my hand. He hesitated for just a moment, then shook it.

"The pleasure is all mine, sir," Jonathan replied.

He was handsome, there was no denying it, but there was more to my initial attraction than that. There was a gentleness about him too, a softness so delicate it was hard to find in other people. That light brought me promise and hope, and I craved it more and more as the days and weeks went by. I didn't even try to stop myself. I wanted

49

so badly to free myself from pain. To feel something other than woe and impending loss. And when I was with him, it was like a shield against it all.

One night in April, when the two of us had been tasked with planning a speech for an upcoming event, it happened. The glow of a lamp warmed the shadows around us as we worked. He'd undone his tie and the top two buttons of his shirt, and there was a wrinkle in his brow as he tried to concentrate. I wasn't even thinking about the speech anymore. All I wanted was him. I suggested we take a break so we could speak about anything but work. He got up to stretch his legs and that was when he noticed the games console nestled under the TV. He immediately made for it, his face kind of glowing as he rooted through the games, finally plucking one out from the bunch.

"The future king plays *Mario Kart*?" he said, a swallowed laugh rumbling his words.

I grinned, standing up too and grabbing a controller. "The future king plays *Mario Kart* and is willing to take on any challenger to his crown. Dare to lose?"

I should've known from Jonathan's silent confidence that I was in trouble. I lost the first race and then the second, the third and the fourth soon after. I was eight races down before I knew it and I didn't care. We laughed as we hunched over our controllers, nudging into each other in the hopes the distraction would give us an edge. I kept stealing glances at Jonathan out of the corner of my eye, catching his half smiles, which would give way to intense concentration. Something about watching him in his element, like I was in on a secret, gave me a shot of pure joy, the flutter of a million butterfly wings rippling outward. like a wave of electricity that reared its head and then consumed me all at once.

When he stood up to go a few hours later, I stood up too. We faced each other, unspoken words daring us to set them free. I hesitated, because if I made this move, it would change everything. But just when I thought the moment might break, I took that step and he didn't pull away. We'd never put a label on our relationship, but neither of us had pulled away since.

⟡

Now we emerged into the living room of my quarters, carefully closing an identical mirrored door behind us. Finally, we were alone.

"I don't want to talk about anything," I said quickly as Jonathan went to open his mouth. I grimaced and tried again. "I mean, not anything to do with today. I want to forget it all happened, just for one night." With Quinn's threat looming over us, who knew how long we had left together? We couldn't waste a second of the borrowed time we'd already enjoyed too much of.

Jonathan nodded and fell onto the sofa, beckoning me toward him. I fought a gormless smile and slipped down beside him, his hand curling around my back and bringing me closer.

"Is pizza too common for the Royal Family? I'm

starving." Jonathan grinned, holding his hands up in mock surrender when he saw my face. I reached for my phone, my stomach suddenly realizing that I hadn't eaten all day.

"I'm sure your mother is onto us, by the way," Jonathan said before I could make the call. A shiver of panic shot through me. "It's the way she looks at me sometimes. Gayle too. If she finds my room empty again, she'll never believe I was just out for another long walk. She didn't believe me the first time I told her."

"That's because you're a terrible liar," I muttered with a roll of my eyes.

"And you're any better? Gayle asks you a question you don't want to answer and it looks like you're ready to swan dive out of the window."

"That's not true! Didn't you hear what Gayle said? It's our job as a family to lie. We've got it down to an exact science now."

Jonathan raised an eyebrow. "Tell me a lie then."

"The sky's green," I shot back.

Jonathan brought his face close to mine, a frown framing his eyes. "Nope, you flinched. Terrible liar, case closed. Try again."

"You're more annoying than Eddie," I said, although even I had to admit it didn't sound convincing.

"That's like telling me the sky's green. Oh, wait…" He laughed and it sounded like home, like something I could wrap myself in and stay safe away from the world around me.

I looked him dead in the eye. "I love you."

He faltered, the ghost of a laugh still etched on his face. We'd never said those three words before, although it'd been building brick by brick since that first night. Maybe it was a desperate desire for comfort, the urgent need for light in the dark. Or maybe I was simply trying to replace the love that'd been taken from me last night, so I wouldn't feel empty. Either way, there was no taking it back. Jonathan didn't give me the chance to, anyway.

"Now there's something I can believe in," he said quietly, and leaned toward me. His lips were about to meet mine when I pulled back.

"I thought I was a terrible liar," I said. He dropped his head with a laugh.

"You could still be better."

I leaned into him to reprise the kiss I'd missed, but he grinned and pulled away. "Nope, not until you've got that pizza ordered. Priorities."

We passed the night talking about things that didn't matter and, for a brief moment in time, I tried to forget—about today, about the Grief Parade and the funeral plans and the speech that could've ruined my reign before it'd even started. To forget that I was now the king, hiding secrets away from those closest to me, ones that could be about to spill out into the open. But I couldn't pretend all night.

"Why didn't you tell me about Quinn Buckley?" I asked quietly, standing up by the window. The remnants of our pizza crusts were scattered on plates spread out on a blanket over the floor.

"I thought you didn't want to talk about today," Jonathan said behind me, still cross-legged on the blanket. I gazed out at the treetops, now draped in the early summer night, the lights of London twinkling just out of reach.

"You should've told me. You've had so many chances to warn me that someone like Buckley wants my head on a plate."

Jonathan fumbled for something to say. "I didn't think it was important. He's just another journalist trying to bait us for a reaction. You've had enough on your plate. Buckley isn't a problem, I promise."

I bit my lip and said nothing. I heard Jonathan get up, moving across the room before he wrapped his arms around my body. He pressed himself into me as we looked out the window together, his chin on my shoulder.

"I'm sorry. I didn't think you needed the stress. Gayle said we were to keep it to ourselves unless it was important. And he's not. He's writing stupid things that don't matter."

"They do matter if they're lies that people believe."

"Anybody with common sense can see it's nothing more than the diary of a racist who's sulking because the new king of the country is Black."

"And what about the people with no common sense who read it and take it as bible?"

"Do they really matter?" Jonathan countered.

"Yes, they matter. It all matters. They hate me for something I am, not for something I've done. And what if Buckley's already found out about us?" Jonathan's body

54

tensed against mine, no doubt thinking of what we could both lose if our secret started to unravel. "People already hate me because I'm Black. If they find out I'm gay too, they'll tear me apart."

I closed my eyes and let my head fall back on Jonathan's shoulder, half hoping that when I opened them again, I'd be in a normal house in a normal room where we could be together without the pressure of secrecy.

"I know this is hard," Jonathan said quietly, his breath dancing across my neck and sending a force field of electricity shimmering around my body. "But you can do this. You're stronger than any person I know. We're all here to support you, the whole lot of us. You'll never have to face this alone."

I couldn't see him, but I could hear a question creeping into his voice. "But...?" I prompted.

Jonathan shuffled, his arm around my body not quite slipping away entirely but beginning to let me go. "We should think carefully about what we're doing here," he said, almost too quiet to hear.

"What's that supposed to mean?" I didn't want to turn around, to see what I knew he was saying written all over his face.

"It means...maybe we should stop this. At least for now. I don't want to be a distraction or get in the way of things, and that's all I'll be doing if we keep seeing each other. And you saw what Quinn said. If he's already onto us, we need to lie low until the dust settles and everybody's forgotten that there's even a secret to uncover. You need to focus on what's important, and that's not me." His words were all pushed up against each other, questions about us creeping around them.

"And what if it is you? You're more important to me than anyone. I can't do this without knowing that you're with me." I knew the stakes, and now they felt higher than ever. But I didn't want to be alone. This was a risk I needed to take. Jonathan went to say something but stopped. I shook my head, clinging on to his arm as if it were a life raft.

"Don't let me go." My voice shook. He hesitated, and in that moment I knew something had come between us. Even when he held me tighter, I knew. Even when he promised to stay, I knew.

CHAPTER FIVE

HIGH SOCIETY DARLINGS

J ames? Get up! We've got things to do."

Eddie came bowling into my bedroom without knocking, of course, because even if I was king and it was the middle of the night, some things would never change. He eyed me in bed, swaddled in covers. "I said I didn't want to be disturbed tonight," I said, forcing my words to stay even.

Eddie waved me off, stepping farther into the room and producing an unopened bottle of champagne from behind his back. "Today has been absolute horseshit, excuse my French, and just because you're *king* now, doesn't mean you shouldn't have some fun. God knows we all need it."

"Isn't champagne for celebrating?" I asked, sitting up to get a better look at my brother. It seemed that the day had finally caught up with him too—there was a manic sort of look swimming in his eyes.

"Cassandra's getting ready, and the rest of the gang will be here any minute," he said, ignoring me. I groaned so hard I could've sworn I felt my organs shift, but Eddie shook his head firmly. "None of that. Up. Now. You're not staying in here and sulking. And besides, it'll reflect badly on me if I've organized a get-together and the king himself doesn't grace us with his presence." Eddie's eyes zeroed in on me. "Unless you've got some secret party of your own going on in here. All this disappearing you've been doing lately and your requests not to be disturbed... I'm starting to grow suspicious." He grinned while I tried to keep a straight face, the irony of which didn't escape me.

"I'm not leaving until you agree, so you may as well just say yes now and make this pain-free for both of us." Eddie plopped himself onto the bed to make his point.

I wanted him to leave—needed him to, actually—but I couldn't help the questions and thoughts scrambling around in my head. "Do you not think it's a bit soon to start this again?" I asked, trying to keep my voice measured so it wouldn't send Eddie off the deep end. "I know they're your *thing*, but Dad..."

I let it hang in the air because even now I couldn't quite bring myself to say the words we both knew out loud. Believe it or not, parties at Buckingham Palace were more frequent than you might think, and I'm not talking about those royal, stately affairs either. Eddie had been

58

throwing them since last year—in secret, of course. They'd become his thing, a way for him to forget the responsibility that was always knocking at our door and to enjoy life like we were regular teenagers without a crown and throne looming over us. I'd just assumed, after everything that had happened today, they'd stop, at least for now.

But Eddie shook his head almost violently, raising his hands to block his ears like a child. "No! No, no, no, no, no," he blurted. "I don't want to hear it anymore."

I reached out for him, but he recoiled from my touch. "We're doing this. We're carrying on as normal. Because if we don't, then we have to stay stuck in this never-ending cycle of pity and grief. I'm not going along for that ride. I won't do it. And if we don't go on as normal, then we have to face *this*." He vaguely gestured toward the rest of the palace. "*They* want us to break almost as much as the people outside do. They want us to get the hell out of this place, back to where they think we belong."

"We belong here," I tried. "This is the only place we've ever called home."

"And does that matter to *them*? To those people who never accepted us here in the first place? To those who told Dad"—his jaw tensed—"to get us all out of here before we brought the establishment to its knees? They bow and curtsy to our faces, but the moment our backs are turned, their knives are out. Do you honestly trust a single one of them?"

"I trust Gayle. Peter. Jonathan. There are good people here too, Ed. They're not all out to get us."

"Then maybe I don't know you as well as I thought I did. I assumed we were on the same page—in this together. I guess being king changes things." I started to protest, but Eddie plowed on. "You're a fool for believing in any of them. You can't trust a single person on *either* side of the palace gates. They'd all pay to see us left in ruins, and I'm not giving them the satisfaction. No fucking way."

How could I say my brother was wrong? Time and time again, we'd woken to see our secrets splashed across the front pages, ones that only people who were sworn to silence could know. The palace—our home—was nothing but a cupped hand trying to hold water.

Eddie shrugged it off, and then the mask that hid his grief was back as if it'd never happened. He was better at burying his feelings than me. "Anyway, it's a Friday night, and what are you going to do instead? Stay in here on your own? We might be royal, but we're also seventeen, so get up before I drag you out from under that sheet."

"All right, all right," I muttered, holding my hands up in the air to show him he'd won. "I don't know why you had to invite the Heir from Hell though."

"You try keeping the parties a secret from her. If I had it my way, she wouldn't live here at all." Eddie snorted and lay back on the bed. "Anyway, if Cassandra says anything tonight, you can have her locked up in the tower and beheaded at dawn or whatever."

I rolled my eyes and made to untangle myself from the sheets, then remembered I'd lost my last shred of clothing before falling into the bed. "Do you mind?" I said, gesturing to the door.

Eddie grumbled but hopped up anyway, clutching the champagne. "Ballroom in fifteen minutes."

"I assume Mum doesn't know about this," I said.

"Know about what?" Eddie smirked. "What she doesn't know can't hurt her. Now, be a good king and hurry up."

He turned and marched out of my bedroom, murmuring something about calling the kitchens for alcohol. Five seconds after the door of my quarters had opened and closed, Jonathan crawled out from under the bed. He always looked so serious and *important* when he was standing around the palace in one of his suits. Now he was in my room, wearing just as many clothes as me.

Keeping our secret had become an instinct, and our guards were never down when we were together. A sound, no matter how slight, sent jolts of fear through us. Eddie crashing into my bedroom wasn't the first near-miss we'd had—Jonathan had hidden in wardrobes to avoid Gayle; he'd waited for the all-clear from behind bathroom doors while I told my mother I'd been talking to myself in the shower. Eddie hadn't even taken two steps into my quarters when Jonathan disappeared under the bed.

"I think I got carpet burn from how fast you pushed me down there," he grumbled, checking his knees before hopping back under the covers, leaving them lingering around his waistline, his bare chest glistening under the lamplight. "I know you're the king and everything, but why is your bed so much comfier than mine? I'm filing a complaint with Gayle. The one they've given me is like a slab of concrete."

I gave him a kiss to shut him up and slipped out of the bed to put on some clothes. "I have to go to this thing or Eddie will never let it go. Are you good in here on your own?" I checked my watch—past midnight. "Nobody should be coming in at this time."

"I can sneak back to my own room if you want?" He asked it casually enough, but the question marks from earlier were still lingering in his voice.

"Stay," I said, trying not to be needy and failing miserably. I felt safe from my own thoughts and feelings when he was there. "I won't be long. I'm just going to pop my head in so Eddie sees me, make sure he's not entirely destroying himself, and then I'll leave before anybody notices."

Jonathan shrugged and nodded, settling back into the pillows with a gentle sigh. "I'll be here when you get back then."

I stepped out of the bedroom, already dreading what might lie ahead. The last thing I wanted was to be inspected like a zoo animal by the diamonds of upper circles I'd never felt a part of. Eddie, always the smooth and confident twin, slotted in just fine, sliding like smoke between sons of earls and daughters of dukes. But he was a prince. As the heir to the throne, they looked at me differently. I never knew if they wanted something from me, or just wanted to see me fall, but their eyes, piercing and unforgiving, were always on me. How would they react when they saw me now, this time with the crown on my head? Metaphorically, of course—I wasn't going to wear that monstrosity unless I had to.

⟨≋⟩

So, picture this—it was the middle of the night and there was a party going down in Buckingham Palace. It was a secret—because according to Eddie, that was how all good parties should be—although not one that was very well-kept based on the noise level alone.

They always took place in the Ballroom, a sweeping space with ceilings as high as clouds. Six sparkling chandeliers bore down on the debauchery below. A balcony took up an entire wall, housing the golden pipes of an organ. Opposite, a white marble archway encased a cascading velvet canopy, its curtains tied back with gold tassels to reveal an antique throne. It was the room farthest away from Mum and Gayle, who would shut it all down instantly if they knew, nervous of the ensuing scandal should the details leak out into the open. If Mum were to find out, we'd be done for, even if I was now king. If Gayle were to stumble upon it, we'd be lucky if Buckingham Palace was still on the map by morning. But apparently that was all part of the thrill.

And then someone smashed the third lamp of the night.

It was a twist of gold with crystal droplets hanging like tears from its stem. A gift from the king of Spain, or maybe it was when one of the presidents came to visit. I groaned when I saw it in pieces on the floor, a crystal droplet lodged under the foot of someone who'd had too much to drink but didn't know when to stop. And why would he? It wasn't like he'd ever been told no before.

It was Louie, of course. White and brutish, no longer a teenager but not quite a man. He was a classmate of mine and Eddie's who'd played rugby when he was at school (as every son of a rich father seemed to) and now prided himself on floating around from party to party without planning to do much else. I wasn't particularly fond of him—he was too loud and brash for me—but Eddie always said he knew how to make a party fun, so he was always top of the guest list. As the heir to a fortune that saw fleets of Rolls-Royces ferrying him from one place to another, Louie also had a cavalry of lawyers on speed dial to clean up the messes he left behind. Believe me, there were plenty.

I watched as he roared like a gorilla, throwing his head back and erupting with a laugh that could've shaken the walls. He thumped Eddie on the back with a boulder-sized hand while Grigor, my brother's best friend, raised his glass with a chuckle, both of them congratulating my brother on something I probably didn't want to know about. Louie was a nightmare, but like I said, nobody could stop him. They couldn't stop any of us. That's why the staff, selected for their discretion, were standing out in the hall like part of the furniture instead of breaking up the party. Unless there were orders to do so, they'd wait until the carnage was over and then start cleaning before sunrise. It was a miracle these parties hadn't found their way into the papers yet.

A group of girls stood close by, throwing furtive glances at Eddie, Louie and Grigor, whispering among themselves and fluttering their eyelashes. They were beautiful and wrapped in furs, jewels glinting from their necks and ears, but the boys were too busy playing cricket with champagne corks and empty bottles to notice.

Ophelia was there too, standing beside Delphine, the daughter of an earl who'd once been the thirty-third richest man in the country, something she never let anyone forget. Delphine proudly held the reputation for being an over-the-top princess after she showed up to prom in a gilded horse-drawn carriage as if it was her coronation. She also had no problem reminding people that she'd been gifted a penthouse apartment in Chelsea for her eighteenth birthday. I smiled when Ophelia's eyes landed on me, and she did an over-the-top curtsy in response, hiding a giggle behind her wineglass. There were worse people to pretend to be in love with.

The Ballroom itself was too grand to host a party as grim and uncaring as this one, but none of the party-goers seemed to agree. Magnificent statues carved for kings and queens centuries ago now acted as nothing more than coat hangers, their spears and swords propping up furs and suit jackets. An enormous table that had hosted some of the greatest names in history had been reduced to a stage, covered in the muddy footprints of public schoolboys too drunk to care. This hall, with its grand and legendary past, was now nothing more than a pub's back room drenched in riches and gold. If only the people outside could see us now.

I'd been there long enough. Eddie had seen me arrive and was too busy jostling with Louie to notice if I disappeared. Call me boring, but sticking around to watch the Ballroom get trashed wasn't exactly my idea of fun. If I could just skirt around the outside of the room while nobody was watching, then...

"And where do you think *you're* going," a silky voice said. "Not trying to escape our little get-together, are you?"

I grimaced as Cassandra's talons dug into my arm, pinching the skin in a viselike grip. I struggled to look my cousin in the eye on an average day, even if my rank said it should've been the other way around. She was all angles and sharp edges, cheekbones slicing across her face like shards of glass, her high eyebrows always arched in a mocking glare.

"I was just getting some water," I mumbled half-heartedly, looking at the tip of her pointed chin so I didn't turn to stone if I caught her eye. She laughed like she had an ace up her sleeve. Knowing Cassandra, it probably involved poison and getting one step closer to the crown.

"I saw your little speech, by the way. Cute. I thought Quinn Buckley's interview was particularly interesting though. I would just *hate* for your secrets to come to light and ruin your reign before you've even taken your oath." Cassandra leaned in closer, her words all fire and ice. "What a shame that'd be indeed."

She did this on purpose, just to prove she could. She got some twisted joy out of playing games with me, even as kids. When I was eight, she tripped me up as I walked down the aisle during a royal wedding that was watched by ten million people. She *accidentally* knocked over Eddie's and my birthday cake when we were ten. Then, when I was eleven, she waited until we were out of earshot and told me that they didn't let people like *me* be king. She'd even spread a rumor, which was false might I add, that I'd once wet the bed after watching a horror movie when I was thirteen.

"I'd watch my back if I were you, *Your Majesty*." With one last scathing look, Cassandra disappeared through the crowd. I breathed a sigh of relief, trying to ignore the fact my hands were trembling—with anxiety or rage I couldn't tell.

"The Wicked Witch of Buckingham Palace hasn't stolen your ruby slippers, has she?" Ophelia slipped into place next to me with a smile, nudging my arm with hers.

"Not yet, but if she starts turning green, I'll let you know." I nodded toward the crowd of partygoers, who seemed to be getting sloppier by the minute. "What's the gossip?"

Ophelia pondered this for a moment. "Well, Delphine's furious because Louie won't show her any attention. I think she has her sights set on Grigor now instead and, to be fair, who can blame her? I'd be in line right behind her."

I held a hand to my chest. "How could you?!" We both burst out laughing. I couldn't lie, it felt good to push everything else aside. For a moment, it felt just like any other day where Ophelia and I would talk and laugh on the outskirts of a party, observing the scandals of the week.

I watched Grigor in the throng as Ophelia shared more

gossip. He was Eddie's best friend, someone who drifted seamlessly between the darlings of high society. He was standing confidently among a group of friends, grinning widely and clearly enjoying the attention. Grigor was the kind of person you'd describe as magnetic. Eyes followed him wherever he went, ears listened to whatever he had to say. I'd known him for most of my life, since he'd been adopted by Lord and Lady Greenwood, who were close friends of the Royal Family and lived in the grounds of Kensington Palace. Grigor had been at our birthday parties and sleepovers, special occasions and state dinners. He'd also been my first crush, although a stubborn one that I'd tried to push away, especially as Jonathan entered the picture. I'd told Jonathan about it as we murmured, under covers, about growing up and realizing we were gay, but I'd assured him, and myself, that the crush on Grigor was old news. Sure, faint traces of it still lingered like specks of gold in my mind, but I told myself it was just memories of that crush playing tricks with my thoughts. Even so, catching Grigor's eye was usually enough to make my head spin a little. After all this time, I had to fight a blush every time he said something in my direction. I think he knew he made me nervous, and probably enjoyed every minute of it.

"Uh, hello? Anybody home?" Ophelia pulled me out of my accidental reverie. "Don't tell me you're not bothered about Teddy Townsend getting pulled out of uni for drugs. That's the best gossip I've heard all night."

"His parents will pay their way out of it, I'm sure," I replied, just as Teddy knocked over a glass, which smashed into smithereens on the floor. He didn't even look at the mess, carrying on his conversation as if nothing had happened.

"I hate to crash a party, but do you mind if I borrow the king?"

Grigor stepped into my line of sight, as if he'd heard everything I'd just been thinking about him. I didn't know what to say, so I said nothing. Luckily, Ophelia came to my rescue.

"Oh, hey, Grigor. Sure. I think Delphine needs me anyway." She slipped away, only turning back to give me an *Oh my god what's that about?* look.

Grigor led me to a corner of the room and away from the baying crowd, stopping by a statue that partly obscured us from view. I was starting to wonder if he was drunk enough to have mistaken me for Eddie, but then I remembered he'd asked for the king. It wasn't that we never spoke to each other—more that we never spoke alone. Until now.

"Uh, hey?" I said into the quiet between us. His face broke into a smile, one that glued me to the spot. Up close, he was even more handsome.

"I just haven't had a chance to say I'm sorry about your dad," he said, his words measured and sure of themselves. "I wanted to make sure you were okay."

"Oh. Yes..." I struggled to look him in the face, but then realized I was staring at the muscles of his chest instead and began to blush. I dropped my eyes farther, before it occurred to me that *that* was hardly a better place to focus on. I was the king of the country, the head of

69

state for several more, and yet I couldn't stand in front of a good-looking boy without crumbling.

"You looked like you were thinking of leaving before Ophelia came over?"

I shrugged, but silently questioned why Grigor had even noticed. "You know it's not really my scene."

Grigor glanced over his shoulder at the room, taking it all in. Louie was standing on the table, pouring champagne into people's mouths. "I guess it's not really mine either," he said with a smile.

"Could've fooled me. Weren't you just playing cricket with corks and empty bottles?"

Grigor laughed, a low and velvet-laced rumble. "So, you've been watching me then?"

Way to go, James. Really smooth. Internally I flailed, trying to come up with a way to save myself. "I was trying to avoid injury by champagne cork."

"It's Louie you want to watch out for. I've got better aim than that."

I fought a smile, dropping my chin until it'd passed. Grigor didn't try to hide his—instead, it was toying with his entire face, reaching up through his cheeks and lighting up his eyes. Why was this conversation happening? What did Grigor want? And why was a wisp of excitement hovering in the shadows?

"I guess I should be heading back to my quarters. God forbid the king should be caught out of bed at this time encouraging deeds such as ... that." I nodded over Grigor's shoulder to where Draco Lewis, son of a diamond heiress

70

and the first student to be suspended from our prestigious school, was betting a stash of crumpled pink notes on something I was sure I didn't want to be a part of.

"You're the king now—doesn't that mean you give the orders around here?" Grigor raised his eyebrows, issuing a challenge or a dare.

"In that case, I order you to let me go to bed."

Grigor took a step closer and a jolt fired through my body, pressing me back into the wall. There was no way to style it out and pretend I hadn't nearly been knocked over by the prospect of Grigor moving into my orbit. He leaned in slightly, close enough that I could smell the rich aftershave on his neck.

"In that case, I bid you a good night. Until next time, Your Majesty." Now he stepped aside to let me pass.

"Good night," I murmured. In my haste to leave, I nearly bowed, forgetting it was supposed to be the other way around. "Good night," I said again in confusion, as Grigor chuckled to himself.

I took a breath, praying my legs still had the ability to at least get me out of the room. But they didn't have to take me far. I'd taken three steps when I looked up to find my way and was rooted to the spot. Jonathan stood by the door, a pained look blemishing his face as he glanced from me to Grigor.

"Jonathan . . . ," I mouthed. But it was too late. Without another look, he turned on his heel, closing the door behind him and disappearing into the palace.

CHAPTER SIX

AFTER-PARTY

A loud crash stopped me from following him, one that demanded attention. The sound of crunching metal meeting marble floor, melded with the moan of a human body in pain, silenced the party.

One of the grand chandeliers, a relic from before the palace was even built, lay in a heap of crushed gold, its precious stones scattered around it. The body of the person who'd swung from it was pinned underneath, squirming and groaning like a wounded animal. When he emerged from the rubble, I realized it was Louie. Of course.

The oak doors bursting open broke the heavy silence. My blood ran cold as people fell back into the shadows, leaving me, Eddie, a bloodied Louie and the wrecked chandelier in the middle of the hall.

Gayle surveyed the room and everybody in it. Her lips

were pursed and rage blazed in her eyes. I no longer felt like the king, but instead like a little boy who was about to get grounded. I had no doubt she'd always known about these parties happening—she had eyes and ears all over the palace, after all—but until now, she'd let them be. And now we'd been caught red-handed.

Gayle took in Eddie and me for a moment. There was something to her stare, a weight that I couldn't describe. I didn't know if she would shout or scream, or simply burn us to the ground with her eyes. But instead, she let the excruciating silence go on, nipping at us like the frozen air of a January day.

"Everybody out," Gayle eventually growled. "Now." She didn't wait to see if her orders were followed, knowing full well they would be. With one last glare at Louie, she wheeled around and disappeared, a line of staff standing in her wake waiting to start cleaning up.

The eyes of every person in the room fell on me like burning spotlights that seared through my clothes, through my very being, waiting for the king to say something. My mouth was dry, but I tried to stand up straight.

"You heard her. Everybody out."

The room descended into quiet chatter as people gathered themselves together and began trickling out the door. Louie looked too beaten and bruised to put up a fight and hobbled out after everybody else. No doubt he'd be on the phone to his platoon of lawyers before the night morphed into day. Ophelia waved in my direction with a grimace and followed Delphine.

Eddie, still in the middle of the room, blinked out of his daze. "What did Jonathan want?" he asked, as if the Ballroom didn't resemble a smoking ruin.

"How would I know?" I batted back, a little too quickly. An internal flame was heating my cheeks. "Probably to warn us about Gayle."

"He didn't look too happy to see me." Grigor appeared at my side and the constant crackle of electricity I felt whenever he was too close sparked in the inch between us. I stepped away, more out of instinct than anything.

The look on Jonathan's face hovered like a ghost in my mind. What had he seen? Nothing had happened, but how bad had it looked? I wanted nothing more than to run to him, to explain that it was just a misunderstanding. But Gayle had reappeared, and her frigid stare was fixed on me. Eddie and Grigor slipped into the trickle of people still exiting the room, leaving me to face her alone. When the final guest had disappeared, an army of staff wielding brushes and bin liners swarmed the room. I hung my head in shame as they got to work.

"Gayle, I'm sorry," I started before she could say anything. "It got out of hand. I shouldn't have let it happen. I'm really sorry."

"Why are you apologizing?" Gayle said, her words carved with a sharp edge. I shifted uncomfortably on the spot, not even sure of the reason myself. It just seemed like the right thing to do.

"Let me remind you of something, Your Majesty. You are the king. It doesn't matter what I think, or what your

74

brother thinks, or even your mother. We're here to support you, to advise you, but the decisions that must be made are yours alone. You're no longer a prince. You're the beating heart of this palace."

I wasn't sure if her words were intended to soothe, but each one felt like an anchor weighing me down. I'd never asked for this. I'd never wanted it. Dad had always said that to be a king was to be an island, and now I understood why.

"And what decisions must be made?"

"They'll reveal themselves over time, but the answer will always be the same," Gayle said, unmoved and unblinking. "The king must always come first. The *crown* must always come first. Anything deemed a risk or a threat to that must be eliminated. There can be nothing that puts us—that puts *you*—in jeopardy."

"So, I'm not allowed to make mistakes?" I said in despair. The well of grief was overflowing, and it wasn't just for my father. It was for me too. For the old me. The one I'd have to bury to be king. "What if I can't do it, Gayle? Then what? What if I want more from my life than to live with a crown on my head? Than to live in an empty room with nothing but shadows for company? What then?"

I didn't give Gayle a chance to say anything more, storming past her and out the door. I already knew the answers to my questions. They filled my head like water, drowning everything else. Only one thought survived, floating above the rest. Jonathan. He was the risk, the threat that Gayle spoke of. I hid no secret greater than him, and I wondered if Gayle already knew that.

My feet steered me down the stairs, toward Jonathan's room, desperate to find him and explain, to tell him that what he'd seen was nothing more than . . . what? What had it even been? I couldn't think of that now. I had to focus on Jonathan and making this right.

Kings and queens of the past watched from their gilded frames as I hurried through the gloom of long and endless hallways. I rounded the final corner, creeping past closed doors until I finally reached Jonathan's. I never came to this side of the palace, except to use the palace gym or swimming pool. If I was caught here in the dead of night, there would be no reason or explanation that'd satisfy the whisperers. They'd know *something* was going on, and in a place like this, it probably wouldn't take them long to figure it out.

I gently knocked on the door, my body tense as the noise galloped down the hall. When there was no answer, I knocked again. "Jonathan, it's me," I whispered. This time, there was a sound like scuffled footsteps. But then nothing.

"I know you're in there, and I know you probably don't want to talk, but it wasn't what it looked like. We were just talking, I promise you. . . ." I placed my palm on the door, waiting for something. Anything. But there was only silence. I couldn't stay here much longer—not without being caught.

"I'll be ready to talk when you are," I said quietly.

With a sigh, I started back up the hallway toward my own quarters, where I'd be safe.

I thought back to Gayle's words. The pressure bearing down on me had always been great, increasing year after year. I'd hoped that when the time came to wear the crown myself I'd know what to do—that a lifetime of lessons would be enough to guide me. But now the time was here, I didn't even know where to start.

I'd watched my dad all my life, trying to learn from him. On the surface, he made it look simple, as if the matter of being king was as easy as breathing. Beneath that exterior, he shouldered the weight of expectations, but he never let it turn him away from what he loved. He never let it come between him and his family.

So why should I? Maybe Jonathan was the answer. Maybe refusing to give up on him was the first step of many I needed to take to fight back. If I let the crown bully me into submission, my future looked bleak. I could have everything I wanted, just like my father, if only I fought for it first.

And so, I turned back.

This time I ran through the halls as if the watching portraits were chasing me, as if the palace walls themselves were closing in and I was running out of time to make it. My footsteps ricocheted around me, echoing around every corner and threatening to give me away. But I didn't care. I needed to see him, and if I had to wait outside his door all night to explain, then so be it.

When I reached the corridor again, the silence felt

off. There was a beat to it now, like it knew something I didn't, or as if something was hiding in the darkness, just out of sight. Watching me. Waiting.

I reached for the door. And then I realized it was already open. Just a crack, like it'd been carelessly shut by someone in a rush. My heart was thumping in my ears, anxiety injecting adrenaline straight into it.

"Jonathan?"

I stepped inside. Everything was still and bathed in nightfall. I hesitated, letting my eyes adjust to the dark.

"Jonathan?" I tried again.

Nothing. The darkness mocked me where I stood.

I crept in farther, the crackle of silence too lifeless and still. I reached for the curtains and slipped them aside, moonlight illuminating everything it touched in a ghostly white. It crept up and onto the bed, the sheets crumpled in a heap and spilling off the other side. It was empty.

Jonathan was gone.

Part II

A Slipping Crown

A POISONED PEN

HIS ROYAL CRY-NESS

REVEALED: How the new king crumbled
within hours of wearing the crown!

By QUINN BUCKLEY, *ROYAL REPORTER*

King James cried. It was the moment he was supposed to announce himself as the reigning monarch, and yet, in his first address to the nation, the seventeen-year-old boy crumbled. We were told by palace press secretaries in the hours before the disaster that our concerns over a boy sitting on the throne were unfounded—that the young king was ready to take his place. But James Albert Arthur Hampton fell apart in his first public address, proving my theory that he is unfit to wear the crown.

His Royal Cry-ness has spent months trying to ingratiate himself with the public, using the protection of the royal machine like a shield. Is it merely coincidence that the king introduced a girlfriend to the world after yet more speculation over his interest, or lack thereof, in finding a queen? After my report of the Queen Mother's demands that her staff not look her in the eye? Or is it simply a transparent tactic from that same royal machine to distract us from the fact that the Hampton family—now helmed by people who have never belonged near the throne, let alone proved their worth to sit on it—has fallen entirely from grace? Sources close to the family tell me King James's relationship is a sham. Based on the pair's rigid appearance when mourning King George's death, it would appear those sources are correct.

It is fair to say that the monarchy has never looked worse. At this point, it seems the footmen of the palace would be better equipped to take on the role. Even the king's brother, Prince Edward, would apparently make a better head of the firm, although my sources tell me he comes from the same bad batch and is nothing more than a spoiled troublemaker behind the scenes.

No—if we, as a country, are to have any hope in the Royal Family again, the crown must be passed on to someone we can trust in. Someone we can believe in. Someone like Princess Cassandra, who has already proved her worth and grace to bear such a burden. She would no doubt steer the House of Hampton back toward its glory days, when those who don't belong in the Royal Family were found

on the right side of the palace gates—that is to say, locked outside of them.

———————————

I could do nothing but look at the newspaper in dismay. A huge picture of me dominated the front page, taken during the speech, my face contorted into an ugly, almost impossible shape. I had to be mid-blink *and* mid-sentence. There would have been a thousand others to choose from, but of course Quinn Buckley had made sure the worst sat above his words like a gloating jeer.

Cassandra's picture stared up at me too, next to my own. She looked beautiful, a halo of grief and soft sorrow radiating around her. She was crying, tears glinting on her cheeks. And yet they wanted her to be queen, as if Quinn Buckley hadn't just called me an unstable wreck for the exact same thing!

To make matters worse, the clip of my accidental outburst during the Grief Parade was being played on a constant loop on all the news channels and social media. Quinn had cleverly framed it as an aggressive response to an innocent question, while also dangling the carrot of Princess Catherine in the faces of those who still favored her over us. People were far from happy that I'd all but said my father loved my mother more than her. So far, in being king I'd only succeeded in one thing—making everything worse.

Gayle stood rigidly by the door to my quarters, having delivered the newspaper herself at the first sight of daylight. Jonathan wasn't at his usual place by her side, and his empty room last night played over in my mind. I'd heard him before I left the first time, I was sure of it. And yet in the time it took me to return, he'd gone. How long could it have been? Five minutes? Four? Less? What could possibly have happened in that time?

Sleep hadn't come easy. In fact, it hadn't come at all as I lay restless in my quarters, consumed by thoughts that pulled me in every direction—toward grief and guilt, then worry and pity, and finally unbridled fear that posed questions I didn't know the answers to. Where was Jonathan? I'd tried to contact him, but his phone had been switched off and it had only made my fears grow. What lay ahead for me as the king? Could things get worse?

"I don't want to see it. And I don't want to see Quinn Buckley's name in this palace again." My hand shook as I pushed the newspaper away. Somebody swooped in to gather it up. "We surely can't let him continue to print these lies."

"We don't fight every lie that's printed. It's not what we do." Gayle smoothed out her blazer, looking as if the paper had merely confirmed it was Saturday. "If things get worse, we'll extend a notice to the papers themselves, maybe call a meeting to see if we can cool things off. But we don't reach down, especially for opinions in a column I'm sure nobody reads. Silence and distraction are the ways we operate. They always have been."

"Well, I'm asking you to please look into it. See if you can get Buckley to stop. I don't need this. I'm trying to find my feet as king and grieve my father. If he won't back down, then we'll fight fire with fire." I thought about it for a moment. "Actually, what's the harm in doing some digging anyway?"

"Your Majesty?" Gayle looked uncomfortable.

"Have someone look into his background, his past—see what they can unearth." I nodded to myself. If Buckley wanted to play this game, I'd make sure he lost. But Gayle looked horrified.

"James, please. We don't want to antagonize the press, regardless of what they write. It's their influence that could be the end of the monarchy."

"In which case, the end must be near. Anybody reading that will think I'm weak and not fit for the throne. I won't stand here and be trashed in front of the entire country. What am I supposed to do? Just wait until they tear me down altogether?"

I sat up a little straighter, sick of being pushed around and patronized. A Black teenager sat on the throne of a country that valued white authority above all else. They were going to villainize me, smear my name in the dirt until they broke me. They wouldn't be happy unless the head that bore the crown was one they deemed appropriate. Well, to hell with that. I was the king, and it was time to start acting like it.

I could tell that the words Gayle wanted to level at me were lodged in her throat, fighting to be heard. But she swallowed them. After all, it was she who'd told me that these decisions were mine to make alone.

"If that's what you wish…"

"It is," I said firmly.

Gayle nodded stiffly, her face giving nothing away. She turned to leave, but I couldn't fight the question that was resting on my tongue.

"No Jonathan this morning?" I tried to sound casual, as if I asked the question every day. It wasn't a strange ask, considering he accompanied Gayle wherever she went. But I felt the weight of the question leave my body and hover between us, lit up with neon signs. Gayle blinked, but otherwise there was no reaction.

"He texted me to say he was ill. He'll be back when he's better, I'm sure."

She was lying. Or at least not telling the whole truth. My instincts blared a warning in my ears. Maybe it was the way she refused to look directly in my eyes, or how she leaned toward the door as if she wanted to escape before I could ask anything else. There was something she wasn't telling me. I would've bet the crown on it.

"He's in his room? Maybe I should send something over to cheer him up. From us all."

"He asked not to be disturbed," Gayle said quickly, her counter framed with a forced smile. Then she bowed her head and left.

I checked my watch. Alfred, my father's senior advisor, was due at the palace at ten a.m. sharp. He'd sent word that he'd be arriving and had requested a private reception with me. He had something to give me—something important—and he was never late. That gave me less than half an hour to search for answers and figure out where Jonathan had really gone. It wasn't much, but it was a start.

⌒௰⌒

For once, I wasn't sheepish about people melting out of my way as I hurried to the other side of the palace. The royal staff had their own maze of corridors and tunnels that looped under and away from hallways where they'd likely cross our path. Tradition ruled that they should simply disappear if they saw one of the Royal Family approaching. If they couldn't escape, they stood against the wall, head bowed, and waited until we passed. I hated it, but right now, it was working in my favor.

I'd packed a small holdall with a towel and swimming trunks, ready to make an excuse if I was seen by someone I was hoping to avoid. There were different, more direct ways to reach the palace pool, but it wouldn't be that strange to find me near Jonathan's room if I was heading for a swim.

The hum of the palace followed me until I reached Jonathan's door. Heart in my mouth, I saw that it was still slightly ajar, as I'd left it the night before. Nobody had been back, or if they had, they'd been careful enough to make sure they left everything as it'd been. Looking both ways, I took a deep breath and ducked through to the other side, gently closing the door behind me.

"Jonathan?" I tried, knowing it'd be met with nothing but silence.

87

The room looked just as it had last night, except it somehow seemed worse in the harsh light of day, its emptiness even starker. It was split into sections, like a studio apartment or a hotel suite. The living area was tidy, except the cushions from the sofa were strewn on the floor and a stack of books had been knocked off the table. With each step, my body wound itself tighter, injecting fear straight into my heart.

As I crept toward the bed, nestled behind a corner, I stepped on the broken pieces of a shattered vase, the china scattered by the wall as if it had been thrown against it. Ornaments on the dresser had been overturned or swiped onto the floor. But one thing raised the hairs on my arms more than anything else—the drawers, which had been flung open recklessly, were empty. I ran my hand over the damage, hoping in vain that something I'd missed might give me answers. But all I saw was rage. Was this the outcome of Jonathan's hurt? Had jealousy really driven him this far?

My eyes raked over the room for answers, but the swirls of a cherished memory emerged instead, taking shape in my mind. It was so vivid that it almost seemed as if the memory were a physical thing I could touch. It filled the room with its color, sweeping me away into the past for a moment, to one of many evenings I'd spent in secret with Jonathan.

It had been the middle of a stormy night and I couldn't sleep, thoughts of my father's health eating away at me as the wind and rain lashed the windows. We were always careful to meet in secret and used the passageways as much as possible, but I craved the comfort he poured into me. And so, ignoring good sense, I left my quarters and headed for Jonathan's room, hoping that at this time of night, the security would be too busy observing the outside cameras rather than those watching our own hallways. I knocked gently, and for a moment, I thought he'd be fast asleep, but then I heard him shuffling and the door opened to reveal him standing there, shrouded in moonlight, as if he'd been hoping I'd come.

"Can't sleep either?" he said. He stood aside to let me in, closing the door softly behind us and then pulling me into a tight embrace, his arms wrapping around my back and bringing me into him. I remembered his breath skimming my neck, how his touch made my body crumple slightly as if it couldn't withstand the temptation.

When we broke apart, we spent hours on the floor of his living room playing silly card games, trying to keep the noise of our laughter down but almost failing and hardly caring. It was what had kept my head above water over those months, knowing that I had Jonathan to rely on. Nights like this were what I held on to, allowing myself to fall ever further for him with every game of *Mario Kart* we played, every David Attenborough documentary or new reality dating show we loved to watch together. With every new discovery of common ground between us, my feelings blossomed. Each laugh inhaled new life into me; each lingering gaze became a held breath; every gentle touch or graze of his hand stirred lust that already simmered barely below the surface. I felt that I could let go when I was with him, like he soothed every pain just by being there.

That night, we eventually fell into his bed, finally exhausted. With nothing but the darkness between us, his lips found mine, then moved to my cheek, my jawline, my neck, each kiss leaving behind the trace of unsaid words. When he found my lips once more, he hesitated.

"Do you trust me?" he whispered.

I didn't think twice. "Yes."

The sound of the door handle creaking dragged me out of the memory, which had left me feeling sick at the thought of potentially hurting Jonathan. But I couldn't dwell on that now. Not yet. Someone was here. Was it him? Someone else? Whoever it was, they were coming in, and I couldn't be caught in this room.

As the door began to open, I fell to my knees and scrambled under the bed. The covers spilling off the mattress hid me from view, but left me blind, blocking whoever it was who'd just walked in.

The door closed behind them.

I held my breath.

A severe silence coated the room for a few seconds, to the point where I thought whoever had come in must have left again. But then there was movement, soft and careful, creeping farther inside. The brush of somebody's hand against a surface. The scuff of their shoe on the carpet. Silence again. Then a breath, shallow and fragile. It was small, yet in the quiet it swept around the room. My heart threatened to expose me, slamming against my ribs like an animal trying to break free of its cage.

The steps moved closer, until they were right next to the bed. If I reached for the sheets, I'd be able to see their shoes. But I couldn't move. I didn't dare.

One beat.

Two.

Three.

And then they moved again, this time to the dresser to close the drawers, and then back toward the door. One last pause, and then it opened, followed by a soft click as it closed once more. I couldn't wait any longer, my body begging to escape. I hauled myself out from under the bed, shaking with fear. I'd give it ten seconds, to make sure the person had gone, then I'd get the hell out of here.

But then something caught my eye. Something that hadn't been there before. A piece of paper rested on the dresser, facing down onto the wood. I knew I should leave it and walk out while I could. But I reached for it anyway, and as I turned it over, a simple typed message sent my world into free fall.

Your secret is safe with me. Or is it?

Without thinking, I grabbed the note and ran for the door, throwing it open in the hope that whoever had left it might still be in the hallway. And there, slipping through a door out into the palace gardens, was the retreating back of my twin brother.

CHAPTER EIGHT

THE PERIL IN TRUST

I watched through a window as Eddie got farther and farther away, moving into the sunlight that bathed the gardens. There was nobody else in the corridor, but surely it couldn't have been him who had left that note. Had another person simply disappeared before I'd had a chance to see them for myself?

The note burned in my hand, igniting yet more questions. Had someone left it for Jonathan having figured out his secret—our secret? Was it intended as blackmail? Was that why Jonathan had come to look for me in the Ballroom yesterday? Was that why he'd simply vanished into the night, pretending to Gayle that he was ill and in his room?

My eyes zoned in on Eddie again, who'd now picked a spot on the grass and was lying back, hands behind his head and face angled up toward the sun. He looked calm, as if last night's debauchery hadn't even happened. He'd always been better at hiding his true self in plain sight, something we'd all been taught to do since birth to protect ourselves. Beneath that calm, who knew how he really felt, but in that moment it was envy that simmered within me.

"Looking for something?"

I whirled around in panic, the note slipping from my hands and floating down to rest by my feet. Grigor stood before me, a bottle of apple juice in hand. The smile that had been flirting with his face quickly evaporated when he saw the fear written on mine.

"I didn't mean to scare you," he said, eyebrows drawing into a soft frown. "Everything okay?" I nodded without thinking, my heart still slamming against my ribs. He didn't look convinced.

"I was on my way to the pool," I said automatically. "Just got sidetracked. What are you doing here anyway?" I shuffled toward the door that led outside. Even though Jonathan wasn't here, I still didn't want to be seen getting too close to Grigor. The last time that happened, it hadn't exactly ended well.

"I stopped by the kitchens for some juice. I'm here for that ray of sunshine," Grigor said, nodding to Eddie over my shoulder. "He's indulged my request to have lunch out in the garden. However, he's once again rejected the offer of a shoulder to cry on as he's still adamant he doesn't actually need one."

I breathed a humorless laugh, glancing back at Eddie. "Sounds like my brother all right," I said. He had a habit of pushing people away until he'd convinced himself he was fine.

"It looks like you could do with someone to lean on too," Grigor said, holding me carefully in his gaze.

"I don't need anybody." The words blurted out of me before I could stop them. I guess my brother and I were alike in more ways than one. I grimaced under Grigor's raised eyebrow. "Sorry. Just stressed, that's all."

"You don't have to go through what you're enduring alone, you know?" He shrugged. "Just think about it. You know where I am if you need me. Or if you need to forget about all of this." I wanted to look away, but Grigor pinned me to the spot with those kind eyes, urging me to believe he was there to help. I didn't trust myself to speak, so I nodded instead.

"I best get out there and see what denials your brother is excelling in today." I smiled despite myself. "But remember what I said, all right? Anytime. I can be a good distraction when it's needed." He reached out, but for what I couldn't tell. My fear kicked my dozing instincts into gear and I met his hand with a fist bump. One that I immediately regretted.

"Uh, thanks, but I was going to open the door." Grigor grinned as I tucked my hand into my pocket, horrified. "Oh, and you dropped something."

Before I could do anything, he ducked down and scooped up the note. He gave it a glance and handed it back, the merest twitch giving away that he'd read what it said. But I was saved from having to explain by the sound of hurried footsteps coming toward us. The butler bowed low, then straightened up with his hands behind his back.

"Mr. Kew has arrived, Your Majesty. He has been set up in the White Drawing Room and awaits your arrival now." I'd forgotten all about the meeting and now I was late, something that wouldn't bode well with a man like Alfred. I nodded stiffly.

"I'll see you around," I murmured to Grigor, and started off up the corridor, forcing my eyes to look ahead as I passed Jonathan's empty room once more, the note clutched in my fist.

Alfred Kew had always been a stern man who stood for no nonsense. He was black or white—never in between or indecisive—and had a (usually correct) opinion on just about everything. He was fair-skinned, wore glasses and had a dash of grey hair adorning his upper lip, matching his perfectly coiffed hair that was never out of place. He always wore a three-piece suit, polished shoes and a tie, his formality never fading no matter the occasion. Eddie always joked that he probably bowed to his plate before dinner every night.

He'd worked as my father's right-hand man for as long as I could remember, first as his private secretary, and then as his primary advisor and closest confidant. Wherever you saw Dad, Alfred was always two steps behind, his probing eyes taking everything in. With Alfred's help, Dad's reign had reignited the popularity of the Hampton House, pushing the monarchy toward another golden era. It was only when Mum entered the picture that the adoration began to dim.

"Alfred," I said, hurrying into the White Drawing Room like a beast was on my tail. "I'm so sorry I'm late. I got caught up in—"

I didn't have time to finish my excuse. Alfred crashed into me, knocking me off balance. I'd have fallen back through the door if his arms hadn't been around me. I faltered, confused. This wasn't how Alfred greeted anybody. He once returned with my dad after a three-month tour of Australia and New Zealand, only to shake my hand at the airport. I was seven.

When he pulled back, his eyes were red and watery behind his glasses, a shadow encasing them. He looked like he hadn't slept in days. I wasn't the only one who'd lost somebody important.

"I'm so sorry, Alfred," I said quietly. He waved me off, like he was insulted I'd said such a thing.

"Don't you dare apologize. It's me who should be consoling you. Forgive me—I forgot myself for a moment." I brushed off the apology as he stepped back and gave me a swift bow. Once he was upright again, his eyes raked over me. I wouldn't have been surprised if they could see through me too, into the cauldron of secrets I was trying to stop from boiling over.

"It's a ridiculous question, but…how have you

96

been?" Alfred nodded to a pair of chairs, waiting for me to sit before taking his own seat. Some habits die hard. He leaned forward slightly to get a better look at me. You couldn't hide in front of Alfred. He was too smart for that.

"I've been doing what I'm supposed to do—holding it together. Duty comes before grief, right? That's the way it works," I said bitterly. Alfred sighed, but he understood. He knew I was right.

"I saw the speech." It was a simple statement, but one I couldn't decipher.

"It was a train wreck, right?" Despite myself, despite the title I now held, I found myself searching for validation, proof that I wasn't already crumbling under the weight of the crown.

Alfred shrugged. "I've seen better, I've seen worse. Your dad's first speech was exactly the same."

"It was?"

"Almost identical. I assume you went off script?" Alfred chuckled to himself when I sheepishly nodded. "That was always a trick your father would pull. It was enough to give me a heart attack. No matter what he promised, he'd always find a way to wedge his own words into the speech. Even when it went wrong and he got a lashing in the papers for it, he always did it again. I think it was his way of keeping some control. Of letting us all know he'd never let this institution run his life."

Just the thought of my father was enough to widen the chasm I was standing on the brink of, desperately trying to stop from falling into its depths. In public—even alone—I had to keep it together, because if I let go of myself for even a second, I would splinter and break into a million pieces. With Jonathan, I'd felt safe to fall apart. Alone, I was terrified I wouldn't be able to put myself back together. My father's shoes felt cold and unforgiving. Had they felt that way for him too?

"I'm scared I'm already messing it up," I said before I could stop myself. "I don't think I'm ready. I thought we'd have more time together to figure all of this out. And I can't step away from it. I can't ignore the duty or pass it on to someone else."

I sighed, dropping my head into my hands. There were too many vines tangling together in my mind—my dad, the crown, Jonathan, Quinn Buckley and his web of lies that were inching closer to the truth. I worried about what Alfred would make of me now that I'd spoken my fears aloud, but his face didn't change. He didn't flinch.

"Every great king and queen has held the same concern. No matter who they were, where they came from, or their circumstances. Every single one of them had that doubt. Your father was no different. George was a man of honor and integrity, of grace and kindness, but there was a time when he didn't believe he could do it either."

Alfred's eyes were looking through me, as if envisioning a past where my dad was nearly thirty and preparing to take his oath as king. He smiled to himself at the thought. But the moment was fleeting, and his face settled into a solemn mask.

"I have something to give you which might help."

Alfred produced an envelope from inside his blazer. It was a rich cream color and perfectly smooth. I could see the royal crest where it had been sealed and my heart lurched when I read my name in my dad's slanted scrawl.

"Your father gave me this a while ago. He instructed me to give it to you only when he was no longer here. He said it was important that it went to you, and to nobody else. He made that last part very clear."

I took the envelope from Alfred's grasp, feeling at once like my father was near. "Why can nobody else know of it?"

Alfred's gaze flickered to the door and back again. "The palace has always been watched, Your Majesty. From outside, and within too. Your father knew better than anybody that deception and greed roamed these hallways." He nodded to the envelope in my hands. "I'm not privy to its contents, but I'm sure answers to your questions will reside in his writing. He wouldn't have wanted to leave you in the dark."

Alfred made to stand up, our conversation almost over. I stood to meet him, mind blooming with thoughts, stomach festering with dread.

"One last thing, James. Your father and I were close. I hope not to speak out of turn, but I'd consider our relationship one he held dear, which is why I speak on his behalf now." He bowed his head for a moment, considering his final words. "Do not trust a single soul within this palace. I can't answer your questions as to why, but it was something your father considered vital to his reign.

The throne is lonely to sit upon. However, those who surround it are not always the allies you believe or want them to be. To succeed as king, you must trust only yourself."

The note from Jonathan's room felt like a sack of stones in my pocket. It proved as much as anything that Alfred was right.

"My dad trusted you," I tried. Alfred snorted.

"You have a lot to learn yet, my boy. Your father never trusted a single person—myself included."

"What about my family? I can't trust them?"

Alfred opened his mouth to speak but was interrupted by a swift knock followed by the Drawing Room door opening without permission being granted. It was Gayle, an agitated look blanketing her features. Her eyes immediately flickered toward Alfred with ill-concealed irritation. As advisors to the two most important people in the palace, they'd never quite seen eye to eye, jostling for their own portion of power. Alfred, for his part, seemed just as happy to see Gayle.

"Alfred," she said in graceless greeting, as if the name offended her.

"What a pleasant surprise," Alfred responded, mirroring her sour tone.

Gayle ignored him and turned to face me. "Your mother is on her way. She wishes to speak with Alfred." Before she could say another word, my mum appeared in the doorway, gliding into the room. She rested a hand on my arm, giving it a gentle squeeze, then moved into Alfred's waiting embrace. Gayle stood stony-faced by the door, glaring intently at the opposite wall.

"I've missed you, Alfie," Mum said, drawing away.

"And I you," Alfred replied with a bow of his head.

Mum's warm smile wavered as the moment passed them by. In a quieter tone, one cushioned with a delicate ache, she said, "Is he home?" It was a punch to my gut. Alfred blinked quickly behind his glasses, his own grief soaking through his resistance. He nodded.

"He's home."

Mum closed her eyes, the traces of heartache she'd been harboring now washing over her entirely. But she wouldn't let the tide take her. Not here. Not yet, when there was still so much to do.

Now she turned to me. "I'll confirm the arrangements for a private vigil this afternoon before the public funeral in a week. You have more than enough to deal with right now. Let us worry about the details."

"We'll have it covered, Your Majesty," Gayle chimed in, her sour note from before forgotten.

Mum made to leave, but drew me into a last hug before she did. "I'm always here when you need me," she said, holding me tight. "You'll never have to do this alone." She kissed my cheek, then broke away, fixing Alfred with warm eyes. "Stay for tea, Alfred? We have so much to discuss. Indulge an old queen, won't you?"

Alfred smiled. "It'd be my pleasure, ma'am."

"James?" Mum cocked her head to one side, imploring me to accompany them. But the letter in my hand begged for my attention, and I couldn't wait a moment longer to read it. And there was also the overwhelming matter of Jonathan lingering around my shoulders. I shook my head, desperate to investigate further.

The three of them left the room together, Alfred with a swift bow and a pointed glance at the envelope. Then they were gone, leaving me alone with the words of my father. I slumped back down into the chair, ripped open the letter and began to read.

My son,

If you are reading this, then I assume that the worst has come to pass—my beautiful garden has been knocked off the top spot by Earl Fraser in the summer issue of Tatler, *and rather than bathe in ceaseless shame, I have simply turned to dust in order to avoid his gloating and put an end to my disgrace.*

Trust Dad to make a joke out of his own death. His friendly rivalry with Earl Fraser was one of the few pleasures he had allowed himself. Focusing on his plants and flowers kept him sane. He used to joke that everything else could go up in flames, so long as his garden survived.

I wish I could be with you now, to talk to you one last time. This letter is the hardest thing I have ever had to do in my reign as king, and it is made all the more difficult by the fact that, as I write this, we have no clue as to how much time we have left together. I hope it is years before you read this, allowing us to make memories that will far outlive us both.

So, you are now king. I wish I could give you a step-by-step, fail-safe guide to wearing the crown and sitting on the throne. It will seem of little comfort now when I say that there is no such thing—that there is no right or wrong way to carry out your reign. But, in time, you will see that to be the beauty. In time, you will figure out for yourself what it means to be king.

James, remember who you are when you wear the crown. Do not let it dim your light. I know better than anybody how the weight of it can wear you down into submission, to leave you a shell of the man you were once destined to be. But you must not let it win. Others will tell you that the crown must always come first. I beg you to ignore them, and to follow your instincts as you navigate this new world. Despite what anybody says, it is you who must always come first, before the crown and its demands. Always remember that you are not one entity fused together under oath and duty. You are separate from the crown, in the same way that it is separate from you. If you are to keep your head, you must always remember that fact. Do not let James Albert Arthur Hampton fade away, to be replaced by King James III. Learn to live with them both in harmony, side by side.

It is not up to me to tell you how to lead. That is for you, and you alone, to decide. But I would remind you of the conversation we had when you were still a boy. I remember how you feared Edward would always make a better king, how you wished you could swap places rather than face a world that might agree with your own worst thoughts. But I hope you will remember what I said then, and how I still feel today. You are the heir to the throne for a reason. While you fear your brother holds the traits most fitting to be king, never doubt that it is you who possesses the qualities that will lead to a long and prosperous reign.

My greatest advice is simple—trust in yourself and nobody else. I admit that allies are crucial, but the title of king or queen falls to one person, and one person only. Give trust sparingly to those you hold dear, and even then, only with caution. It is not the enemy you need to be wary of, but the friend who schemes with a smile. Trust laid in the wrong hands can prove perilous. Be sure of who you let in.

Please, do not mourn for what you have lost. I will always be with you, and I will always be your dad—no matter what. Remember that above all else.

I love you. Long live the king. Long live my son.

The tears fell freely, landing on the page in my lap and smudging some of the words. Just holding the letter felt like he was by my side again—like me and Eddie were kids in the garden playing football with Dad in goal, while Alfred waited patiently by the door with a phone call on hold. The weight of his words cascaded like a waterfall over me, relentless and yet freeing. It opened something inside me, a seed that had begun to flower.

I could do this. Fear and grief had threatened to keep me captive, but they wouldn't hold me back. I wouldn't disappoint my father. I couldn't. And I wouldn't let secrets or blackmail stand in the way of making him proud.

CHAPTER NINE

THE EYES OF
THE PALACE

The security office in Buckingham Palace hid in the heart of the building, tucked away like a secret. It was a small fortress that housed the team tasked with protecting us at all costs. Few had access beyond its metal doors, which could only be opened with verified identification cards that had to be signed off by the head of security and the monarch. Even as a prince able to go anywhere in the palace, I'd never been down there. But it was there that I was heading now, with only the vaguest beginnings of a plan in mind.

"You don't want to tell me what this is about?" Peter said, throwing me a sideways glance as we marched quickly through the palace. I was desperate not to be caught, to keep my cards close to my chest, so I'd chosen a longer route with quieter hallways. Every time we saw a member of the palace staff, I ducked my head, as if that was going to hide me from sight. It hadn't escaped Peter's attention that we were clearly doing something he should know about.

"The less you know, the better," I whispered, although that wasn't quite true. I needed to know what had happened to Jonathan, and Gayle had proved that I couldn't rely on her to tell me. She was keeping something to herself, and I wanted to know what. Peter, one of the few I trusted with my life, could be my only ally.

When we finally reached the formidable doors, Peter produced a card from his pocket and swiped it. There was a beep and a green light, followed by a hiss as the doors slid open to reveal an almost empty security office. One man lounged in front of a bank of TV screens and controls, his feet up on the desk. Each screen cast a different view of the palace both inside and out. There were few places that weren't in the eye of security. If you weren't inside someone's personal living quarters, you could bet that you were being watched. Peter cleared his throat and the guard leaped up from his chair, his face draining of color when he laid eyes on me.

"Nice to see you hard at work, Hutchins," Peter muttered.

"Your Majesty," Hutchins said, snapping into a stiff bow and trying to rearrange his crinkled shirt. "How can I help?"

"I need to see CCTV from last night and this morning," I said, ignoring Peter's frown. "Everything from around midnight onward."

Hutchins grimaced, looking down at the floor. "I'm sorry, that's not possible," he said, barely audible. If he looked pale before, he appeared frighteningly ill now.

"What do you mean, not possible?" I replied.

Hutchins's jaw was so tense, I feared his teeth might shatter in his mouth. "The CCTV was switched off, sir."

"Switched off? For what possible reason were the cameras cut?" Peter demanded sternly.

"There was a request from up high that they be switched off until morning." By now, Hutchins looked like he wanted to swan dive off the palace roof rather than continue this interrogation.

"From up high?" Peter turned to me. I shook my head. "Well," Peter continued, "if the demand didn't come from the king, who did it come from?"

Hutchins hesitated. "I was instructed to keep that to myself."

I stepped farther into the room, closing the space between us. "And you're now instructed to speak by the king. So, I'll ask again—who requested that the cameras be switched off?"

Hutchins still refused to meet my eye. "Prince Edward, sir."

I swallowed hard, trying to hide my emotions. "Eddie gave the instruction?"

"It's not a rare request, sir. He instructs that they be turned off every time there are guests invited to the palace for one of his gatherings. If footage of those parties was to ever get into the wrong hands, it would be worse than bad news."

I breathed a sigh of relief. Eddie was just being cautious. You didn't know who you could trust on either side of the palace gates—it was better to be safe than sorry.

"Who else knows that the cameras are switched off on these occasions?" Peter said, glancing at the screens. "That information could be a massive security breach if the wrong person found out."

"Only Edward," Hutchins said immediately. Then he sighed. "There are a few others too. Apparently, His Royal Highness has been known to tell other guests at the party, although I can't be sure of who exactly. And Gayle knows, although she didn't seem to mind so long as there wasn't any trouble."

Of course Gayle knew. I'd always guessed that she was aware of the parties, and she would've made it her business to gather every detail about them.

"So there's no footage from last night?" I blew out a breath. There went my plan.

"No, but there is from this morning, sir. The cameras were switched back on at five a.m. and have been running as normal ever since." Hutchins gestured to the screens, each one blinking into a new scene every few seconds. He pulled out a chair for me and sat down at the controls, waiting for my instructions.

What did I want to see? If there was nothing from last night, then it was impossible to know where Jonathan had gone. But what had happened before that? And would there be anything of interest afterward? The person who'd left that blackmailing note had surely been caught.

"Pull up the footage outside my quarters from last night, before the cameras were switched off," I said, making up my mind. It was a long shot, but maybe there was something.

Hutchins fiddled with the controls, replacing the pictures on-screen with different angles from the corridors surrounding my quarters. The time stamp in the corner said eleven p.m. He turned a dial in the center of the desk and time began to skip forward, the corridors remaining empty until eleven forty-five when Eddie appeared. Hutchins slowed it down and we watched as my brother swept into my quarters without knocking, bottle of champagne in hand. My mind flicked back to pushing Jonathan out of bed as the sound of footsteps approached.

Again, Hutchins moved the dial and the screens jumped forward to eleven fifty-six when Eddie left. Several minutes later, I followed. And then nothing. The corridors remained empty until the screens went black. I sighed. There was nothing that I didn't already know.

"Okay, try this morning," I said.

"Not so fast." Peter came up behind my chair, peering more closely at one of the screens. "Back it up just a fraction." Hutchins obliged and the empty corridor leading up to my quarters flicked onto the screen again. "There, in the corner." Peter pointed to where the shadow of a person had appeared. Another second, and they would've walked right into the frame.

"Was that you returning to your quarters?" Peter looked at me and I shook my head. I hadn't returned until

110

after I'd gone to Jonathan's room. Besides, this was before the cameras cut. Jonathan had still been in my bed.

"Then what business did anybody have to be in this corridor at that time of night? There's only one place they could be going, and that's straight to your door." I leaned in closer, but there was no use in trying to decipher the shapeless shadow. It was barely a silhouette—just a smudge in the corner of the screen.

Shrugging, Hutchins clicked a few buttons and the screens changed, this time showing the corridors lit up by the breaking of day. He began to move the dial, but I stopped him.

"Not my quarters this time. I need to see the corridor leading out into the gardens, where staff quarters are based." I kept my eyes locked on the screens, ignoring the glance Peter and Hutchins exchanged with each other. They might not question my instructions out loud, but their curiosity floated in the air around us.

If I wanted to back out, keep myself and my secrets hidden, now was my last chance. A few more seconds and Hutchins would bring up the footage that showed me creeping down the corridor and entering Jonathan's bedroom. But I needed answers.

Hutchins found several angles of the hallway and began dialing through the footage. Jonathan's door was easy to spot since I'd left it slightly open the night before, exactly as I'd found it. I focused on it as the morning wore on, cleaners, maids, butlers and aides roaming the halls. They all passed the door without a second glance.

And then there was me. Hutchins slowed it down, letting the tape play at regular speed. It was the least of my problems, but it was nothing less than mortifying to see myself shuffling down the corridor like I'd stolen the crown jewels and was plotting to scale the garden walls to sell them on the black market.

"It's lucky you're the king, sir. I'm not sure we'd have a place for you in our ranks," Peter said with a smirk, as the me from this morning looked over his shoulder to check he wasn't being followed.

Peter and Hutchins grinned, until they watched me do one final check and then slip into Jonathan's room. Peter's eyes narrowed, darting from the screen to me and then to Hutchins.

"Want to give us a minute here?" Peter said in Hutchins's direction. Hutchins wheeled his chair back and slinked out of the room, probably breathing a bit easier now we weren't on his case about the cameras.

"Isn't that Jonathan's room, sir?" Peter asked, taking Hutchins's seat and hitting pause on the controls. I fought the urge to lie, but I was too far gone now. There was no going back.

"Yes. I think we might have a problem."

Peter sat up straighter, locking me in place with dissecting eyes. "What kind of problem, exactly?"

Snippets of my father's letter floated around my head, drifting in and out of my grasp. As far as Dad and Alfred were concerned, I couldn't trust anybody. But I had to lay my trust, or at least part of it, in someone else's hands, and Peter was at the top of my list. His job was to keep me safe from harm. And so, I explained it all.

I made a long story short, skipping past the fleeting glances and long nights alone that had led to our first kiss; skirting around the promise that it'd never happen again, only for the thrill to draw us back together. I'd never publicly shown an interest in boys before—although I hadn't shown an interest in girls either, until I was forced into a situation with Ophelia—but I maneuvered myself around any shame, because why should I be embarrassed? What indignity should I feel? I wouldn't bear an anchor of disgrace over who my heart had chosen to fall for. I refused.

Peter's face remained impassive, taking in every word. But his jaw tensed as I explained what had happened the night before, and how Jonathan was now nowhere to be found.

"You heard someone inside his room when you were at his door last night? But you don't know if it was him or somebody else?" I nodded. Peter stared at the screens, no doubt cursing Hutchins for allowing the cameras to be turned off. "His drawers are empty. The place is a mess. And somebody left a note. It's not much to go on, but I guess we better start with finding out who left it behind."

Peter turned the dial and the screens leaped into action once more. We didn't have to wait long. I tensed as I saw the shadow move into frame, sure I was about to see my brother appear on the screen. But it wasn't Eddie. It was Gayle. She hurried down the hall, clearly in a rush. I held my breath as she drew close to Jonathan's door, only breaking her stride to check behind her before she grabbed the handle and disappeared inside.

Peter leaned forward on the desk, moving the dial fractionally until Gayle reappeared, hastening back the way she'd come just as Eddie came into frame on another screen. They missed each other by half a second, Gayle ducking through a door as Eddie rounded the corner. He strode along the wall, disappearing through the garden door as I exited Jonathan's room, whipping my head round in time to see him go.

He hadn't left the note. Gayle had.

I felt stupid for thinking for even a second that he might have anything to do with it. What would he want with Jonathan? The blank I drew was answer enough. But what did Gayle want with him? Why would she leave a note that said his secrets were safe with her, and then all but threaten that they weren't? And what secrets was she referring to? Answering one question had only opened a door to reveal a swarm of others.

"I guess we've found who left your note then," Peter said, leaning back into his chair and running his hands over his face. He blew out a long breath. "I don't want to dive off the deep end here, but if he's simply disappeared into thin air, that doesn't look good."

"You don't say," I muttered. "I've tried to call him but his phone is switched off. Gayle told me that he'd texted her to say he was ill. But what—"

I was interrupted by the screens, which had kept playing the footage in the background. My conversation with

Grigor had flashed by and we'd headed off in different directions. But as the time ticked by at double speed, more people appeared in the hallway, gathering by Jonathan's door.

Peter slowed the footage back down and we watched as four cleaners shared bin bags out between themselves. They propped open the door and disappeared for a moment, before one of them returned with a bag now full and tied. This went on for a few minutes, more and more bags piling up in the corridor, until eventually, the last one was added and the door was closed and locked.

"Follow them," I said, perched on the edge of my seat. Peter didn't hesitate, flipping between cameras on various screens and keeping up with the cleaners' movements until they disappeared through a door.

"There aren't any cameras there, but I bet I know where they'll end up," Peter said, hunching over the controls. He hit a few buttons and a screen on my left flickered to show the back of the palace. Sure enough, the cleaners came into shot, struggling to fit through the door with the bags in their hands.

"The bins are out there," Peter said, tracing the screen with his finger. "But why are they throwing those bags out?"

"They're making sure they've got rid of Jonathan altogether," I realized out loud. "They're cleaning up every last trace of him." An unnerving chill crept up my spine as I watched the bags being tossed into a dumpster, which was then slammed shut.

"I don't know what's going on here, but Gayle isn't telling the whole truth, that's for sure. If he's ill, why would they clear his room out?" Peter rested his chin in his palm, thinking hard. "Have you got anything to do this morning?"

"Oh, you know, just the small matter of enduring my second day as king and wondering if every nightmare I've ever had about the crown will now come true."

Peter hopped up from his chair. "Perfect, it sounds like you've got all day then. Let me make a quick phone call." Without any further explanation, he stepped out of the room, leaving me alone with the bank of cameras and a million questions I wasn't sure I wanted the answers to.

Things were falling apart around me. I'd been king little more than twenty-four hours and my kingdom was already in jeopardy. There were too many things stacked up against me—the grief, the fear, the confusion and the questions. The emptiness. The chasm was opening wider and wider, and I feared if I fell into it, I'd never be able to climb back out of its depths.

Jonathan's door was frozen in time on one of the screens. I stared at it, looking for something obvious that I'd missed. I only had half the story, and what little I did know made no sense. But I knew Jonathan. I had to believe that, or the last few months had been nothing less than a fantasy. He wouldn't just leave. Even if he was hurt or angry, he wouldn't have walked away from me in my darkest hour. So where had he gone?

Peter pocketed his phone as he came back into the room, his face giving almost nothing away. But I could see the tension in his jaw, the slight darkening of his eyes, the crease of his brow.

"That was the head of staff on the phone. He confirmed that they've emptied Jonathan's room." He dropped his gaze for just a moment—long enough for me to feel the world tilt on its axis. "Apparently there was an order made by Gayle to have it cleaned out. Jonathan isn't coming back."

It didn't make sense. Nothing about it did.

Peter sat down in his chair, hands folded in his lap and head slightly cocked to the side. "I don't mean to be blunt, Your Majesty, but do you think Jonathan's in danger?"

I blanked, each breath I took shallower than the last, as if the air in the room were running out. My mind was in overdrive, racing around in circles.

"I think if Gayle is involved, then he can't be in danger. He *can't* be. There's got to be an explanation behind this." It sounded like I was trying to convince myself and doing a terrible job in the process. Peter, eyes glued to the screens, seemed to be weighing something up in his head.

"Do you trust her?"

"With my life," I said immediately. It was only after they shot out into the room that I realized those words would've been true yesterday—today I wasn't so sure.

Peter nodded toward one of the screens, where a camera now showed a live feed of the hallway leading up to my quarters. Gayle had just arrived at my door and was knocking impatiently. The urgency of it spiked an instinct in me that something was wrong.

"Don't tell her that you know what's going on," he said. "Not yet. You'll be showing your hand too early. I'll do some digging to see if I can find Jonathan, or at least any more information about what happened last night."

Peter glanced at Gayle on the screen. "If she said Jonathan was ill, then she can only use that excuse for a short while longer. Eventually she'll have to switch to something else, or she'll have to confess the truth. Let's just bide our time until we know more."

It was too much to take in. One of the few people I could trust inside these hellish walls had been thrown into doubt. The list was already short, and now it was threatening to be nothing but a blank page. Peter made for the door, but another question occurred to me before he could reach it.

"Should I be worried?" I squared my shoulders as the question I really wanted to ask formed on my lips. "Am I safe?"

Peter let the silence take charge of the room for a moment before he met my eyes and nodded. "As long as you have me, Your Majesty, you are safe."

I wanted to hug him. Right then, he was the closest thing I had to a father. It gave me comfort to know I had someone by my side, no matter what.

He held the door open as I prepared to face whatever Gayle had in store for me. "Remember, Your Majesty— act normal. You're the king. Nobody can hurt you."

I let my legs begin to steer me down the corridor, away from the security office and toward my quarters, wondering if what Peter had said was true, and if I now walked in the heart of the palace . . . or stood alone behind enemy lines.

CHAPTER TEN

THE KING AND THE JESTER

The last person I wanted to see was Cassandra, but I'd barely walked two corridors when I bumped into the Princess of Faces herself, her eyes glinting as she cast them over me and saw that I was alone.

"If it isn't the darling king himself. Keeping a firm hold of those secrets you're hiding, I hope? I'm surprised they haven't all just spilled out into the open, one by one." My skin crawled as Cassandra maneuvered herself so she was blocking my path. "Why in such a rush? You're not hiding something this very minute, are you?"

I tried to convince myself she was bluffing, that all she knew was what Quinn had said in his interview. But my instincts prodded my suspicion. If she knew anything about me and Jonathan—or even the situation with Ophelia, a secret that had been kept inside a tight circle—it wouldn't take long for it to become public knowledge. Cassandra had her own gains to be made by casting me in a bad light, and I had little doubt that she'd go further than anybody else to see me off the throne altogether.

"You can trust me with your secrets, you know," she went on, a smirk pulling at her lips. "I won't tell a single soul."

"I'd rather try my chances with Quinn Buckley than let you anywhere near my secrets," I snapped.

"Ah, the lion has found his roar. Such a shame it's little more than a feeble bark." Cassandra was enjoying this too much, the smile on her face twisted by wicked intentions. "For a moment, I thought you were admitting that there were indeed secrets to hide...."

I couldn't hold her eyes. They were burning hot and searing into me. But I knew as soon as I'd looked away that she smelled blood in the water and was circling for the kill.

"So, there *is* something to hide. How terribly exciting. What a shame it'd be if those secrets found themselves in the wrong hands. A canary might sing inside these palace walls if it heard a song worth telling."

The ominous threat retreated as Eddie came bowling around the corner, pausing when he saw us, before coming to stand by my side with a cool smile. "Which face did you wake up and put on today then, Cass? I'm just dying to know."

Cassandra didn't even blink. "If it isn't the eternal deputy, destined to always be the spare to the heir. Tell me, how does it feel knowing you'll always be second place? You should start charging him rent for living in your shadow, James."

Eddie tensed by my side, and my body felt the blow too. As brothers and heirs to the throne, we were fated to be jealous of each other—him for always having to come in second, and me for craving the shade in which he could live out his private life, mostly in peace and away from the scrutiny of a billion eyes.

"Well, as much as I'd love to stand around watching you two play king and jester, I've got places to be," Cassandra said dryly, slipping past us with her head held high. "Oh, and, James? Keep my spot warm for me, won't you? And don't worry, Eddie—you can still be my jester when I take over."

Eddie wheeled around just before she turned the corner, barely containing his fury. "That tiara will slip someday, and I just hope I'm around to watch when it happens."

Cassandra paused, drinking in the moment with a smile on her face. "You wish, deputy."

And with a cruel laugh she disappeared.

Eddie's hands were balled into tight fists as he stared at the empty spot where she'd stood. When I tried to reach for him, he pulled away, snapping out of his trance. I didn't want to pile more troubles onto him, but I needed to tell him about Jonathan and Gayle. I didn't know how to navigate this alone. Dad had said I needed allies, and my brother didn't seem like a bad place to start.

"I need to speak to you," I said, but I was interrupted by my phone buzzing in my pocket. Heart in my mouth and every other thought abandoned, I reached for it. Jonathan? But then Eddie's phone buzzed too, and when my own screen lit up, I found a text from Gayle.

> Sorry to interrupt your day,
> Your Majesty, but we need to
> talk again. It's urgent.
> We'll be in the Conference Room
> when you're ready.

"What now?" I sighed. I was still unsure if I could trust myself to be within a meter of Gayle when her deception was fresh in my mind.

"I don't know why I have to be there," Eddie muttered darkly. "It'll only be about you. What does she need me for?" Before I could answer, he stalked off in the direction of the King's Conference Room, leaving me to trail in his wake.

Mum and Gayle were already seated when we arrived, huddled around one end of the large table, untouched glasses of water before them. Eddie looked as if he'd rather open the window and tumble out of it than sit down, something I could relate to. Mum wore a shadow of exhaustion mixed with nervous tension on her face. She stood up to hug me and then Eddie as we entered, and I took the seat at the head of the table that had been left empty for my arrival. Gayle sat on my left, opposite Mum, while Eddie took the seat next to her.

"What are we celebrating now then?" I tried to joke. Eddie breathed a laugh, but otherwise it was met with silence. And I soon realized why.

"We have reason to believe that Quinn Buckley is gearing up to write an exposé on the Royal Family to follow his article in the *Daily Eye* this morning," Gayle said. My heart plummeted to my stomach. "We have our own moles inside various publications, to keep us abreast of what's happening and beat negative stories to the punch. But it's been impossible to get ears within the *Eye*. They run differently from all the newspapers. They're backed by a billionaire who couldn't give a flying hoot about the monarchy and what it stands for. If anything, he'd love to tear it down himself. Buckley has the full weight of his support behind him, not to mention his money too. It's why Buckley's stories have been picked up over the last few months."

Mum shifted in her chair, sitting a little straighter. Until recently, most of those stories had been about her. Now Quinn's pen was circling me instead.

"Although we don't have direct ears within the *Eye*, we do have them elsewhere. It seems that Buckley has been bragging among his peers, promising that this story will be the start of something explosive." It was Gayle's turn to fidget uncomfortably in her chair. A promise from Buckley was enough to set all of us on edge.

"Okay, and what is it?" I said, trying to bury my nerves.

Gayle shook her head. "We don't know exactly. All we

do know is that it's about you." Of course it was. Why else would Gayle be looking at me like I was a ticking bomb waiting to explode? But what had Buckley unearthed exactly, and why was it supposedly so damning?

"We're doing more work to uncover whatever story will be coming out of the *Eye*'s offices, but until then, we need to sit tight and figure out a strategy. We'll keep our code of silence for now, but we must have a backup option in case we need to distract or deny." Gayle sighed, the day wearing on her shoulders already. I would've felt sorry for her if it wasn't me in the firing line. Or if the footage from this morning wasn't playing on a continuous loop in my head.

"What could it be?" Mum directed her question at me, as if I'd be willing to lay bare everything so we could better prepare to deflect the missile heading our way. We all knew each family member had secrets purposefully kept in the dark. Family or not, some things needed to be kept closely guarded, and I wasn't about to shed a spotlight on them now.

"It could be anything," I said with a shrug. "How do we even know that what's coming will be true? It's not like Buckley or the *Eye* have ever concerned themselves with separating fact from fiction before."

Gayle nodded half-heartedly. "True, but this feels different. Usually, these stories are floating around before their publication, so we can get hold of what's to come. But whatever Buckley's up to, he's made sure to cover his tracks. Anything that secret can't be good."

"What if it's Ophelia?" Until now, Eddie had sat still, eyes cast down into his lap, his hands locked together. We all turned our heads to him and he finally looked up. "It's the obvious one, isn't it? Quinn's already said that his 'sources' have called the relationship a sham. What if he's confirmed it? All of those public appearances will be outed as a lie, and then the country will turn on James even more than they already have."

I swallowed the panic that reared its head, knowing there was little use for it now. It had never been my idea to begin with, and I'd never wanted to put Ophelia in that position, but I'd selfishly gone along with it to hide my own truths. Now everything was tilting, threatening to come crashing down—not just for me, but Ophelia too. Her father, Richard Budd, was one of the wealthiest business-men in the country. Or had been anyway, until his gam-bling stranded him in deep waters and debts threatened to drown him. The Budds had been seen as a respectable fam-ily with connections in high places. Now, their names had been dragged through the mud for all to see and they were quickly plummeting from their high society pedestal.

"Ophelia's the only possible story it could be, right?" Eddie went on. "It's not like you're hiding a body in your closet." A body, no, but we all had skeletons.

"Okay, so we should talk to Ophelia, make sure she's all right and prepared for what might be to come before Buckley can get ahold of her," said Mum.

I couldn't hide the alarm on my face. "You think Buckley's going to track her down and use her against us?"

"Oh, without a doubt. Someone like Ophelia would be useful to Buckley. I'd be surprised if he hadn't got his claws into her already. There's no telling how much money they'd offer her to turn informant, and we all know the Budds are somewhat struggling right now. House on the market and furniture up for sale, are they not?" Mum flicked her eyes to Gayle, who nodded soberly. No doubt she'd known all about that before approaching Ophelia to be a part of this scheme in the first place. She'd have known that our family's status would offer a life raft to the Budd's tattered reputation. Ophelia might've agreed to the ploy because she was my friend, but I couldn't ignore the fact that she might've also gone along with it for her own gains too. However, if this blew up in smoke, then her family's reputation would be obliterated entirely. Ophelia needed this to work as much as I did.

There were three sharp knocks at the door, and Peter walked in when Gayle called for him to enter. I felt some relief to have him close again.

"Ah, Peter, right on time." Gayle gestured to a seat, which Peter took, resting a reassuring hand on my shoulder as he passed. "You've assembled a team together?"

Peter nodded. "A small group. Nobody outside of the team knows a thing."

"*I* don't know a thing," I pointed out.

"We need to keep on top of this. If the story is as explosive as Buckley says, then we have to move first." Gayle paused, collecting her words. "I recommend using Peter and his team to launch surveillance on both Ophelia and Buckley. To keep an eye on them both, so we're not blindsided should he manage to weasel his way into her favor. If anything, shadowing Buckley might help to shed some light on whatever he's planning."

It didn't sit right with me. Buckley, I could understand, but turning on Ophelia as if she were already the enemy when we hadn't even given her a chance, when we'd been the ones to drag her into this mess in the first place, smelled rotten.

"I agree we should keep an eye on Buckley. But I want protection *only* for Ophelia—no surveillance." Gayle went to open her mouth, but I plowed on. "She's a friend before anything else. If that is the story Quinn's writing, then it's about her as much as it is about me, and she'll need protection too. We can't just leave her to fend for herself. So, give Ophelia a protection officer, watch Buckley, and I have one more request." I hesitated, glancing at Eddie.

"I want surveillance on Cassandra."

My demand was met with a tense silence, one that overwhelmed the room. Gayle looked as if I'd just slapped her across the face, Mum's eyes had narrowed at the mere mention of her name and Eddie couldn't help but offer a fleeting smile. Peter jotted it down in his notepad.

"Your Majesty, with all due respect, why Cassandra?" he asked.

"I don't trust her. I never have, and I'm not about to now. She desperately wants to be queen and I believe she'd do anything to move me and Eddie out of the way."

"But, James, she's your cousin," Gayle blustered. "She

127

wouldn't jeopardize the crown for her own selfish gains. She wants to see it succeed as much as we do." Mum snorted, drumming her nails on the table.

"I want Buckley and Cassandra under surveillance," I said with finality. Mum gave me a reassuring nod of her head, telling me that I was doing the right thing.

"And send word to Ophelia that I'd like to see her tonight. We should talk about all of this, *together*, and figure out what we're going to do next." I stood up, ending the meeting. "Anything else?"

Gayle shook her head woodenly.

"Perfect," I muttered, and left the room.

CHAPTER ELEVEN

FROM ONE KING TO ANOTHER

The one thing I'd yet to do since becoming king was leave the confines of the palace itself. As dangerous as staying within its web seemed, it paled in comparison to being beyond its protection. As a royal, I had one of the greatest protection services in the world, headed up by a man I trusted wholeheartedly. But something about stepping outside of those gates and away from the royal bubble filled me with dread.

"It's okay, Your Majesty. We're going to take it one step at a time," Peter said as I checked myself over in the mirror once more. It was late afternoon, and the moment I'd been dreading had already arrived. It was time to go and see my dad.

"You'll have me and Walsh in the car with you, plus two cars of security ahead and behind us at all times.

Police motorbikes will provide the escort and other police units will be on standby along the route too. It's a short trip down the Mall, a quick right and we'll be at Westminster Hall in no time. Once you're inside, you're as safe as can be." Peter listed it all off as if we were going to the supermarket for a loaf of bread and some milk. But I'd known him long enough to hear the slight edge to his voice, each word straining to hold itself together.

I needed to focus on something else, something to take my mind off what was coming, and as Peter held the door of my quarters open, his shirt collar moved to reveal a gold chain around his neck.

"I didn't know you wore a necklace," I said, clinging on to this one small and unimportant detail.

Peter straightened up abruptly, falling into step next to me as we made our way down to the east entrance where our cars were waiting. The afternoon sun slanted in through the windows of the corridor, patches of shade separated by blemishes of golden summer light.

"It's a locket," he said.

"Don't they usually have pictures inside them?" It was taking all of my strength to focus on the necklace and not head straight back to the safety of my quarters.

Peter seemed hesitant but stopped and reached inside his shirt to retrieve the locket, opening its clasp. It contained two black-and-white pictures, one on either side, small and delicate and faded with age. Both were of Peter, holding a baby. He wasn't smiling at the camera, or smiling at all—in both, he was looking down into the baby's eyes, the only thing in the world he could see at that exact moment.

"I didn't know you had a family," I murmured, hating myself for not knowing that fact about someone I spent every day of my life with. But Peter shook his head, closing the locket and tucking it away once more before continuing down the corridor.

"I don't, Your Majesty. Passed away," he said tightly. I went to open my mouth, to apologize for being so stupid and reckless, but he cut me off before I could. "It's okay, sir. It was a long time ago now."

Two people stood on either side of the main doors as I approached, opening them wide to reveal a squad of suited security guards lined up outside by the cars, awaiting their mission. One guard held open the door of my vehicle, a sleek black Bentley kitted out with reinforced steel and bullet-proof windows, with a miniature flag—a Royal Standard, the symbol of the sovereign—flying from its roof. Another stood idle behind it for Mum and Eddie, along with a huddle of Range Rovers that would make up the security in our motorcade. Leaving home for anything, big or small, was an operation, and not one that was ever taken lightly.

Before I could climb into the car, the voice of my mum called out, stopping me in my tracks. She walked through the doors of the palace as if she were floating, dressed up in black as rich as a starry night sky. Her hair had been swept back into a low bun and a string of elegant pearls was wrapped around her neck. Eddie, in his suit, followed her out into the sun.

Even though I was slightly taller, Mum placed her hands on my shoulders, peering up at me. "It's just like any other trip, you hear me? Don't pay any attention to what the crowds are doing, or what they're saying. Focus on getting there, and we'll be right behind you the whole way."

It sank in then that for the first time, I'd be riding alone, as the monarch often did when they weren't married. Sure, I'd have Peter and the driver with me, but they'd be sitting up front, leaving me alone in the back. I could request Mum or Eddie, or even both, to ride with me, but I didn't want to look like a child who needed their hand held. I'd already been slated by Quinn Buckley for breaking down during my speech. Too many people still saw me as a boy, instead of the king. An impostor wearing a crown. It was time to stand up straight and prove to them, to my country and to my dad that I could do this.

Mum gave me a squeeze and a reassuring smile before slipping into the car behind, Eddie already in place. The doors were closed behind them as another guard jumped into the passenger seat next to the driver.

"Ready, sir?" Peter coaxed, standing by the open door of my car.

"As I'll ever be, I suppose." I slid into the nest of comfortable leather, the seats cooled to just the right temperature against the August heat. Peter closed the door after me and jogged around the back to get into place next to the driver, Walsh.

"Afternoon, Your Majesty," Walsh said, starting the

car and gently revving the engine. "I had a quick peek out front about an hour ago. Just a small gathering, all holding flowers and the like. Nothing to worry about, sir."

"Thank you," I murmured, watching the palace slide away past the window as we edged up toward the gates. I twisted in my seat to see Eddie and Mum's car following a few meters behind, the security vehicles on their tail.

The Range Rover in front blocked my view as we approached the gates, but I knew they were already open for our departure. As the security car ahead slipped through them, flanked by police motorbikes and their flashing blue lights, I saw the waiting crowd for the first time.

It was much like the day before, when we'd stepped outside an eternity ago to conduct the Grief Parade. Except there were even more people lining the roads, stretching down the Mall as far as I could see. Some clasped bunches of flowers, while others held signs; some cried while their neighbors held up phones with outstretched arms to take pictures as we passed. I couldn't help but look as we drove by them, the sudden weight of the moment pinning me to my seat. These people were here because of my dad, but they were also here to see me.

I couldn't define the sensation wrapping itself around my spine, creeping into every crevice of my body it could find. I didn't know whether to smile and wave or just burst into tears. Some waved, calling out for me, trying to reach me through the car window, even though they were separated from the road by metal barricades. Some settled for throwing their flowers so that petals rained down on the windshield like velvet tears.

As we reached the end of the Mall and drove through the Admiralty Arch, I saw the crowds standing together as one in Trafalgar Square, a handful of people having scaled the lion statues for a better glimpse of our cars. They waved and cheered, throwing their signs up in the air.

OUR KING!

THE KING FOR US!

RIP KING GEORGE!

GO BACK TO WHERE YOU CAME FROM!

I recoiled as I read the last one, sweeping my eyes over the signs to try and find it again, but the car crawled on past Downing Street, heading for Westminster Abbey without pause. I turned the words I'd thought I'd read— *known* I'd read—over in my head.

I would never be king for some people because I was different. Not by lineage or anything else that would make me unfit to wear the crown, but by skin color. The brown of my body was an insult to them, as if being darker than any king or queen before me made me illegitimate. I could wear this crown for a hundred years, cure the country of every pain and rid it of every evil, and it would never be enough for those who refused to accept that their king was Black. That the first heir to the throne was Black. That their Queen Mother was Black. That wouldn't change, no matter what happened now.

And I could sit and wish with all my being that they'd change their minds, that by some great miracle they'd see the truth: that being Black didn't make me lesser than. But it would be in vain. So, I was left with two options. I could beg those people—I could get on my knees and plead with them. Or I could continue being king for those who already accepted me as I was. For people like Michael, the kid who'd given me the flowers during the Grief Parade, who saw someone who looked like him sitting on the throne and wearing the crown. I could stick two fingers up at the rest of them and get on with my reign.

"We're here, sir," Peter said evenly as the car began to slow down.

The aura of Westminster Abbey lay like a fine fog around Parliament Square, its splendor peeking through glimpses behind the trees. But we weren't heading there. Not yet. That would be where the funeral took place the following weekend, but my father's body now lay in rest across the street in Westminster Hall. It would be open for people to come and pay their respects, but this afternoon it would just be us. This was the last time we would be able to share a private moment with him.

The car slipped through a security gate and was welcomed into an internal carpark attached to the hall. Peter jumped out of the car while it was still moving, sweeping our surroundings for any signs of danger. Even though the dozens of armed security placed around Westminster should've kept any risk at bay, he was never one to get too comfortable. When Peter confirmed the coast was clear, he opened my door. I unfolded myself from my seat, straightening my blazer and tugging on my cuffs as I headed for the open doors that'd take us into the building itself. Mum and Eddie's car pulled in behind ours, both of them following in my wake.

There was a somber mood inside that clung to every brick, drifting up into every corner of the magnificent, vaulted ceiling. And there, on a stone plinth, lay my father's coffin, draped in the royal flag and adorned with flowers and wreaths. My breath caught in the back of my throat, gluing me to the spot. Mum and Eddie came to stand beside me, taking in the scene before us. A gentle melody played by a hidden organ filled the silence, summoning my emotions to the surface, and I let my tears flow freely.

"Let's do this together," Mum said quietly, her own grief tugging at every word.

We walked through the hall as one, alone but for each other. I couldn't see anything but the coffin, the edges of everything else blurred by my tears. When we reached the plinth, I paused, a shiver of existential dread washing over me. I knew my dad was dead. I'd known that fact, repeated it over and over in my head to make sense of this new hand that life had dealt us. But now, standing before the coffin, it felt final.

He was gone. He wasn't ever coming back. There would never be another moment shared, not another embrace, unique to him, that I'd find comfort in. Grief bloomed from the poisonous seed that had been planted in the deepest part of my soul. It threatened to engulf me from the inside out. To break me.

Eddie went first, taking the few steps up to the coffin.

He clasped his hands together behind his back, looking down on where our father lay, his shoulders rigid and still. He murmured something we couldn't hear, just a breath on the wind. Then he turned, head bowed, ducked past us, and strode out of the hall.

"He'll be fine," Mum whispered, taking my hand and giving it a squeeze. "Shall we?"

I nodded, thankful that I didn't have to do this alone. We approached the plinth and took the steps together. I urged myself forward, resisting the impulse to back away.

Mum lay her hand on the coffin, a small gasp parting from her lips as she made contact. It opened the floodgates, a sob wrenching itself from her body. She pitched forward with the next one, splaying herself over the coffin's lid as if she could reach my dad within for one final embrace. My heart ached with misery as the sobs of my mother struck my ears, beating down the last of my defenses.

The moment was too intimate, shared between partners who'd lived a life together in love. So I stepped away, retreating to the back of the hall. I stood with my head lowered by the doors, the murmurs of my mother's final goodbye lost in the gulf between us.

After a few minutes, she leaned down and gave the coffin a last kiss. "I will always love you," I heard her say defiantly. Then she peeled herself away without another glance, floating back to me with tears glistening on her cheeks, her eyes shimmering pools. She fell into me, wrapping her arms around my back. We stayed that way for a moment before I felt her take a deep breath and she pulled away.

"Have your time—as much of it as you need. We'll be waiting outside."

"You won't wait with me?" I asked.

Mum reached for my face, stroking my cheek. "This is a moment you need alone, just the two of you. From one king to another." She gave me a look, one that insisted I could do this, then stepped around me and disappeared through the doors, leaving me alone in the hall.

I approached the coffin, that current of existential crisis lapping at me once more, triggered by a life reaching its end. This time I didn't hesitate to mount the steps. The coffin was cold to touch, unforgiving and unyielding, nothing like the man and the once-beating heart it encased.

"Hi, Dad," I said out loud, my words drifting up into the air to gather with the notes from the organ. I didn't know what to say. How did you say goodbye one final time? How did you let that person know just how much you loved them? How did you make sure that you left nothing unsaid?

"It's been a couple of days since I spoke to you last, and I keep running that conversation back in my mind, over and over again. You were telling me about your visit, how something about the rolling greens outside the city made you feel like you were at peace, but how you couldn't wait to get back. And I didn't tell you how much I missed you, or how much I loved you, and that regret sits with me now. I can't remember the last time I said I loved you. I always thought you'd know that, and that we'd always have the chance to say it again another time. But I wish I'd told you at every opportunity just how much you mean to me, because now I'll never be able to tell you again."

I gathered a breath, needing to get everything out before I let myself be submerged by the sadness.

"I hope you're watching down over me, over all of us, and that you're smiling and proud and just happy to see us holding each other up. But if you can hear me now, I want you to know that I loved you before, I love you now, and I always will. Everything I do as king will be to make you proud. Everything I do as your son will be to keep your memory alive. You'll live on through us, I promise."

The dam burst before I could finish, bringing me to my knees with a cry that reverberated through my body, through every fiber of my being, until all I could do was cling to fragments of myself, no longer whole but fractured. I held the coffin, letting each cry drag itself out into the open, until I had nothing but an empty void left inside me.

Still on my knees, I heard the door at the other end of the hall open. I assumed it would be Mum, or maybe Eddie, but when I finally turned, exhausted, to see who it was, I was surprised to find Peter standing there, looking regretful.

"I'm sorry, Your Majesty. I didn't want to interrupt, but we need to leave."

His words immediately raised alarm bells, but I didn't question why or ask what had gone wrong—unspoken words between us said enough. I heaved myself up to my feet, unsure and unsteady. Peter bowed his head as I rested my hand on the coffin and then stepped down off the plinth, ready to face whatever lay in wait.

CHAPTER TWELVE

HUNTING LIES, HIDING TRUTHS

The crowds waiting in Parliament Square had doubled over time. Peter had warned me about it when we got back to the car. He gave a sideways glance to Walsh, who nodded, flexing his hands around the steering wheel. Behind us, Mum and Eddie sat in their car, their driver and protection officer peering out of the window to see ahead.

"It's a protest, but no cause for concern, Your Majesty," Peter said. His tone, tight and strained, belied his words. "We're going to whip straight out of here and be back at the palace in a matter of minutes. Just keep looking ahead and let us worry about what's going on outside."

"If you've got something to worry about, then it sounds like it *is* cause for concern," I muttered, clipping my seat belt in place. My hands were clammy, tucked into my lap, and my heart was picking up pace at the prospect of leaving the safety of Westminster Hall.

Ahead of us, the motorcycles leading the way turned on their blue lights, accelerating forward. One of our cars followed suit, mine revving its engine and pulling away after it. Daylight hovered around the entrance of the car-park, welcoming us out of the gloom. What a shame that mayhem waited to greet us.

The crowds in the square seemed to get wind that we were on our way back, the rev of the motorcycles giving us away. Few families revealed their entrances and exits with such fanfare. As we reached the street, they surged forward, signs thrust up in the air. I didn't need to read them this time to know they were bad, but one caught my eye—ABOLISH THE MONARCHY, RETURN THE JEWELS, EAT THE ROYALS! Even through the reinforced windows, I could hear the crowds. Their rage spewed out into the air, entwining together to create a monstrous beast that bellowed fire right at us.

"Come on," Walsh urged, itching to push the car into another gear and get us home to safety.

As if on cue, the car ahead accelerated and Walsh followed suit, gripping the wheel tightly as we shot around the square, heading for Parliament Street. Before we could make it, something slammed into the car roof, followed by another pellet exploding on impact against the window.

"It's just eggs, sir," Peter said calmly. "They'll need a lot more than that to break it." Despite sitting in one of the safest and best-protected cars in the world, I still didn't want to tempt fate, and was only too glad when we started speeding up the road, past Downing Street and down the Mall, the palace glinting at the end of it. Once we crossed the boundary into our protected bubble, I breathed a sigh of relief.

"They must really like me," I said sarcastically as Peter held open my car door and escorted me inside.

"Quite," Peter retorted. He looked behind him to check nobody was there, then took a step closer. "I've had Hutchins looking into Jonathan. He's checking if he can be located at home without raising the alarm. He's camped outside his mum's house right now to catch sight of him and should be back this evening with any news."

Out of the corner of my eye, I spotted Mum and Eddie about to step through the front door. I lowered my voice, speaking quickly. "Bring any news to me as soon as you have it. Ophelia will be here to discuss the situation tonight, but I want to know *everything* as soon as Hutchins is back."

Peter nodded. "Yes, sir," he said, and disappeared off into the palace.

"Are you all right?" Mum said, rushing over and enclosing me in her arms. When she broke away, her eyes flitted over my face, searching for damage or pain as if the eggs might've shattered the car windows.

"I'm fine, Mum. Honestly." She didn't look convinced, but she accepted the answer.

"Ophelia's due this evening?" she asked, and I nodded. "Perfect. I'll go and freshen up."

142

Dropping a kiss on my cheek, she glided toward the Grand Staircase, calling orders for a scorching-hot bath to be run, which would no doubt be ready by the time she reached her quarters. That left me and Eddie to stand together in the foyer, his eyes refusing to meet mine.

"Eddie?" I tried to pull him out of whatever ditch he'd dug himself into, but he seemed to be getting further and further away, retreating into his grief. I took a single step toward him and he met it with one of his own in the opposite direction, keeping that same distance between us.

"Don't." He shook his head sharply as if he were trying to dislodge a sour thought that had taken residence. "Just don't." He stalked away, leaving me to stand alone and observe the growing distance between us.

⌘

As night engulfed London, a black Mercedes purred down the Mall, followed by a rusting Ford with flaking paint. The passenger in the Ford leaned out of the window with little concern for his own safety, intent on getting his job done. A camera hid his face as the driver swerved out into the other lane to pull up alongside the Mercedes, a spatter of flashes lighting up the vehicle before the Ford overtook it and accelerated up to the railings of Buckingham Palace.

The photographer had already leaped from the car before it could stop, his camera poised to get the money shot. When the car carrying the girl reached the gates, slowing down to slip through them carefully, the man ran for the back window, wielding his camera like a weapon.

The flashes illuminated the girl for a brief moment, alone and petrified in the back seat, before the car cleared the gates and glided into the safety of the palace courtyard. The gates slammed shut behind them. The man quickly checked the screen of his camera, grinning when he saw that he'd gotten exactly what he wanted. He jumped back into the car, racing off toward the city.

⁂

Ophelia nearly fell through the door as I descended the stairs, Gayle hot on my tail. Tears streaked her face and her hair was flying in all different directions. She spotted the pair of us and tried to pull herself together, dipping into a curtsy before realizing that pretending was fruitless when she already looked so distressed.

"They're awful," she sobbed as I crossed the foyer to give her a hug. "They were waiting outside my house, a whole mob of them, and they all but chased us across the city. One of them sped ahead and cut us off just before we got here. They're monsters."

Gayle made to step into our orbit, but I waved her off. *Not now.* Gayle's mode of attack would always be practicality first—emotion never came into it. She'd want to figure out a way to make sure this never happened again, and while her cool head and decision-making made her perfect for the job, what Ophelia needed right now was a friend.

"We'll meet you upstairs," I said pointedly. Gayle acknowledged my discreet order with a nod and disappeared.

I let Ophelia cry, waiting until she looked up at me with red-rimmed eyes before guiding her into a small room by the stairs. It was an office for staff, empty at this time of the evening. Ophelia perched on the edge of a sofa, dabbing at her eyes with a tissue I handed her from the desk.

"I'm sorry. You must think I'm such a mess," she said with a shaking voice. "It's just never been like that before. It took me by surprise."

"Don't be silly. My heart still beats a hundred miles an hour whenever we leave this place. If you're taking my example, then you're doing a top job." I grinned and Ophelia giggled, but a dark cloud soon passed over her face.

"They know about us, don't they? They know it's not real."

"Why do you say that?" I asked, even though at this point it had to be obvious. The paparazzi would behave like that for an engagement or a scandal, and as far as I was aware, I hadn't gotten down on one knee recently.

"One of the photographers shouted it as I left the house. He asked me if it was true that we were putting on a show for the cameras. When I didn't answer, he called me a bitch and said he was only trying to help me get my side of the story out there before someone else had their say first." It didn't take three guesses to know whose side of the story would be coming out soon. Quinn Buckley loomed over us all. Ophelia shuddered as if she could read my mind, peering up at me with big, wide eyes.

"I should've never let this happen in the first place. I'm so sorry." I sighed. I could've prevented this, but instead I'd let Gayle and my family throw us out there in front of the camera's glare, selfishly hoping it would shield me. Now it looked as if it might be about to do the exact opposite.

"Everyone is upstairs now, waiting to try and fix the problem. But I just want you to know that whatever happens up there, I'm on your side. I'll give you every last protection I can to make sure you're kept safe. You won't have to go through this alone."

"Thank you," Ophelia said, her voice close to breaking again. She sniffed and took a deep breath. "I guess we should go and see what they've got to say, right?"

I led us upstairs to the White Drawing Room, where a mixture of family and staff lay in wait. I knew the room had been chosen on purpose to fool Ophelia—to fool us both—into feeling comfortable. Something as important as this would normally take place in the King's Conference Room, but its stiff chairs and formal table gave off an air of strict business. In the Drawing Room, with its plush sofas and chairs, golden frames, intricate ornaments and family photos, you could be forgiven for thinking that you'd been invited to relax in the monarchy's living room. But nothing here was ever done by accident.

Gayle stood stiffly by the fireplace, itching to start. Mum had changed into comfier clothes and looked soothed by her bath, her face smooth and soft. Peter stood opposite Gayle, his arms folded across his broad chest.

"No Eddie?" I asked, thinking about how we'd left things earlier. His presence wasn't necessary for the meeting, but it would've made me feel better to see him. Gayle shook her head.

"He's requested that he not be disturbed."

"Of course," I mumbled, taking a seat. I wondered if he'd finally let his own grief pour out. "Can we sit down to discuss this? Watching you all stand over us is making me feel like I'm in the headmaster's office." Peter, Gayle and Ophelia took their seats as I squirmed back into the sofa to make myself comfortable. "Okay, let's get this over with."

Gayle cleared her throat. "Well, let's not beat about the bush. I think we can agree that the next few hours and days are critical." She leveled her glance at me first, then Ophelia. "We still don't have a definite answer on what the *Eye* is producing, but based on the attention Ophelia received tonight, and the whispers coming out of various other newsrooms, I think it's clear to see that the story pertains to the pair of you."

Ophelia looked pale, as if she might throw up on the rug. Mum's face remained passive, but I knew she'd be spinning the information around in her head, deducing what options we had left.

"It's stating the obvious, but this isn't good. My moles tell me Buckley's story is coming with backup from a bunch of anonymous sources. Unless someone was silly enough to go on the record, we can use that to our advantage and fight back, label the whole story as nonsense and carry on as normal."

I leaned forward. "I'm sorry—as *normal?* You mean carry on with this ludicrous ruse just to prove that it's not made up?"

Gayle didn't blink. "That's exactly what I mean. This attention is unlikely to die down any time soon, and even if it does, the lies we were trying to counter in the first place will only resurface."

I tried not to squirm. I'd wanted to shut down those rumors about my sexuality, to hide away behind a lie of my own, but Gayle was right—if we gave in now, they would only return, and probably worse than before. Yet I couldn't just think of myself anymore, not when there was someone else involved.

"The attention won't ever go away if we keep feeding it," I said. "We've put enough pressure on Ophelia and now it's backfired. We can't keep pushing blindly through in the hope that everything will go to plan."

"James is right," Mum said with a nod of finality. She reached out for Ophelia, laying a gentle hand on her knee. "I'm sorry we dragged you into this mess, but it's our responsibility to get you out of it. From my experience with those beasts—and believe me, I have plenty—they'll only persist if you're giving them something to work with. When they realize you won't budge, that you won't give them that comment or picture they so desperately need, they'll find something else to be fascinated by and leave you alone."

I nodded my agreement. "For now, we lie low and let the attention fizzle out on its own," I said. "When

Buckley's story drops, we'll deny, deny, deny and wait out the storm that follows. Ophelia will have a protection officer twenty-four seven until everything dies down."

But Gayle had the bit between her teeth and was refusing to let go. "It's your call, Your Majesty, but as your advisor, I must admit that Ophelia's hand provides a distraction from secrets we hope will never see the light of day."

The thought of Jonathan materialized in my head, quickly joined by the note Gayle had left in his room. My eyes narrowed. She knew about us. The threat, as vague as it may be, lingered behind her words, attempting to scare me into submission. But I wouldn't flinch.

"I said what I said," I replied firmly, meeting Gayle's stare head-on. "We're not using Ophelia as a puppet to distract from anything. If they have secrets to expose, then let them. Acting out this lie won't stop them from telling the world, and I'm sick of hiding behind it."

Gayle hesitated, but she didn't quit. "Hiding in plain sight is what we do. We've done it for centuries, keeping every secret we can behind these walls. To let them spill out into the open now could spell the end of the monarchy as we know it. It could spell the end, full stop. I know it's a great ask, but I have to strongly advise that we—"

"We?" I spluttered. "This isn't about *we*. This is about me and my family, and we're people just like the rest of them. I refuse to play these games. I will not be wheeled out like some party trick, waving with one hand to distract from whatever we wish to hide in the other. How can you expect me to live a life like that?"

"Because it's what kings do."

A fleeting shadow of regret passed over Gayle's face, but there was no taking it back now. Ophelia looked like she'd rather drop dead than remain in this conversation. Peter stared into his lap. I could tell by the tense knot in his jaw that he was desperate to say something, but he knew it wasn't his place. Mum went to cut in, but I held up my hand, standing up to leave.

"My dad wanted me to find my own way to wear this crown. In case you hadn't noticed, I'm not like any king or queen before me. For one, I'm Black. Any mold created by the monarchs of our past will *never* fit me, no matter how hard you might try to force me into it. So, to hell with tradition and whatever else the past has to offer. It's of no help to us now, and it never will be."

Gayle went to apologize but I'd heard enough. I left the room, only Peter jumping up to follow in my footsteps. He trailed me like a silent shadow all the way back to my quarters. I waited for him to cross the threshold, then slammed the door for good measure, desperate to shake off some of my rage.

"How dare she talk to me like that?" I ranted. Peter stood back, letting me get it all out. "All my life I thought she was out to protect me and my family, but it took two days of the crown being on my head to see that she puts four pounds of solid gold above anything else." I picked up a cushion and launched it across the room. Its soft thump against the opposite wall infuriated me even more.

When I'd calmed down, my heightened rage reducing

to a simmer, I looked at Peter. "She knows about me and Jonathan. All of that back there about Ophelia helping to hide our secrets? She as good as admitted it, and she'd rather sweep it under the rug than let the shame of having a gay king get out into the world."

As the words left my mouth, the fight left me too, allowing the grief from earlier to clutch me in its embrace once again. I slumped down onto the sofa, covering my face with my hands and letting my thoughts run in wild circles.

"Hutchins returned to the palace about an hour ago, Your Majesty," Peter said gently, and I immediately sat bolt upright.

"Why didn't you tell me?"

"It seemed like you needed to let that out first." I sighed and nodded for him to continue. "Hutchins reports that there's been no sight of Jonathan at all. He was staked out by the house all day and didn't catch a glimpse of him. His mother and sister appeared, but no Jonathan."

"He has a sister?" There was a pain developing behind my eyes. All this time I'd been with Jonathan, and I'd never once asked about his family. I didn't know he had a sister. It was only just starting to dawn on me that I barely knew anything at all. Whenever we were together, it was always about me, my family, the palace, the staff. Anything and everything, but never about him and his life away from here.

"A younger sister, yes. She's fifteen and lives with

their mother. His father died a few years ago when he was fourteen."

How could I have never known that either? How could I have shared a bed with him, shared my darkest secrets and fears, but never known that he'd suffered the same loss I was now going through? My mind raced back over all the times I could've asked those questions, every missed opportunity to know more about the boy I was supposed to be in love with. There had been months of hiding in plain sight under the disguise of work, and then nights spent together in secret, each one a moment I could've used to ask more. I recalled one time he'd delivered flowers to my room as if they were purely for decoration, but the note buried in the stems had said: *For you, always.* At the time, I'd thought those few words to be romantic. Now I thought of them in a different perspective—everything had always been for me, leaving nothing for anybody else.

I pulled all the information we had together, but there were too many questions still unanswered. It left me with one glaring option and little else—I had to talk to Gayle and reveal the missing pieces of the story. Fortunately, I didn't have to go very far, because as if by magic, there was a frantic knock on the door.

CHAPTER THIRTEEN

A ROYAL SCANDAL

We've got the story," Gayle said immediately when I opened the door. Mum and Ophelia stood behind her, their faces pinched with panic.

Gayle held up a newspaper and I saw my own face, exhausted and scared, looking back. It was a picture I hadn't seen, one from the Grief Parade, and I was clearly paralyzed by fear. The headline above it screamed: *THE KING IS A LIAR*. My heart responded before my head, slamming against its cage like it was begging to be let free. I reached for the newspaper to get a better look, but the more I saw, the worse it got. Pictures of Ophelia arriving at the palace tonight for "crisis talks" exploded to the right of the page. The press was always quick, and they'd moved with exceptional speed to print this story. But it was a smaller headlinc, below the first, that stole my breath like a silent thief: *REVEALED: The secret the king is so desperate to hide!*

I staggered to the dining table and spread the newspaper out over the polished wood. Peter came to stand by me, taking in the front page over my shoulder. There was one picture I'd missed at the bottom of the page. It sat next to the article, as if it were nothing but a simple addition to the piece. But its placement wasn't accidental. It was me and Jonathan, side by side at a public event, back when he'd first joined the palace. And when I saw that picture, taunting me from the front page of a newspaper hundreds of thousands would read, I felt my world begin to shatter.

THE KING IS A LIAR
REVEALED: The secret the king is so desperate to hide!

By Quinn Buckley, *ROYAL REPORTER*

King James, the fragile and seemingly unfit teenager, who this week became the first Black monarch to wear the crown, has been seeking solace in a palace confidant. But the *Daily Eye* can exclusively reveal that the arms he has fallen into are not those of Ophelia Budd, the young socialite whom the royals have been parading before the cameras for months, but another close friend working within the palace itself.

This explosive revelation comes after the seventeen-year-old and his family, including the

154

Queen Mother herself, Alexandra Hampton, tried to hoodwink the nation into believing his relationship with the young woman was genuine, when in actual fact it was anything but. The decision to wield Ms. Budd—daughter of disgraced financier Richard Budd—as a weapon of distraction has now dramatically backfired, with a source close to the Royal Family telling the *Daily Eye* that the pair came to a mutually beneficial agreement to cover up the king's true relationship in exchange for paying off the Budd family debt.

"King James has been living a lie for months," our source told the *Daily Eye*. "His secret palace romance started back in April. In fact, although James has been keen to keep matters private, his immaturity and his disrespect for the history he is supposed to preserve have seen him conduct moonlit trysts in various rooms of the palace, including one such passionate meeting in the White Drawing Room."

The Drawing Room mentioned, built in the 1820s, is one of huge historical significance and has since played host to a number of important figures past and present, including monarchs, various heads of state and international royalty. It even provided the backdrop for the engagement of King George and Princess Catherine before her untimely death.

The new king's complete disregard for its historical importance, as well as his deception of the whole world, begs the question: Should he not only abdicate the throne, but also remove his entire immediate family from the institution he swore to serve? Recent reports suggest he wouldn't be missed. The latest public polls show King James's approval rating sitting at a dismal 16 percent, the lowest percentage for a king since records began. His mother, Alexandra Hampton, fared little better with 17 percent. First heir to the throne, Prince Edward, saw the highest in the immediate royal circle with 26 percent. Princess Cassandra proved to be most popular, however, with an approval rating of an almost perfect 92 percent, the highest of any royal since records began.

FURTHER STORIES CONTINUE ON PAGES 4, 5, 6 and 7.

There was no mention of Jonathan by name, but the picture of us together was all that needed to be said. Quinn Buckley knew it was him. And now every person who picked up the *Daily Eye* come sunrise would know it too. Something more sinister revealed itself to me in glimpses, unfolding in my mind as I made sense of what I'd just read—whoever had spoken to Quinn knew fact from fiction. They knew the truth.

"It's not true," I said automatically, although it sounded unconvincing at best. It was Mum who came to stand beside me, resting a hand on my arm.

"We know what's been going on between you and Jonathan, sweetheart," she said, nodding toward Gayle. Ophelia's eyes widened for just a second, but I saw that look, the one I'd been desperate to avoid. It was one of panic, like suddenly she didn't know me anymore. My body tensed up of its own accord, my mother's hand feeling like the unforgiving bite of winter air on my bare skin.

156

I wanted to lie, to say I didn't know what she was talking about. But instead, I turned to my mum, the tears in my eyes multiplying, and whispered, "How?"

Mum's face floated closer, her eyes as warm and kind as ever. She stroked my arm with her thumb, letting me know that she was there. She gestured to the sofas and guided me over to sit down. I let her, allowing the plump cushions to swallow me up. Everybody else took a seat, Mum next to me, her hand never moving from my arm.

"Gayle came to me a few weeks ago," Mum said softly. A twinge of betrayal twisted my stomach. Of course. That was why Gayle had been so adamant the lie with Ophelia must continue—anything that threatened the monarchy had to be eliminated, or at least covered up.

"I've known about you and Jonathan for a little while," Gayle said. She picked her words carefully, gently delivering them like a wrong choice could blow up in her face. "The times I found his room empty were a giveaway, because if he wasn't leaving the palace, then he had to be sleeping elsewhere. And a simple check of the cameras to see where he might be disappearing to confirmed it."

I cringed at the thought. We'd always been careful to use the secret passageways to avoid being seen together when we shouldn't have been. But for someone like Gayle, it would be all too easy to piece together where Jonathan was going.

"Those kinds of relationships are strictly forbidden, and they always have been," she went on. "Nobody who works for the palace can conduct a relationship with somebody else within these walls, especially when that person is a member of the monarchy itself. It's a conflict of interest and the first rule of our institution."

It was too mechanical. Our relationship was being reduced to its technical parts, the color of the emotions that had fueled it diluting until they were black and white, but Gayle kept going.

"I didn't want to have this discussion with either of you and hoped you'd figure it out between yourselves. But, with the passing of your father, and your ascension to the throne, I knew that it was time to make a decision, and Jonathan did too. He would be a distraction, one salaciously welcomed by the media if it were to be discovered. So, I spoke to him."

It was a punch to my gut, one of many tonight. Gayle was sitting up straight, talking evenly as if she wasn't dissecting my relationship—my *life*.

"I spoke to him on the morning your father passed, to tell him that your relationship had come to a crossroads and a decision would have to be made. He agreed, and promised he would end things, at least while he was still a working member of the palace."

I remembered Jonathan holding me that night, before the party, his unsaid words crackling over the growing chasm between us. He'd wanted to end it there. But he'd stopped himself, or at least backed away from the ledge. Maybe he was hoping he could let me down gently.

"I came to your room last night to find him alone in your quarters. I had no choice but to tell him that his services were no longer required, and that he needed to pack his things and leave by morning. If anybody else had found him there, the secret would already be out in the open, and who knows what would've happened then?"

"You did what?" I couldn't believe what I was hearing. I couldn't make sense of the fog falling around me, leaving me directionless in the midst of its confusion.

Gayle didn't flinch. "I found him in your quarters past midnight, while you were downstairs at the party, and I told him that he needed to leave. That if he really cared for you, he would step away while you found your feet as king. He tried to fight back and said that the decision lay with you. And then he stormed out. But when I found him again, he was leaving the party, furious at something."

I pictured the vase in pieces on his bedroom floor, the ornaments turned over—a result of that same rage.

"I assumed his conversation with you hadn't gone well," Gayle continued. "He said he'd pack his things and go. There was no further explanation as to what changed his mind, and I didn't have time to ask. As you might recall, I had other matters to attend to...."

The chandelier. It had fallen as Jonathan left the party after seeing me and Grigor together. The scene from last night was starting to unblur, but it still didn't make sense, whichever way I tried to look at it. Gayle leaned forward, a serious look on her face.

"Did Jonathan have any reason to be angry with you, James?" she asked.

Grigor's name clawed its way into my mouth, but I swallowed it back down. "None. When I saw him last night, he was fine. Everything between us was fine." I tried to keep a straight face, but I could feel flickers at the corner of my mouth threatening to give me away.

"Well, something upset him, and now he's clearly trying to retaliate."

I jumped up from the sofa. "Retaliate? You think *Jonathan's* behind this story?" It was almost too ludicrous to say out loud. Of all the people in the world who would want to hurt me, Jonathan would be the last. He'd hurt himself before he'd turn the tables on me. He was selfless, a man who'd always made me feel safe, and I was certain he couldn't be behind this.

But the image of his face, twisted by hurt and pain, floated into my head. And was it just my memory adding brushstrokes to the picture, or was his face colored with rage when he'd seen me and Grigor together? Peter had already given me the proof that I didn't know Jonathan as well as I thought I did. Could I really say he wouldn't want to hurt me back?

"Well, let's eliminate the suspects here. When did your relationship start?" All eyes flicked from Gayle to me.

"April," I said, throat dry and voice cracked.

"And the White Drawing Room? You...met in there?" The way Gayle skirted around the suggestion in the article made my skin crawl, shame flooding my chest and splattering outward like a broken wave. I couldn't deny it, so I stayed silent.

"And if those two things are true, then who else would know about them?" Gayle went on, her tone softening as she tried to land the final blow without destroying me altogether.

"It *can't* be him," I said, although my brain was telling me otherwise.

"Why not?" Gayle pushed.

"Because if it was him, then I didn't really know him at all."

Gayle sighed, shaking her head slightly. "And maybe that's the case."

It was impossible. I couldn't comprehend for even a second that the person I'd put all of my trust in would do this. I'd loved him, and he'd loved . . .

I felt the thought crumple before it was finished. Last night, before the party, I'd told him I loved him. But he hadn't said it back. He'd not said anything at all.

Sitting down, I turned to Mum for help, as if she could right all these wrongs with the swish of a magic wand. She squeezed my hand, but she could do little else. She couldn't sweep out into the world and delete Quinn Buckley's words. She couldn't go back in time and tell me to step away from Jonathan. She couldn't fix what he had seemingly broken. I turned to Peter, to Ophelia, back to Gayle, but all I was met with were sympathetic eyes.

"The note," I blurted, forgetting that Gayle didn't know I was in Jonathan's room when she'd left it behind. Peter tensed but said nothing. "I found your note in his room this morning."

Gayle simply nodded, eliminating my last hope that this nightmare wasn't real. "I went to Jonathan's room to find it a mess and already half-cleared out. I assumed he'd be back to collect what was left behind. I'm not proud of it, James, but I needed to make it clear that this secret was one to be kept buried. I wanted to protect *you* from all of this." She gestured at the newspaper.

"It was my way—our way—of reminding Jonathan that we know his secrets too. It was an attempt to stop him from doing anything stupid. But he texted me almost as soon as I'd left his room saying he wouldn't be back. I tried to call, but he'd turned his phone off." From my own attempts to get in contact with him, I knew that much to be true. Gayle shrugged. "I made orders to have his room cleaned out and secured since we no longer had use for it."

She finally sat back, her cards all on the table, giving me space to digest everything. This whole time I'd been placing the blame everywhere else, determined that I would find out what had happened to Jonathan. Even now, I wasn't sure that I could believe it.

But what other choice did I have? Gayle was right—who else would know those details? They were secrets only Jonathan and I knew, and I certainly hadn't run to Quinn Buckley to tell him about them. If Quinn really did have eyes in the palace, maybe he'd picked up on Jonathan early, knew that he was a good target. The *Eye* would have offered untold amounts of money to get a source like Jonathan on their side. If he was angry or hurt, wouldn't he want payback? Wouldn't I?

Through all of this, Ophelia had remained silent, tucked away in the corner and almost forgotten about. Her being there went against everything Gayle had ever taught us about letting outsiders into our secrets. But we'd dragged her into this, so she was as much a part of it as any of us. In fact, we'd probably just made her life a living hell.

"It's late. We should think about getting you home, Ophelia. Unless you'd like to stay, of course." Mum cocked her head in Ophelia's direction, but she frantically shook her head, as if it were unsafe to be anywhere near us. I guess she was right. The mess we caused wherever we went rarely hurt us the most. It was somebody else who always paid the price.

"We'll get you home, sweetheart, don't worry. Peter, could you organize three cars to escort Ophelia home. They're to travel with four guards in each. And instruct them to be careful out there. There's nothing those animals won't do for a picture, especially now."

Standing, Peter nodded and held the door open while Ophelia got to her feet.

"Ophelia?" Mum called before she could leave. Ophelia hesitated in the doorway, reluctantly turning back to face us. Mum stood up tall, her face unchanged apart from her eyes, which narrowed slightly. "The plan is the same as it always was. I implore you not to break our trust. We can't protect you otherwise."

The threat was clear, lingering over the room with unsaid menace. Ophelia shrank away from it, wilting under my mother's watch. She nodded, taking one last fleeting look at my family in all its broken mess. She looked as if

163

she might say something, but the words caught on her tongue and died on her lips. Instead, she bowed her head, murmured, "Of course," and all but ran from the room.

"So, now what?" I asked once Peter had shut the door behind them.

Mum had replaced her softness with armor, her tenderness with rage. "We fight back."

"No code of silence?" That was the way we always operated. Fighting back was against everything we'd ever been taught.

"That doesn't apply here," Mum said, and Gayle nodded her agreement. "The code of silence is reserved for stories that simply aren't true. When it comes to something rooted in reality that could leave us in ruin, we don't lie down and wait for the coffin lid to close."

Gayle's cogs were turning as she ran through our options. "We have allies at other newspapers, people who will help to not only get our story out, but also discredit the *Eye* and Buckley at the same time. So, we go to them—we deny everything Buckley has written and try to spin this back in our favor."

Although it was important, I couldn't focus on the press wars and royal manipulation that we were planning to use to clear my name. My attention was fixed solely on a single question, one that scorched every other thought in my head with its ferocity.

"And what about Jonathan?"

Gayle stood up, fixing her face into an unforgiving expression. "We find him, and we make sure he stops talking."

Part III

TWO STARS CROSSED

CHAPTER FOURTEEN

DON'T SHOOT THE MESSENGER

The morning was even worse than I could've antici-pated, the news not so much seeping out into the open as crashing through the gates and sweeping around the world like a gust of unforgiving wind. Every news channel displayed pictures of me and Ophelia, news anchors sitting before them with grim looks on their faces, pointed words and glares sharpened like pitchforks. Before daylight had fully splintered the night, a small hud-dle of protestors, just like the ones from the day before, had gathered outside the gates. As the morning wore on, their number only grew.

"Grigor's going to have a nightmare getting through that mess," Eddie murmured, twitching the curtains once more for another look outside, as I tried not to react to the mere mention of Grigor's name. We were tucked away in a room attached to my quarters that acted as our barbershop for our weekly haircut.

"They can't get in here, can they?" Eddie asked. "We're identical twins—if they see me first, I'm done for. It'll be my head rolling down the hallway."

It was a joke, one to dilute the acidic mood that had drifted over us like a poisonous fog, but I was hardly in the mood for it. I was too tense, my body aching from holding myself together. I was paranoid, every small and insignificant look from the palace staff morphing into something I was sure had to be about me. I didn't know who I could trust anymore. Jonathan had been my safety net, and now it'd been cut wide open, sending me into free fall.

"Look, it's not really *that* bad, is it?" Eddie tried, falling into the chair opposite mine. Kevin, his personal barber, turned his clippers on, narrowing his eyes as he got back to work. The soft but firm hands of my own barber, Lee, guided my head in one direction, the scrape of his blade running over my skin.

Too ashamed to even glance up from the floor, I couldn't meet my brother's eyes. Eddie carried on. "You've been found out and the world hates you for a few days. Big deal. This family has survived worse, right? Remember when Cassandra's dad was called a Nazi sympathizer for throwing the Hitler salute? If we can ride that storm out, we can get through anything."

"He was white," I muttered. "It's not the same."

Eddie opened his mouth, but nothing came out.

He knew it was true. Cassandra's dad had been loved by the likes of Quinn Buckley, racist outbursts and all. He was given a tap on the wrist in the newspapers before he showed up at a charity event to make a grand gesture that would prove he was really nothing like how he'd been painted to be.

And people fell for it every time. Every. Single. Damn. Time. His whiteness excused his bigotry and allowed him to get away with it, over and over again. When he questioned how dark our skin would be before we were born, it was twisted into an offhand musing made by an uncle curious about his nephews, and eager to learn of their culture and background. But when Eddie got suspended from school for punching a classmate, the *Eye* promoted a petition to get him removed from the line of succession altogether. It was conveniently left out that said classmate had just moments before called us "half-breed princes." One hundred and eighty thousand people signed it.

"All I'm saying is, don't let this be what breaks you. It's a small misstep, and they'll be onto the next thing in no time." Eddie paused, a smile creeping over his face. "If you want me to step outside wearing nothing but the breeze, I'll gladly do it. That should distract them from discussing your love life."

I laughed, despite everything. "We need some good press—I don't think that's going to cut it."

Eddie held his chest. "Wow, that one cut deep."

We fell into a familiar silence, one I'd missed since the crown began to wedge its way between us. Ever since

Dad's health put the wheels in motion for my ascension, Eddie had retreated away from me and toward Grigor and Louie. It felt good to be back together, things seemingly calm and, if I dared admit it, normal.

My eyes felt heavy, lulled by the gentle hands of Lee as he moved my head one way and then the other. Unsurprisingly, I hadn't slept all night, fear of what had already happened colliding with my anxiety about what would be coming. Gayle had assembled a small team, including Peter, to find Jonathan at any cost. If he'd started talking now, there was no telling how far he'd go. Maybe this would be it, his one strike aimed at me. But he knew enough palace secrets to cause concern, and if Quinn Buckley *did* have his claws in Jonathan, it could spell disaster.

Only a small circle of people had been entrusted with knowledge of the search for him. We didn't want to expose ourselves to anybody who could start a game of whispers. But when we found Jonathan, then...who knew what would happen? I'd pulled Peter aside and said I didn't want him to get hurt in any way. But I did want to talk to him, face to face, to ask him why he'd turned informant. An uncomfortable energy was churning in my gut at the thought of seeing him again.

"Do you think he did it?"

I snapped out of my thoughts, glancing up at Eddie, who was watching me carefully. It was obvious who *he* was, and it was something that had been playing on my mind through the night hours and into the day. I flicked my eyes up at Kevin, but neither barber broke the rhythm of their work, clearly accustomed to tuning out of private conversations.

"I don't know." I dredged it all back up again. "It's the only reasonable explanation, isn't it? Nobody else knew about us. It was just him and me. He told Quinn those details knowing I'd see it as a form of revenge."

Eddie frowned, and I realized I'd said too much. "Revenge for what?"

He didn't know about my conversation with Grigor. Nobody did. And yet, it occurred to me that anybody at the party could know. Anybody could've turned and seen us, standing in the corner, too close to be friendly. I looked down at the floor, averting my eyes from Eddie's blistering stare that asked all the questions I didn't want to answer.

"You could've told me about Jonathan, you know?" Eddie let his words hang over us. They hurt to hear, piercing my skin over and over again. They shined a spotlight on the shadow that the throne had cast between us.

"I couldn't," I said, barely above a whisper.

"Why?"

"You wouldn't have understood it."

"Understood what? There was nothing to understand. I'm your brother. You can tell me anything." It hurt to look Eddie in the eye, to see the pain that lived there. But I forced myself to meet his stare. "You're telling me that after almost eighteen years of being side by side, of doing this whole thing together, that you didn't trust me?"

"I wanted to trust you, but I couldn't. I didn't

understand it myself, so how could I have expected you to get it?" It was feeble and weak, a cop-out, but it was true.

"What's there to get?" Eddie countered, not letting the beast lie. "What, you wear a crown on your head now, and suddenly I wouldn't get what you're going through? I wouldn't understand because you're the king and I'm the spare?"

"Eddie, I never said that."

"But you want to. I can see it. You think you're above everybody else now." Eddie's mouth was twisted around all the words he was flinging at me, words he'd probably wanted to say for a long, long time. They stung, but I refused to let them best me.

"How could I ever think I'm above anybody else? When I'm reminded every single day that it's you who'd make the better king. Everybody knows it. Everybody wishes it was *you* who was born first—they wish it was *you* who'd come into this world eight minutes before me. Don't sit there and tell me that I think I'm above everybody else when I'm below even you."

"*Even me*," Eddie spat, the smoke from his rage swirling around the room. It was years of pent-up fury, of being constantly reminded that he was the second heir. "God forbid you think yourself below the fool whose entire life is supposed to be devoted to upholding *you* and *your* reign. Below the person whose life is meaningless unless you step down or die. You stand on *my* shoulders. Don't pretend it's the other way around. Not when you're sitting comfortable on that throne."

"Comfortable?! On a throne that's ruined our lives? That's pushed us out into the world to be torn down by people who don't want us here? How could you ever think that I'd be comfortable, sitting alone, bound by duty, restrained by honor? I will *never* be free of it. *Ever*. I'll be a prisoner to this crown for the rest of my days. You'll always be free to live your life, to make mistakes and fall in or out of love, to do whatever the hell you want, because you're the prince. The one who would've made a better king, but never got the chance."

Eddie opened his mouth to utter some spiteful retort, but I beat him to the punch, my rage submerging me entirely. "And you're damn right you wouldn't understand. You wouldn't understand what it's like to have every single pair of eyes on you, waiting for you to trip up and fail. You will never understand what it's like to sit on this throne and wear this crown, to have everybody around you dissect your life, your relationships, your secrets. There will never be an ounce of my life that will ever just be mine. I have to give every part of me to a country, to a world, that may or may not want me here, strictly based on the color of my skin and who I choose to love. You get to live a *life*. So, no, you wouldn't understand any of it. And you never will."

Maybe it was the grief for our father clashing. If he could see us now, he'd be ashamed. But my anger and pride wouldn't let me fill the bloated silence that rose between us, born out of the jealousy that we harbored toward each other. The irony that a king wanted to be prince, while a prince wanted to be king, had become tall and mocking, an uninvited guest in the room.

"We're done, Your Majesty, Your Royal Highness." Kevin's smooth drawl tore us out of the moment, reminding us that we weren't alone—that we never had been. We'd just fought our ugliest battle with witnesses present.

"Thanks, Kevin. Thanks, Lee," I murmured, as my barber removed the gown from around my neck.

Kevin and Lee both bowed, then made for the door like they couldn't get out of there quick enough. In the space they left at the threshold stood Grigor, his eyes darting between the two of us.

"Everything all right...?" he asked cautiously, stepping into the room like it was an active minefield ready to explode in his face.

"Yup," Eddie said, standing up and brushing himself off. "Just hearing some home truths, that's all." With a sarcastic smile, he barged past Grigor and stalked off down the corridor.

"What was all that about?" Grigor said, checking over his shoulder to make sure Eddie wasn't still standing there.

"Nothing," I muttered, getting up myself.

Grigor seemed to contemplate probing further, but decided against it, instead holding his hands behind his back. "I've got something for you," he said, a smile lighting up his face. Even filled with rage, my heart skipped a beat. This was immediately chased by a confused guilt as Jonathan's name stepped out of the shadows at the back of my mind.

"Lucky me," I said, trying to keep my tone even. It

flicked up at the end, giving me away. Grigor raised his eyebrows teasingly, producing an envelope and a small rectangular box wrapped with a bow from behind his back.

"Now, last time I checked, I wasn't a messenger, but one of the maids was trying to deliver this letter to you. I don't think she wanted to interrupt whatever was going on in here, so I offered to do the honors myself. After all, you can't fire me. I'm unsure if I should've charged for the service but, hey, I get to see you, so maybe I'll let it go." He said it so casually, his words leveled out by a confidence that made it seem like he was in on a joke that I hadn't figured out yet. I bit the inside of my cheek to stop myself from smiling. I nodded toward his other hand instead.

"And what's in the box?"

Grigor held it up, shrugging to himself. "I couldn't just show up empty-handed, could I? What kind of loyal subject would I be if I didn't arrive with gifts of my own?" He dipped into a low and graceful bow, hiding a playful grin. I couldn't help but laugh this time, my anger from moments before all but fluttering out of the window like doves coasting on a breeze.

Grigor handed me the envelope and the box, his hand brushing mine. It was brief, only a fraction of a second in time, but it felt like a shower of sparks raining down around me.

As the expert on how to play things cool, I immediately opted to open the gift-wrapped box, almost too desperate to know what was inside. Grigor had a glint in his eye as I tore the paper. The words *Buckingham Palace* beamed up at me in gold lettering above a picture of the gift on the packaging—a teddy bear, dressed in the red tunic and bearskin hat of the King's Guard.

"Is this…from the gift shop outside?" I asked, and Grigor burst out laughing. It was the only joy I'd heard inside the palace in days, and its warmth made me laugh too.

"I had limited options, and unless you wanted me to steal some of the china on the way up here, I thought this might be the next best thing," he said, grinning.

"You couldn't have at least got me some of the short-bread instead? What am I meant to do with this?" I held up the box, which Grigor took from my hands and opened, releasing the teddy bear within. He turned it one way and then the other, smirking, then tossed it in my direction. Thankfully, my hand-eye coordination didn't let me down and I managed to grab the teddy out of the air.

"It's a guard, right? He'll keep you safe."

I frowned at the teddy as a thought occurred. "If I ask you a question, you're not allowed to lie…."

Grigor held up one hand and placed the other over his chest. "Yes, Your Majesty."

"The teddy was for my brother, wasn't it?"

Grigor folded his lips, trying to keep a laugh from escaping. "No comment, sir." He winked, then nodded at the envelope that I'd forgotten was still grasped in my other hand. "Something important?"

I looked down at the envelope, a distinct and rich forest-green color. "I guess we'll find out," I murmured, flicking it over and tearing it open.

Inside was a simple white note, no bigger than a post-card. One side was completely blank. The other had a short, typed message, which warped the room around me as I read it.

Meet me on the bridge in St. James's
Park at midnight. We need to talk.
Come alone.

My whole body came alive, prickling with apprehension from head to toe. It was Jonathan. It had to be. I read the words again—twice, three times, four—drinking them in like they'd reveal something more. But there was nothing else. No explanation as to why or what any of it meant. But I knew in my heart, without doubt, I'd go. I wanted answers.

"That must be one killer note," Grigor chipped in, dragging me back down to earth. He pointed to the teddy on the floor by my feet. "Next time it'll have to be the shortbread if I want to keep your attention, huh?"

I couldn't even pretend. I'd spent years rehearsing how to paint a smile on my face, so it was an instinct I could trust in when I needed it most. But now everything went out the window. All I could think about was Jonathan.

"From anybody important?" Grigor asked, bending down to pick up the teddy and pressing it back into my hand. This time when his hand brushed mine, it felt like salt in a wound.

"A friend," I said stiffly. "Just an old friend."

CHAPTER FIFTEEN

THE PARK AT MIDNIGHT

Time seemed to drag its heels as the day wore on, morning seeping into afternoon, afternoon crawling into evening, evening bleeding into night. With less than a week to go, final preparations for the funeral were coming together. It was a miserable topic to focus on, but at least it distracted me from all my other thoughts. I wanted my dad to have the final send-off that he deserved and I wouldn't let anything stand in my way. As king, I had the final say, but the responsibilities were shared out between me, Mum and Eddie.

Eddie wouldn't even look at me as plans and final amendments ricocheted between us. The words from earlier still stung, a gentle rage hiding beneath the surface. If Mum and Gayle noticed the tension between us, they chose not to say anything about it. Instead, they focused their attention on the matter at hand, making sure that anything we wanted to happen was possible. It was all coming together, which gave me a feeling of grim satisfaction. Dad's funeral would be our final goodbye, and I'd do anything to make sure it was perfect.

I was back in my quarters just after eleven p.m. when there was a gentle knock on my door. I called for the person to enter and Gayle appeared, the weight of the day resting on her shoulders. I muted the TV, a program playing in the background that I hadn't been paying attention to anyway. There were other things on my mind. Midnight was just an hour away.

"The Queen Mother has requested to see you tomorrow morning to discuss the final guest list for the funeral," Gayle said, her voice strained with exhaustion. "Sometime around ten, after she's attended to other matters."

"Of course," I said. Gayle bowed her head and turned to leave, only pausing in the doorway when I called out to her. I gestured to the seat next to me, trying to pass off a smile. She hesitated but closed the door again, shuffling over to sit beside me.

"You look how I feel," I said lightly.

She leaned over to slap my arm with a weary laugh. "It won't always be like this, you know? Being king has its perks, even if it doesn't always feel like it. Getting started is the hardest part."

I pulled my legs up onto the sofa, folding my knees up against my chest. "It'd be exhausting enough if it was just the funeral to think about. I could do without everything else on top."

179

I wasn't looking for a pity party—more just stating facts out loud. Gayle looked like she wanted to offer me some help, some kind words that I could believe and trust in. But I'd heard it all before. It wouldn't solve the problem until the problem solved itself. So, I jumped in before she could say what was on her mind and asked the question I was desperate to find answers to.

"Is there any news on Jonathan?" Even his name made my skin prickle. The clock ticked in my ear, counting down to midnight.

Gayle shook her head slowly, glancing down into her lap. "Not a thing, sir. He's not home; he's not anywhere that we'd suspect him to be. It's like he's just vanished into thin air." For the first time in my life, I was looking at a Gayle who was close to breaking. She was the rock of this family and always had been, but this raging tempest was proving difficult to weather—for all of us. Looking at her now, trying to hold the pieces of our family together, I saw how stupid I'd been to suspect her in the first place.

Gayle leaned into the sofa, letting her head fall back slightly. "Part of me thinks that he'd never do this. It seems so unlike Jonathan, so out of his character, to go running to Quinn. But if you could've seen the look on his face when he left the Ballroom that night...He was hurt about something. I just wish I knew what."

I folded my lips together, refusing to meet Gayle's eye. But she was in a world of her own, trying to piece everything together.

"I've asked Peter to keep an even closer eye on Quinn,

too. Jonathan leaving the palace, talking to that para-site and seemingly disappearing? It reeks of Buckley. I wouldn't be surprised if he's offered him a safe house to hide out in until all of this blows over."

I sat forward. "You really think that?"

Gayle sighed. "I don't know what to think anymore. This is completely new ground."

"We've had leaks before though, right?"

"Harmless ones, sure. But the press have never really known anything. The royal circle has always been tight for that very reason. It's impossible to keep everything behind closed doors, but what matters is that we keep the *right* things inside the palace, so what could really hurt us will never have the chance to see the light of day." Gayle lifted her eyes, their gemstone blue clouded by a simmer-ing panic. "Jonathan...he knows too much. If he really has turned to the other side, then we're playing a danger-ous game indeed."

I wanted to tell her about the note. That by tonight, we'd have answers. I was almost sure of it. If he'd asked to see me, it could only mean one thing—he wanted to talk, and surely that meant he wanted to make things right. But I knew if I said anything, Gayle would demand I not venture into the park at all, or at the very least not alone. She'd want to make sure that I had every protection the palace could afford. As king, you never went anywhere alone, but I needed to tonight. I needed to do this by myself.

"Anything on Cassandra?" I asked, trying to steer the

conversation past Jonathan so my guilt wouldn't trip me up into confessing.

Gayle shook her head. "Not a thing, unless you count the ungodly amount she spends in various restaurants around the city. Anybody would think we don't have kitchens in this palace."

I breathed a laugh. "Well, keep me updated. On Quinn too—I don't want any more surprises."

When Gayle left, the door clicking shut behind her, I felt my nerves begin to swirl with anticipation for what lay ahead. Answers waited outside the palace, hidden within St. James's Park, and I couldn't wait a second longer. I changed into dark clothes, my hands shaking as I pulled on a black hoodie, something I hoped would help me blend into the night.

With one last glance at the clock, I turned off the lights and opened my front door, only to find Peter standing in the hallway, hand ready to knock. I yelped, jumping back with my hands raised to . . . protect myself? It was hardly a demonstration of self-defense and I quickly lowered them when I saw who it was.

"I was just checking everything was okay before I signed off for the night. I saw your light was still on . . ." His eyes jumped over my head and scanned the room behind me. "Everything okay in here?"

"Couldn't be better!" I said cheerily, my voice a notch or two away from hysterical. My throat felt like it was closing up, the explanations and excuses that I'd rehearsed stuck and desperate for air. My head was blank. Peter glanced back to me, sizing up what secrets I was hiding now.

"Going somewhere?" He looked like he might be seconds away from rugby-tackling me to the floor, reading the lies and intentions behind my awkward pauses.

"Just wanted to go for a walk. You know, alone. Clear my head. It's been a long day and I need the air. A moonlit walk in the gardens might be the medication I need to actually get some sleep tonight." Peter didn't look convinced, but he stepped aside anyway, falling into stride with me as we started toward the palace's west wing.

"Something interesting came up on Jonathan," he said just as the silence was beginning to gnaw at my eardrums. The familiar shiver I felt whenever I heard his name came over me. I didn't trust myself to speak, so I waited, hands scrunched into tight balls and stuffed into my pockets.

"I had Hutchins check the CCTV on the night he left the palace."

"I thought all the cameras were switched off?" I said, hearing the tension in my words.

Peter cleared his throat. "They were turned off, but that was inside. Our outside cameras stayed on. It's security policy, in case of a trespasser. We're no good at our jobs if we're working blind, and the threats we focus on come from outside."

"And?" I asked, my heart starting to beat faster.

"I haven't been able to comb through all of the footage just yet. Gayle's had us running around the city trying to find him at any cost, while also keeping tabs on

Buckley and Cassandra. But I did check the camera out front and..." He paused, weighing something up as we descended the stairs, passing the watchful eyes of monarchs in their gilded frames.

"I'll need to look again properly, but I'm almost certain—if Jonathan left the palace, he didn't leave through the front door. I checked the cameras in the courtyard and there's nothing. I asked some of the guards on patrol and they reported nothing out of the ordinary. Staff came and left, and Jonathan could've been lost in the crowd, but nobody reports seeing him that night."

I couldn't make sense of it, not while I was already thinking about so much already. I was on my way to see Jonathan—if I could shake Peter anyway—so what did it matter if he'd left through the front door, the back door, or abseiled off the roof?

"It might not mean anything," Peter said, reading my thoughts as if I'd said them out loud. "It's just interesting. If he chose to leave the palace by avoiding the main entrances, it makes me wonder why he didn't want to be seen—or what he was trying to hide." He nodded toward the glass doors at the end of the hallway, leading out to the steps that would take me down into the gardens.

"You sure you want to be out there alone? I can wait here." I could tell Peter wanted to accompany me. It was his job, and one that he took very seriously. I had no doubt that, if it ever came to it, he'd lay down his life to protect mine. But I shook my head quickly, hoping that I was masking any of the feelings that were trying to dance around my face.

"Well, if you're sure, I'll be retiring for the night." He looked again at the doors and the night beyond. "Just call me if you need anything." With a bow, he strode back the way we'd come, toward his own apartment in the palace.

The summer night air was light, a slight breeze floating over the garden. Moonlight, pure and angel white, crept up the immaculate grass, making it look almost silver in the dark. I tried to keep my steps even, like I was taking the midnight walk I'd said I was. Every instinct told me to retreat into the safety of the palace, but I wouldn't forgive myself if I didn't go. So I kept on, out into the dark, toward a spot that only few knew about. The old wooden door was hidden within the pruned shrubs and bushes of the gardens, a part of the perimeter wall and long since abandoned. It was nothing spectacular to look at. In fact, you might even miss it if you didn't know what you were looking for. It hadn't been used properly in decades— a century, even—but its locks were always checked and maintained to make sure it was secure.

Without a backward glance at the palace, I zipped through a gap in the trees, stepping over flower beds and then on through more wild shrubbery to reach the wall itself. The door looked solid, sealed in place, but it was the only way to get in and out of the palace without being seen. Fortunately, as a member of the Royal Family, I knew where to find the key—in a collection of old artifacts kept in the Guard Room, which I'd rifled through earlier in the evening as Peter worked out in the gym. I inserted it into the lock, praying it'd give way. With a firm budge of my shoulder, it began to move. I inched it open, peering out into the street beyond. At this time of night, there was nobody on the pavement, but there were cars streaming up and down the road. I paused to draw my hoodie up over my head, took a deep breath and slipped outside, away from the shield and protection of the palace.

I started off up the street, head bowed against the headlights of passing cars. Every rev of an engine felt like a gunshot, every light like it was exposing me for who I really was. I was wearing the blandest clothes I could find, but walking out in the open, it felt like I'd left the palace wearing the crown and carrying the scepter. With every step, I waited for someone to shout, to recognize me, or to have realized that I'd escaped. But I kept on going, my body tensed against anything that might stand in my way.

I hurried around the palace walls, keeping my head low, passing by the railings and crossing the street. The lights were bright to my left, but I ignored the calling of home and kept walking on toward the dark. When I finally reached the cusp of St. James's Park, I breathed a small sigh of relief, the shadows now immersing me, hiding me from sight.

The sound of the street fell away as I hopped over a small barrier and started up the gravel path, the car engines lost on the breeze. There were no streetlights here, just the glow from the road, and the darkness soon held me in its grasp. My heart hammered against my chest, skipping a beat at the sound of rustles in the bushes. The deeper I went into the park, the more my instincts screamed at me to turn back. To run. Even in the dark, I was exposed. If anything happened, nobody knew where I was. Nobody knew that I'd left the palace at all. Every step reminded me how stupid this idea had been, but instead I focused on the thought of Jonathan getting closer and kept on going.

The bridge was deserted, stretching over the expanse of black below. The pond appeared like a sheet of mirrored glass reflecting the night sky above. Every one of my senses was heightened as I stepped onto the bridge, my body warning me of dangers I couldn't yet see.

He wasn't here. It was midnight, like the note had said. Maybe even a few minutes later. But there was nobody on the bridge, or apparently in the park at all. The seconds ticked by, mocking me as they did, the sounds of the park morphing into beasts and demons that lurked just out of sight. Prowling in the dark. Ready to pounce.

With my heart beating in my ears, I didn't hear the first few footsteps, but I saw the shadow move out of the corner of my eye. It seemed to be a part of the pitch black, as if the night itself were bearing down on me. It froze me to the spot, the shadow slipping closer and closer, stepping onto the bridge and moving fast. I wanted to scream, but the air in my lungs was trapped. The shadow was too close to run from now. It was upon me. It was...

"Fancy seeing you here," a familiar voice said. But it wasn't Jonathan speaking. It was someone else—the only other person who could send a thrill like a lightning bolt through me.

"Everything okay? You look like you've seen a ghost," Grigor said, stepping out of the dark so I could finally see him. His russet-brown hair was hidden by a hood of his own, but his eyes seemed to attract the moonlight, twinkling back at me.

"Grigor?" I said, as if I'd never seen his face before. What was he doing here? He had to go, before Jonathan arrived. If he saw us together again, things would go from bad to worse.

"Uh, yes, that's me the last time I checked." Grigor frowned, bending a little so his eyes were level with mine. I stared back, dumbfounded, mouth slightly open. "Are you sure you're okay? I know sneaking out at night is a thrill and everything, but you look like you're about to pass out."

"What're you doing here? You have to go," I said, the words falling over themselves. Grigor cocked his head to one side, that same frown deepening until his eyebrows nearly touched.

"What do you mean, what am I doing here? You told me to meet you... *Midnight, on the bridge in St. James's Park. Come alone.* Remember?"

The darkness pressed in on me from all sides. "No, I didn't," I said. My mind began to race my heart as if they were in competition with each other. What was he talking about?

"Then why did I get a note telling me to come here? It was even signed with a *J*. I assumed it was from you, but..." Grigor trailed off. "Apparently not."

I shook my head. "I didn't send you that note. The envelope you gave me this morning told me to come here too."

Grigor seemed to be weighing something up. Despite the fact I had no idea why he was here, I still wanted to take a step closer, to protect myself from the night around us.

"Well, I didn't send you that note either. But if you snuck out of the palace and came all the way here, then who were you expecting to meet?"

I bit my lip. Jonathan's name felt like a sour sweet on my tongue. I didn't want to tell Grigor I was here to meet him. It would require too much explanation about something I could barely make sense of myself. Instead, I bowed my head, thinking quickly, but Grigor's next question came on the heels of his last.

"If I didn't send the note to you, and you didn't send the note to me . . . then who did?"

My note had come without an initial, without any sign of who'd sent it. I'd stupidly assumed it was Jonathan— who else would request to meet me in the dead of night, alone, and away from the glare of the palace?

"Your note was signed with a *J*?" I asked, thinking out loud. Grigor nodded, watching me carefully, like I was the one behind this plan to get us both here together. Could it be from Jonathan? Would he be stupid enough to sign his own initial on a note like that? And why would he want us here anyway?

"Do you still have the note?"

189

Grigor patted his jacket and shook his head. "I threw it away, just like the note told me to."

My thoughts were threatening to overwhelm me, but something stood out to me among the blur. Grigor had given me that note, supposedly passed on to him from one of the maids. Now he was here, telling me that he'd been sent the same note, but he'd apparently got rid of it, so I'd never be able to see it for myself. Convenient? Or just the truth?

"Look, I'm not exactly sure what's going on here, but you looked creeped out when I arrived, so I'm going to..." He stepped back, hands slightly raised as if he wanted to prove that he came in peace.

"Wait!" It shot out of me before I could stop it. The night surrounding us seemed dangerous, and I didn't want to be alone. Standing with Grigor was like shining a torch into that darkness. No matter who had sent the notes, I wanted him to stay. I fidgeted uncomfortably, hoping I wouldn't have to say it out loud. But Grigor took his cue with a raised eyebrow.

"Shall we?" He nodded in one direction and started slowly walking, letting me catch up to his side. "The palace looks nice from here," he said, stopping in his tracks before we'd gone more than three paces.

I looked up, and sure enough, home glinted back at me through a space in the trees. The lights twinkled, a beacon of hope, something to guide me. It still felt miles away though, even if it wasn't all that far, so I stepped closer to Grigor, feeling the air come alive in the centimeters between us.

We began walking with no real aim, picking a path at

random and wandering into the dark. For a brief moment, I forgot that I was king and why I'd snuck out of the palace in the first place. All I could focus on was Grigor. The way his body leaned into mine with each stride, the glances he gave me out of the corner of his eye, a smile never far from his face. He talked to me as if we were equals, as if we were just two teenagers going the long way home so we could keep walking together, neither one of us wanting to cut the night short. There was nobody else around—nobody else in the world—except us, lost in a moment, away from everything.

"How did you even get here?" I asked, holding my arms around myself.

"A cab, of course. I was already in the city, so it wasn't far. Some of us can still be seen in public, you know." He grinned as I rolled my eyes. "I bet you've never even taken public transport before."

"I have!" I countered, immediately defensive.

"Riding a train one stop to promote the opening of a new line doesn't count." I fought for something to say, but I had nothing. He was right. Of course. He burst out laughing, the sound skipping off into the trees. "I'll have to take you out one day. For a proper day out, not one of those *Your carriage awaits, Your Majesty* days out."

"Like you can talk. How many bedrooms is your manor again?"

"You should know. It was a gift from your father, after all. But, hey, we don't have a throne room...." He paused dramatically. "Oh wait, we do—it's just that us commoners call it a bathroom instead."

Grigor's family lived a few miles away within the grounds of Kensington Palace in a townhouse gifted to them by my dad. Lord and Lady Greenwood were close friends of the family, our histories intertwined over generations. They'd adopted Grigor as a baby, finding their last piece of happiness to make their family complete.

We kept wandering, talking about everything and nothing at the same time. It felt like we'd been walking for hours, and yet it wasn't long enough. The rustles of the park didn't scare me anymore. I was too focused on Grigor's words, the way they dipped low, then rose as he fought a laugh. I could listen to him talk all night, clinging to the growing warmth it gave me as it spread through my body. I liked him. I hadn't had a chance to realize that before.

But with it came the pinching thought of Jonathan and the urge to push Grigor away. I loved Jonathan. Or I had. Did I still? Was I letting Grigor cloud that, or was it Jonathan's actions that were pushing me into his arms? My secrets had already cost me too much. Could I really afford to take that risk again?

"I guess we should think about getting you home, huh? God forbid someone discover that the king is missing at this time of night." Grigor checked his watch and sighed. "It's past two. How are you even getting back in there without getting caught?"

"I have my ways," I said, touching my finger to my nose.

We stopped in a patch of darkness, close enough to the road that the amber pools of streetlights were barely out of reach. The wide stretch of the Mall was almost empty except for the odd car, purring past us every now and then. Grigor turned to face me. The moment stood between us, begging one of us to grasp it. A smile tugged at the corner of his mouth, his eyes never moving from mine. He started to lean in and the world around us melted away, my heart counting the milliseconds. All I could see was him.

Click.

The sound in the silence burst the bubble, the moment fluttering up into the air, out of our reach. We'd both heard it. In the dead of night, the smallest noise echoed like a gunshot.

Click.

Again. I cast my eyes around us, over the pond, through the trees, trying to find the source. Grigor did the same, still only a step away from me.

Click.

This time the sound was accompanied by a rustle as part of the night separated itself into a lone shadow. It was a little way behind us, slipping through the dark, slowly at first, then faster and faster.

Click.

I couldn't move. I couldn't breathe. The shadow had become a hooded figure, and there was no mistaking that it was coming straight toward us.

"Run," Grigor whispered, grabbing my arm. He pushed me away, toward the palace. "Go!"

"What? I'm not leaving you," I uttered, trembling.

"You're the king! Don't worry about me, just go!"

He pushed me in the opposite direction, and this time

I let him. I nearly fell over myself in my haste, but then I was running toward the light of the Mall. Toward safety. Who cared if I was seen when there were shadows chasing us in the dark?

I hit the pavement and didn't stop, tearing up the street, my eyes on the palace at the end of the road. I wanted to scream out for help but my lungs were burning. A car revved by me, beeping its horn as I fell into the road. A small group of teenagers, sitting on a fence smoking, hooted as I darted past. Then one of them said, "Wait, isn't that…"

But the rest of their words were ripped away by the sound of another engine, this one angrier than the one before. Its tires screeched as I reached the memorial outside the palace. I could feel the car's presence by my shoulder and the shouts of a passenger. I didn't have time to get back inside the palace the way I'd left, so I ran straight for the front railings.

"OPEN THE GATES!" I yelled. I slammed into them, but they didn't budge. "OPEN THE GATES! LET ME IN!"

There was the slam of car doors behind me, followed by the stampeding footsteps of people in a hurry. Dread trickled ice-cold through my veins as I heard the unmistakable click of cameras.

"SOMEONE OPEN THE GATES!" I shouted again, this time trying to clamber up them. Several guardsmen appeared at once and I breathed a sigh of relief.

But it quickly turned to horror when I saw their guns raised and pointing at my chest.

CHAPTER SIXTEEN

I YIELD

HANDS WHERE WE CAN SEE THEM! NOW!"
I stepped back from the gate as the King's
Guard—my guard—edged forward, guns mounted. The
gates remained shut as they charged, moving as one orches-
trated squad. I didn't want to move a single muscle, not
when their guns were trained on me, but every fiber of my
body screamed, a torturous adrenaline slithering over my
skin. I wanted to step outside of my body and run—keep
on running far away, until I could never be found again.

"Step away from the gates and get down on your
knees," one of the guards said from behind his gun, his
voice gruff and deadly. The flashes of a million cameras
went off behind me, a murmur spreading between people
I couldn't see.

I wanted to speak, to shout out that it was me, the person who this palace swore to protect. But this guard had seen me up close, looked me directly in the eye, and seen somebody else. He didn't see the king. He saw a trespasser trying to break into the palace. Fighting back tears, I raised my hands and sank to my knees.

"It's the king!" somebody behind me shouted out. Each word felt like a burn on my back.

The guard's eyes narrowed as he took another step toward the gate, his nose centimeters from the railings as he looked down at me. I lifted my head up so the lights of the palace could find their way beneath the hood I'd forgotten I still had up as a pathetic protection. He leaned down, nothing but the bars between us. Then the realization spread over his face, slowly at first and then all at once. After a few seconds, the guard's face fell completely, eyes widening, his mouth dropping open.

"GET THE GATES OPEN!" he shouted, his gun now hanging limply by his side.

The other guards scattered as the gates inched forward. I felt nothing but shame, kneeling before the palace. The cameras trained on my back were just as intimidating as the guns that had borne down on me. It took all my strength to stand back up under their glare. I didn't stop to explain to the guards. I couldn't even look them in the face. Instead, I ran through the gates, into the palace courtyard and through the waiting door, which had been flung open to receive me.

"What on earth is going on?" I heard Gayle say before

she appeared round the corner, wrapped in a pale green dressing gown with slippers on her feet and a scarf hiding her hair. Her face dropped when she saw me, standing there in my hoodie.

Peter wheeled round the corner too, still in his suit and tie. Gayle looked over my shoulder to see the guards running around like headless chickens, the front gates now closed, but the flashes from paparazzi cameras still illuminating the forecourt.

"What have you done?" she whispered.

I didn't have an answer to that. I could barely comprehend what had happened tonight, how it had started with so much confusion and ended with so much chaos. Only now, back inside the palace, it was starting to dawn on me what a mess I'd made.

Gayle and Peter ushered me upstairs into my quarters. Gayle quickly drew the curtains, even though nobody on that side of the palace would be able to see in. I fell into a chair with my head in my hands. Each second that passed offered a different snapshot in my mind of the night's events, and then a glimpse of new disasters that would now lie ahead.

Mum nearly fell through the door, Eddie in her shadow, breaking me away from my thoughts. They both took one look at me, then flicked their gazes to the solemn faces of Gayle and Peter. The worry entrenched on Mum's face made the guilt in my gut flare.

"Dear God, what's happened?"

I didn't know where to start, or how much I should

say. The more I thought about it, the worse it seemed. There was no point in keeping secrets—the cameras outside had made sure that at least part of my night was documented. Possibly the worst part. Only when I thought of the pictures that would grace the front pages in the morning did the pieces of the puzzle begin to fall into place. The paparazzi hadn't just been waiting for me outside the palace—they'd been watching from the shadows before I'd even escaped St. James's Park. Someone had tipped them off.

I couldn't admit the whole truth. I had to mention Grigor, since our picture was probably already on an editor's desk, but I didn't mention the note, or what I'd been in the park to do. I kept my head low, ducked in shame and guilt, and simply said I'd broken out of the palace so the two of us could go for a walk. I couldn't decide if it sounded better or worse than what had actually happened. Peter dropped his head into his hands as I explained, no doubt kicking himself for allowing me to wander the gardens alone when he'd been so reluctant to let me go in the first place.

"How could the guards not recognize him? He's the king!" Gayle spluttered.

Mum laughed bitterly, coming to stand beside me. She grabbed my hand and pulled me up to my feet.

"Tell me who you see," Mum said, her words dark and shadowed with rage. Gayle drew back, but Mum pulled me forward into the middle of the living room, swiping the hood from my head. "Tell me who you see," she repeated.

"I see James," Gayle said quietly, eyes flickering between me and Mum.

"Now, tell me what *they* see?" I could feel Mum's hand trembling on my arm. This time, she didn't wait for an answer. "They see a Black boy. They don't see a king. They don't see somebody who sits on the throne they swear to protect. They were close enough to see his face. Close enough to look into his eyes and see who was standing on the other side of that gate. But they saw what they wanted to see—a Black teenager, wearing a hoodie, trying to gain access to a place they think he has no business being inside of, and they raised their guns."

"Your Highness...," Gayle tried, but Mum cut her off before she could get any further. She pointed to me, to Eddie, to herself.

"They will never see us. *Really* see us. They will only ever see our skin first—anything else comes second. They prove that even when we occupy space we have every right to be in. Whether we are doctors on a ward, drivers on a bus, or royalty sat upon thrones, we will *never* be gifted their acceptance. What would've happened if the guard had fired before they'd realized their error? No apology in the world, no amount of regret or pleading that it was a mistake, would've been able to change the outcome."

Every word was a bullet in itself, punching straight through me and leaving me in pieces. The sneer of the guard looking down at me on my knees played back in my mind, taunting me with the thoughts I'd been trying to drown within me—that I would never be king. I could have the title, but what use was that when nobody else believed in it?

Mum let go of my arm, her face cracked by the sadness and overwhelming fury that her words had inflicted on all of us. It was the truth. We all knew it. She turned to face me, the rest of the room falling away so that we only saw each other. What she had feared had come to pass, and no matter how hard she fought, she would never be able to protect me. But she would try.

"Leave us," Mum said, not taking her eyes off me.

Gayle cleared her throat. "Your Highness, we must—"

"Sort it. I don't care how." Mum was past being polite. She never let that front drop, knowing that if her mask slipped in front of the wrong person, she'd find herself at the mercy of someone like Buckley and his venomous pen. But right now, she didn't care.

Gayle and Peter left the room, leaving the three of us alone. Eddie's hand found the small of my back, guiding me to the sofa, our argument a distant memory. I looked at him, to say sorry or thank you or *something* to tell him how much I needed him right now and always would. But he just shook his head before I could speak.

"I don't care what was said before. We're brothers."

It was enough to push me over the edge. I fell onto the sofa beside Mum, the emotions I'd been suffocating finally rushing up for air.

"Let it go," she whispered.

And I did. The cry that escaped my lips was tight, restrained, like I was still trying to cling to myself. But it was quickly followed by another and then another, until I couldn't hold on anymore.

Mum pulled me close and I collapsed into her, every sob nourished by what I had tried to bury. "I've got you," she said, stroking my head with trembling hands. "I've got you."

As I cried, the night outside settled into a tranquil peace, the waters of chaos stilled by the purgatory between darkness and light. But as morning crept into the sky, a new storm was already brewing.

KING HELD AT GUNPOINT AFTER MOONLIT RENDEZVOUS

REVEALED: Exclusive pictures expose secret dates in St. James's Park

By Quinn Buckley, *ROYAL REPORTER*

In a dramatic turn of events that unfolded in the early hours of the morning, King James was held at gunpoint at the gates of Buckingham Palace and refused entry to the grounds by his own guard. But perhaps stranger still is the king's reason for breaking free of the palace in the first place, a secret the *Daily Eye* can exclusively reveal.

After reports yesterday revealed that the king has been conducting a secret relationship behind the smoke screen of a fake romance with Ophelia Budd, it seems that the seventeen-year-old is continuing to lay his focus on his personal relationships. Rather than tend to matters such as the planning of his father's upcoming funeral, the king instead spent the night wandering St. James's Park on a midnight date.

These exclusive pictures show King James and his mystery companion roaming the park well into the early hours, the king seemingly without a care in the world. In one snap, he was pictured throwing his head back to laugh, an action at odds with his charade of grief over the last few days.

But more alarming still is the small detail that the king's close friend, who accompanied him for his moonlit walk, was not the person he is said to be in a secret relationship with. In fact, sources close to the Royal Family, and to King James himself, have now claimed that his initial romance has soured following a new candidate entering the picture.

These complications offer yet more proof that King James, sitting on the throne as the first Black monarch, is not ready to live up to the title that he has been given. If the funeral of a father and duty to this country pale in comparison to immature matters of the heart, then what hope can we possibly have in His Majesty?

FULL STORY AND EXCLUSIVE PIC-TURES ON PAGES 4, 5, 6 and 7.

<hr>

I threw the paper away in disgust. Just holding it felt like touching a scorching hot iron. It skidded across the table, falling off the other side and landing in a crumpled heap on the carpet.

How could things be getting worse?

Every front page that morning was splashed with blown-up snapshots of the palace drenched in darkness, the guards standing at the gates with their guns pointed at me, kneeling with my hands raised.

One of Gayle's moles revealed that the newspapers had been tipped off about a "situation" in advance, meaning their cameras were waiting for it all to unfold. But it was the *Eye* that had clearly been in on the games, hiding their photographer in the bushes of St. James's Park while the others waited at the gates. They'd known I'd be there with Grigor. Whoever had sent those notes to us and told Buckley that my relationship with Jonathan had turned "sour" had to be behind this. I didn't want to believe it was him, out to ruin me in some vain attempt at petty revenge. But right now, looking at the pictures of me and Grigor, purposefully selected to make it look like we were all over each other, I didn't have much choice.

The *Daily Eye* were painting a sleazy story, replacing actual fact with their own fiction. Buckley and his parasitic racism had decided I was not fit for the throne, and so now he was doing everything in his power to swipe the crown from my head. He wasn't even trying to be subtle about outing me anymore. The gloves had never really been on in the first place, but they were officially off now.

A butler materialized at the door of my living room, scooping up the newspaper from the floor and tucking it under his jacket in one swift move. "You have a visitor, Your Majesty. He refuses to leave the palace until he's seen you."

I looked up, expecting…I didn't know who. It could've been anyone. But there, a mask of worry pulled tight over his gorgeous face, was Grigor. My heart fluttered into a frenzy at the sight of him, standing there with his hands in his pockets, his piercing eyes on me and me alone.

"Thank you," I said to the butler, and he vanished within a second, leaving us alone. The air in the room suddenly felt thick and heavy, weighing down on both of us.

As soon as the door closed, Grigor crossed the room in easy strides. I stood up to greet him, but he swept past my pathetic outstretched hand and wrapped me in a fierce hug instead. My arms stretched around his back, the urge to let him hold me taking over. His body sighed into mine, an escaped breath dancing across my neck.

I pulled away reluctantly. His hand lingered just a moment longer on my back and it sent desire rippling through me. Even lost within my own torment, I couldn't deny my attraction to him.

Grigor refused to take his eyes off mine, holding his ground and searching for something. He wasn't so much looking at me as through me, into me, unfurling every thought buried deep in my mind with gentle curiosity. I shied away, taking a seat on the sofa.

"So, this is what it's like to be the center of attention then?" He chuckled darkly to himself as he took a seat next to me, leaving barely any space between us. He stretched his arm across the back of the sofa, letting his head fall so he could stare at the ceiling.

"I'm sorry." I couldn't say anything else. Here was another person's life I'd successfully ruined without even trying. They were beginning to pile up, left in my wake. Ophelia, Jonathan, Eddie, Grigor. So many people were getting hurt as a result of me sitting on the throne.

Grigor sat up straight, turning his body toward mine. A loose strand of copper hair curled down onto his forehead as he met my eyes again. "Why are you sorry?"

I threw my hands up in the air, gesturing at the door and the windows and everybody outside of them who was gunning for me but taking down others at the same time. "I have everything to be sorry for," I said. "I've dragged you and your life into the newspapers for everyone to see and now they know that you're..."

I trailed off. I hadn't even thought about what Grigor might be. I didn't actually know if he was interested in me, or just trying to provide a comforting, friendly shoulder. I'd let myself assume, to feel better about this mess, but now I couldn't be sure if I'd been dreaming up fantasies that were better than the reality before me. Grigor scooted closer, his knee touching mine. It might have been nothing more than an accident, and yet I hoped it answered my question. That small touch, insignificant as it might be, made me feel alive.

"You have nothing to be sorry for. Why would I ever think that this is your fault? I couldn't care less what they say. I'm fine. But this isn't about me—this is about you."

"It's always about me," I snapped. "Everybody else is expected to stand behind and live in my shadow. I'm tired of making the people around me feel like they're nothing more than collateral damage. They deserve to live and to feel and to see the light too."

"In fairness, I'm living in the light today, and it's not all it's cracked up to be." Grigor's grin dissipated my rage like water through a sieve. It lit up parts of me that'd been shrouded in darkness for days. It gave me just a flicker of hope. But beneath that hope, or maybe even within it, was Jonathan. Every thought and feeling I had about Grigor always led back to him. I couldn't separate the two. All I knew for sure was that my feelings for Jonathan were wilting in the face of each new story he seemed to be telling Quinn Buckley. The way I'd felt about him before belonged to another lifetime.

"We still need to figure out who sent those notes," I mumbled, picking at a thread on the cushion beside me to stop myself staring gormlessly at Grigor and his stupidly beautiful smile.

"How about this? If I actually write you a note, I'll make sure to sign it with something. A little code, so you know it's me."

I couldn't stop my own smile, which escaped too quickly. "You're going to be writing me notes now?"

"Only if you write me one back," he said, not once looking away. "I was thinking about all of that in the *Eye* today, making out that we were up to no good in the park. We surely can't let that be our first date."

"Since when was it a date?" I countered, looking slightly below his eyeline so I wouldn't completely buckle while trying to . . . flirt? Was I flirting? In the predicament we were in? Wasn't *that* what had got me in trouble in the first place?

Grigor pretended to mull over the question, raising his eyebrows while I sucked in my cheeks to stop myself from laughing. It felt ludicrous to experience even a droplet of joy right now when everything else was going from bad to worse. But being in proximity to Grigor made it impossible to wallow in sadness.

"Maybe if this king stuff doesn't work out, you'll humor me for an evening," he said. He was now so close to me that it felt like a kind of sweet torture.

"You'd still want a date if I'm not king?" I half joked.

Grigor leaned in even closer, a whisper away. My heart stopped and then started once more, lust erupting from within it with each thunderous beat. But as his lips parted to deliver the killer blow, there was a sharp knock at the door. I exhaled the breath I'd been holding as Grigor ducked his head to chuckle to himself. He murmured something I didn't hear and then moved back to an appropriate, friendly distance.

"Enter," I called.

Gayle, of course, was behind the door, her narrowed eyes taking in Grigor. Her lips pursed as she looked at me. "There are some private matters to attend to, Your Majesty," she said bluntly.

There was always *something to attend to* as king. I sighed, pulling myself up to my feet. "I guess I'll see you around then," I murmured to Grigor, wishing more than anything that Gayle would leave us so we could say good-bye away from her glaring spotlight.

"I'm sure of it." Grigor sprung up, dipping into a swift bow. He angled his head just right so only I could see him smirk as he did so.

Of course, the matters to attend to would be about Grigor, the night before and how we'd defend ourselves. Have you ever tried evading questions about someone you might have a crush on? Well, try that when you're the king of the United Kingdom and your mother, senior advisor and seemingly every other person in the entire world want answers. All while pictures from your first *kind-of-a-date-but-is-it-actually-a-date-or-are-we-just-friends* are being passed from hand to hand with glee.

It struck me then, as I watched him go, that I wanted nothing more than to leave the palace with him, maybe continue where we'd left off. But I shook the thought away. I needed to concentrate. There were enemies circling, dark threats that loomed just out of sight. And away from Grigor's glow, they reared their ugly heads once more, intent on orchestrating my demise.

CHAPTER SEVENTEEN

DISMISSAL

As the days passed by and the funeral quickly approached, Quinn Buckley and the *Daily Eye* continued their relentless attack, using any nugget of information they could get their hands on. It felt like my whole life was on display for the public to dissect, turn over in their fingers and toss away when they were done, only to pick up the next morsel and repeat the cycle.

And it was no longer just me they were hunting with their pens—it was Mum and Eddie too. Lies about Mum had been prevalent since she first stepped into the royal spotlight, but Eddie, aside from the school suspension hiccup, was often looked at as the fun and whimsical brother—the one who would've made the more natural king over me. Now, even his faint halo was skewed, tarnished by association.

Mum was a bitch who conjured up new ways to make her staff's lives hell on a daily basis. She'd spat in a maid's food for not running her bath at the right temperature, reduced another to tears by screaming at her for wearing the wrong shade of tights, taken up firing staff on the spot for sport. None of it was true, and she didn't care. Or, if she did, she kept those feelings buried where even we couldn't see them. But people were starting to believe that no matter how ridiculous the rumors were, there couldn't be a plume of smoke without a single flame. If the newspapers and anonymous social media posts said it, then it simply had to contain an element of truth.

As for Eddie—he was a drunk. His underage drinking had escalated out of control and an intervention had been made, various rehab facilities investigated behind closed doors. Again, the stories weren't true, although these ones weren't necessarily an attack—instead, they were painted as a cry for help and somehow used to reflect on how careless our mother was, and how drunk on my own power I'd become. A source close to the family had apparently told Quinn that my arrogance had driven a wedge between us and forced my twin to find other forms of escape.

The articles had sent ripples of anger through the entire country, rousing every racist from their slumber. Now that they had an instrument to channel their bigotry through, they weren't even trying to keep it subtle. Gone were the insults tied in bows so they'd appear as something else. Now there were signs waved outside the palace gates in growing numbers, telling us to go back to our own country, to admit that we'd scammed our way into the palace through lies and deception. There were think pieces and conspiracy theories about how Mum had hoodwinked Dad by tricking him with some kind of witchcraft to orchestrate a devious plan to overthrow the monarchy and lead a Black uprising. Apparently, if she wasn't stopped, white people would become slaves in their own country.

It was ridiculous. So ridiculous, I was sure that nobody could possibly stretch their imagination far enough to believe any of it. And yet, something was happening. The tide wasn't so much turning as rising, inching up the golden legs of the throne. We needed to do something, or we would sink.

On the night before the funeral, Peter appeared in my quarters. The day had been exhausting and it sat deep in my bones. It was past midnight, but final preparations were still being made. Tomorrow, we'd step out in public and say our goodbyes. Who knew what would happen when we appeared out there?

"I know this is the last thing you want to talk about, Your Majesty, but I have some updates. They're too important to wait." Peter's tie was slightly crooked, a detail I shouldn't have noticed but now couldn't take my eyes off of. I sighed and nodded, gesturing for him to take a seat. Peter shook his head and remained standing tall, his hands behind his back.

"It's Ophelia, sir. I've received word that she's dismissed the protection officer we gave her."

Ice crept through my veins. "She did what?"

Peter's face remained passive, but I could see the effort it was taking him to keep it that way. "The officer returned to the palace today. When I asked him why he wasn't with Ophelia, he said she'd ordered him away and instructed him not to return. She told him, 'You people have done enough. I don't need your help.'"

The weight of Ophelia's words, even if spoken more kindly by Peter, pushed me back into my seat. *You people.* She didn't mean the protection officer, or even the press that had been hounding her. She meant us—the family who'd used her as a shield to hide my secrets behind.

I dug out my phone and found my text chain with Ophelia, searching for answers. But one I didn't want to see glared back at me. She'd messaged me twice—yesterday and then again this morning—asking to talk. In a blur of Grigor and Quinn and every demon that now hunted me, I'd missed them both. And so Ophelia was wrong about one thing—I clearly *hadn't* done enough.

"She's not herself, sir," Peter said softly. "From what he *did* see, the protection officer says she's become increasingly upset, especially when the officer explained he needed to go with her if she was leaving the house."

I buried my head in my hands. "We're not protecting her, we're smothering her. Maybe she just needs space." I wasn't sure I believed it, and Peter clearly didn't either, but he nodded and moved on.

"One last thing. It's about Cassandra."

I sat up a little straighter. She'd been quiet lately. What was she up to?

"It seems that Cassandra has been leaving the palace without *her* protection officer too. At first, we didn't know she'd been leaving at all, which is why the officer hadn't been alerted. But while I was scouring the CCTV, a car registered to one of her friends arrived at the back of the palace, parking in a blind spot just away from the cameras' reach."

"And...," I pressed.

Peter smiled. "Their plan might've succeeded, but unfortunately for them, the palace has rather a lot of windows. I zoomed in on one and, in the reflection, saw Cassandra skip outside and hide herself in the boot. The friend then drove out of the palace, returning a few hours later with Cassandra, once again, hidden out of sight."

I shot up from the sofa, pacing the room to let my sky-rocketing adrenaline come back down. "If Cassandra is going to all of that trouble to leave the palace undetected, then she doesn't want to be seen for a reason," I mused out loud. "What is she hiding?" I stopped in my tracks and looked at Peter, who shrugged.

"That remains unclear, Your Majesty. But, rest assured, we'll find out."

CHAPTER EIGHTEEN

UNMARKED GRAVES

The horses stood as still as shadows, heads held high and craned slightly up toward the morning sky. The soft light caught their rich black manes, streaking them with slivers of silver. A line of guards in military uniform stood beside them, next to a row of the King's Guard in their red tunics and tall hats. In the middle of it all lay my father's coffin, a singular wreath mounted on the middle of its lid and surrounded by bunches of the finest white lilies and delicate roses.

I looked down on the courtyard from my window, taking it all in. There was an eerie silence that had crept out of the palace and onto the pavements beyond, wrapping itself around the city like a held breath. The day before, the coffin had been driven in its hearse to lay in rest for one last night at Buckingham Palace. Now, it was preparing to make its final journey, leaving the palace behind forever.

The door behind me opened without a knock, Eddie striding into the room in his tailored suit. Whereas my grief shrouded me like a morbid cloud, Eddie's was restrained, held back behind his defenses. He'd always been better at slamming down the shutters. I was too sensitive. He was too apathetic. But we met in the middle to cancel each other out and bring the balance back to zero.

We stood side by side, staring out of the window together at the coffin below. This would be the last gift of privacy that we'd be granted before we were thrown out under the cameras and asked to dance for the public. The seconds ticked in my ears, counting down like a bomb.

"I don't think Ophelia's coming," I murmured to fill the silence so I could ignore that ominous tick.

"No?"

I shook my head. "Peter says she's dismissed the protection officer. I've tried to call her, but she won't pick up."

A dozen unanswered calls from the night before sat in my phone, each one telling me I'd left it too late to make things right. It worried me. Ophelia was a part of our inner circle, but someone who ultimately held no real allegiance to us. I couldn't help but wonder if she resented me—all of us—for getting her into this mess in the first place. Would her life ever be the same again, or would she now always be tainted by the lie we'd used her to create? I could understand why she would want to keep her distance, but that didn't stop the anxious questions in my head from creating disasters that might lie in wait. But for now, I had to push those thoughts away. I had my father's funeral to focus on.

"Are you ready for this?" I asked quietly.

Eddie shook his head. "You?"

"I'd rather walk through fire."

Eddie breathed a laugh. "Funny, because that's exactly what we're about to do."

I nodded down below, where Gayle had just stepped outside dressed in a neat black skirt and blazer. "I guess this is it then," I murmured.

Somewhere in the distance, the tenor bell of Westminster Abbey tolled a single, mournful chime, as it would every minute of the procession. It was time.

"Let's get this over with," Eddie said, and headed for the door.

The silence within the palace was deafening, bolstered by the still blanket that had lain itself on the streets outside. The only sound was the shuffle of our feet on the burgundy carpet as we reached the Grand Staircase and descended to face whatever lay ahead.

In the courtyard, the rest of our family waited. Cassandra stood detached from them all, disinterested in the commotion around her. Instead, her fingers flew over the screen of her phone, her face set in concentration. As we stepped out into the sun, I thought about what Peter had told me the night before and wondered what she could be up to now. My suspicion only grew as she raised her phone to her ear and moved farther away, turning her back. I wanted to know what could be so important that it couldn't wait until *after* a funeral, but now wasn't the time to focus on that.

Mum had stepped through the guards to rest her gloved hand on the coffin. She was dressed in immaculate black, a matching veil sweeping down to the ground and engulfing her. She murmured her final words, then stepped back. I could just about make out her sparkling eyes, shining with tears, but otherwise she'd be hidden from the public's sight, granted one small slither of privacy to mourn.

She placed a hand on my arm and the other on Eddie's, taking us both in. "Together," she said. Her voice was strong, but notes of grief underlined it.

As a family, we stepped through the arches of the palace, out toward the gates. Beyond, thousands of people stood in silence, the cloud of grief looming overhead. The crowds were half a dozen deep, stretching down the Mall and disappearing through the arches on the other side. They'd lined the streets all the way to Westminster Abbey, flowers in their hands and sorrow in their hearts. But all I saw were enemies, or potential ones at least. They could be hidden anywhere in the crowd, waiting to impale me with their cries. As if she sensed my reservation, Mum reached for my hand as the clip of hooves sounded and the coffin was pulled forward.

It came up through the gates and began its long and lonely journey to the abbey. As it passed us, we bowed our heads in unison. I folded my lips hard, forcing my tears to retreat for a moment. After everything that had happened, I wouldn't give the world the satisfaction. Even if it was my father's funeral, I wouldn't let them see me break.

"The car's ready, Your Majesty," Peter murmured in my ear. I gave one last look at the procession as it retreated from the palace. The roads had been closed, the pavements separated from the route with metal barriers and lined with armed police. The path was clear for my father's final journey.

Our cars waited for the coffin to make its way farther down the Mall before starting their engines and pulling away from the palace, veering in another direction to take us directly to the abbey. The whole way, I kept my head bowed, the only sound the murmur of Peter and Walsh discussing security arrangements for our arrival. The crowds flashed past me, throwing their flowers on the road as if they were guiding us with petals. Maybe the occasion had quieted the drama, at least for today. For the first time, people seemed to be trying to hold me up rather than tear me down, and I welcomed the support.

As we arrived, the Great West Door of Westminster Abbey lay open for us, the notes of an organ floating through it to meet me as I stepped out from the car. I climbed the few steps and shook hands with the Dean of Westminster, an old and withered man who'd be helping to lead the service. His pearly white mustache curled around his full cheeks, and his glasses were so thick that his eyes appeared to be bulging out of his head.

"Your Majesty," he groaned, his voice one long drawl. He bowed, then stepped aside to welcome us in.

The abbey itself was cavernous, packed out with thousands of guests from around the world. I spotted Louie and his parents seated a dozen rows from the front, Delphine and hers not far behind. In fact, almost everyone who graced the palace for Eddie's parties was there, craning their necks to catch a glimpse of my family as we entered. We kept our backs straight, eyes trained on the altar at the end of the aisle, ignoring every whisper, every shuffle to get a better look. We walked forward without missing a step or breaking our ranks, me at the head of the pack, followed by Eddie and Mum, then everybody else. But just before we took our seats, my glance was pulled into the pews as if by magnetic force, and I locked eyes with Grigor. He sat up tall next to his parents in the sixth row, hands folded in his lap. His face was smoothed of any emotion, calm and uninterrupted. But, before I could look away, he gave me a small nod. It punctured the bubble of tension that had been blooming in my stomach. Yet, as I took my seat next to where the coffin would be laid, a new and bitter anxiety began to sprout in its place.

The music stopped, instantly replaced by a chorus of angelic voices. A choir dressed in white robes appeared at the end of the aisle, walking slowly toward the altar, every note of their mournful call fluttering up into the vaulted ceiling. Goose bumps prickled my skin, a lump forming in the back of my throat. Behind the choir, the pallbearers entered the abbey, my father's coffin resting on their shoulders. They shuffled forward in uniform movement as they made their way toward us.

The choir's song washed over and through me, pulling up the emotions I'd tried to bury so I could get through this public moment. Eddie looked pained, staring straight ahead, his eyes never touching the coffin in the minutes it took to reach us. A gentle, fragile sob escaped from under my mother's veil. In turn, I could feel myself tumbling, falling into a void of despair as the voices of the choir ceased and the coffin came to rest on its plinth. The Dean of Westminster joined my father, his movements slow and particular. He opened his Bible, ready to speak.

I shot up out of my chair. I couldn't do it. I couldn't sit here in front of my father's coffin and pretend. I needed to breathe. I needed to escape, to collect myself for a moment.

"James...," Mum started. But I'd spotted a small door close to us and had already charged for it, thankful that it opened so I could fall through to the other side, away from the searching eyes and cameras.

I bent over double, hands on my knees, gasping for air. My entire body trembled as if it had been overtaken by a new entity that it was trying to reject. Every gulp of air made me feel like I was drowning. I focused on the stone beneath my feet, the only thing keeping me rooted to the earth. One slow breath in. One slow breath out. Repeat. One slow breath in. One slow breath out. Repeat.

"James?"

I flinched. I hadn't realized I wasn't alone in the

corridor. Grigor stepped out of the shadows, tucking his phone into his pocket. Unlike before in the pews, his face now told a different story—one of concern and worry. Pity too, or was that just my imagination? I straightened up, the sickness churning in my stomach barely calmed.

"What're you doing out here?" Each word quivered on my lips.

Grigor waved off the question and came in close, resting firm hands on my shoulders. His eyes bore into mine, strong and reassuring, willing me on. "An hour and you'll have got through this. Take one step at a time. It's just you and your family out there. Forget everybody else."

He placed a finger under my chin, pushing my face up to meet his.

"You can do this. I know you can."

The door into the abbey opened and beyond it I could hear the murmurs of people hunting for me. It was Eddie. He didn't even blink when he saw Grigor standing there, comforting hands still on my shoulders. His eyes were only on me.

"They're waiting out there. For you. So they can start." He'd let his defenses take over, hiding himself behind them.

"I'm coming," I muttered. I took one last glance into Grigor's eyes and followed my brother back out into the abbey, ignoring the whispers as I reappeared. I took my seat and nodded to the dean, who took his cue and interrupted the quiet babble.

"We are gathered here today to celebrate the remarkable

life of a king," he began in that slow inflection that made every word three times its usual length.

I zoned out, the abbey falling away around me as I concentrated on my dad, my mind filling with memories. Of playing football on the palace lawns. Of sharing inside jokes at the tables of important state dinners. Of him shouting and whooping louder than any other parent at our primary school graduation, and again as we finished secondary school. Of those private moments, few and far between, when I didn't have to share him with the entire world. When he wasn't the king but was simply my dad.

A glimpse of movement out of the corner of my eye snapped me back to attention. Something was wrong. My heart started to race before my brain caught up with what was happening. It was at the other end of the abbey, unseen by the guests who were facing the Dean of Westminster, his drone still commanding their attention. But I could see Peter and a swarm of guards huddled together, deep in hurried conversation before they dispersed and headed for the outskirts of the church.

Eddie saw it too, his head whipping around to see what was going on. Mum sat up a little straighter, her body rigid. Gayle sat unmoving, but her eyes swept over the guests, finding small pockets of subtle chaos beginning to slowly unfold.

I found Peter again and watched him edge around the abbey, slinking closer to us at the front. He had a hand over his ear, listening to his radio. When he moved it away again, he was striding faster until he was behind my chair, ducking to whisper into my ear.

"Your Majesty, we need to get you out of here." The gentle breeze of his murmur didn't mask the urgency beneath the words. I didn't move, aware that hundreds of eyes were already on me.

"What's happened?" I murmured.

"There's been a threat on your life, sir. We need to move you to safety."

It was like I'd been plunged into freezing cold water and held under its surface with no air in my lungs. Time slowed down while my heart sped up, pounding in my ears. I tried to remain placid in my seat, those eyes all around burning through me, but inside, my body was screaming.

"No threat will make me leave my father's funeral," I whispered shakily. "We're in the middle of Westminster Abbey surrounded by guards and armed police—we must be safe here."

The dean glanced in my direction, briefly stumbling over his words as he saw Peter crouched behind me. I nodded for him to continue.

"I understand, sir. But..."

"But what?" I pushed as the dean began to wind down his speech.

Peter held his breath, and then let it go. "We've received an anonymous call that says there's a plan to bomb the abbey."

Fear sliced its way through me. Although I remained still, my body was itching to run. But I refused. I wouldn't be pushed away from grieving my father.

"That's ridiculous. Impossible. It's a hoax." I couldn't be sure if I meant it, or if I was just trying to convince myself. A bomb in what was currently one of the most well-guarded places on earth? It couldn't be true.

"Hoax or not, sir, we have to take it seriously," Peter tried one last time, but I'd already made up my mind. How would it look if we suddenly stood and exited the abbey when the funeral had barely begun? We'd look like cowards, made to run. And what would Quinn Buckley make of that? Threat on my life or not, he wouldn't let me live it down. He would twist the truth to fit his own narrative.

"No," I said with finality. "We're not running away. I want to grieve my father. And *then* you can do whatever you please."

Peter hesitated, then nodded and pulled away. "Yes, sir," he said. Like smoke, he disappeared back into the shadows of the abbey.

In the back of my mind, the threat sat like a brooding shadow, throwing everything else under its shade. Every slight movement pushed me closer to the edge. Every small sound was an eruption echoing in my ears. I clenched myself tightly together, my body groaning under the pressure as the speeches wore on, as the hymns were sung and the final words uttered. The whole time, security guards and protection officers circled at the edges of my vision, even more of them than before.

As the service came to an end, the coffin was lifted by the pallbearers, who shifted off into a different direction, farther into the abbey. Dad would be buried in the royal tomb alongside his family. It made me shudder to think that my place was also reserved in the vault, alongside my father. I couldn't bear to think of my body, rigid and cold, preserved underneath the solid stone floors.

The guests filtered out into the afternoon sun as our family followed the coffin toward the vault. The names of kings and queens were etched into stone to mark where each lay. I ignored the empty spaces past my father's, where Mum, Eddie and I would rest when the time came, and concentrated on my dad one last time. We stood over his coffin, which had been laid in its place to be lowered into the ground, finally in private once more.

"May the king forever rest in peace and rise in glory, where grief and misery are banished and light and joy evermore abide." The dean bowed his head, and the coffin began to move down.

"Ashes to ashes. Dust to dust."

My mother wept openly now that we were away from the cameras. Eddie couldn't fight the tears he'd been holding in, and finally, they silently fell as we watched our father's coffin disappear. The tears in my own eyes refused to wait a moment longer, streaming down my face. Cassandra stood back from it all, a blank expression giving nothing away, her mother stony-faced beside her. A silence hung over us, only interrupted by splintered grief. The ceremony was over. We'd said goodbye for the last time.

My tears were quelled when I saw Peter again, this time standing alongside several other guards in the abbey. Others were scattered out behind him, tense faces sweeping over every dark corner. We locked eyes. His told me what I needed to know. I wiped my tears and nodded, letting his guards surround me. It was time to face whatever waited outside.

We hurried toward the Great West Door, me in the center of their shield. I fell into the back of my car, its engine already running. Mum and Eddie, who wore confused expressions but had long ago learned to follow our security's lead without question, had protection shields too (although from what they didn't yet know) guiding them into their own vehicle. The flashing blue lights of a police escort kicked into action and we sped away toward the palace.

"What's happened?" I asked from the back seat.

Peter didn't turn his head, too busy assessing our surroundings as they flashed past. "We received a warning that your life was in danger. It was a quick call—too quick to trace—but they warned a bomb would be detonated in order to claim your life."

I felt sick. I didn't believe for a moment that the call held any truth to it, but someone was clearly out to scare me. My mind wandered to Jonathan, but I knew it could never be him. If he wanted to hurt me, then he'd done it already. He wouldn't go this far.

"Considering the circumstances and the temperamental nature of the public right now, we can't risk not taking the threat seriously," Peter said as we skidded around a corner and the palace came into sight. "We just need to make sure that you're safe, and there's no place safer than here."

The cars flew through the gates, which immediately shut behind us. I jumped out from the back seat before Peter could even open my door and bolted into the palace. A wake with hundreds of distinguished guests was scheduled to happen in the Ballroom, but we needed to regroup.

"Everybody to my quarters," I said as the rest of my family were rushed inside.

We crashed through my door and assembled in the living room. I threw myself down onto the sofa, my head in my hands. Now the adrenaline had worn off, I felt as if I were seconds away from crumbling apart. Mum, Eddie, Cassandra, Gayle and Peter, along with a small contingent of guards, filed in, shutting the door after us.

The silence stretched on. I realized they were waiting for me to speak. But I couldn't. What did I say? How could I take charge of something I couldn't understand?

"So . . . ?" Cassandra said, tutting under her breath.

"Someone wants me dead," I muttered.

Cassandra didn't flinch. "Who doesn't?" Several mouths dropped open, but she just rolled her eyes, bored. "We're the Royal Family. If they don't love us, they want us dead."

"What was the threat?" Gayle asked faintly.

"A bomb," Peter said, and Cassandra burst out laughing.

"A bomb? Oh, *please*. As if anybody could plant a bomb in *Westminster Abbey*. On the day of a royal funeral no less!" I hated her—more than hated her—but in black and white, it sounded ridiculous. "There was no bomb. It's just somebody trying to scare u—"

She was cut off by the tone of a mobile phone. Peter dug into his pocket, clicked the screen and held it to his ear. His face stayed neutral as he listened. And then it fell.

"Evacuate everybody now. There's something in here." He looked wildly around, eyes roaming over every inch of the room.

"I'm not going anywhere," I said, ignoring my instinct to run. Mum nodded next to me.

"What do you mean, there's something in here?" Eddie said, looking around too.

"There's been another call," Peter said. "Someone's been in this room. They've left something behind."

We all moved as one, everybody jumping up to their feet. I scanned the room for anything out of place, but with so many people in it, it was hard to see anything. Peter and the guards flitted from one place to another, swiping things out of the way, stooping to look under the tables and sofa. Some of them disappeared into my bedroom, others to my bathroom. Everybody else spread out.

"Nothing here, sir," one guard called from the bathroom.

"Bedroom's clear," another said.

Cassandra was looking exhausted by the commotion. "You don't *seriously* believe somebody could just waltz into *Buckingham Palace* and leave James a present, do you?"

"I don't know what I believe," Peter growled.

"Have these always been here?" Gayle asked, holding up a stack of letters in the air. "They were in a pile by the door." We all looked over at her, then everybody switched their glance to me.

"It must be this morning's post," I replied. "It's nothing."

"What about this one on the floor?" Eddie straightened up next to Gayle, holding a forest-green envelope in his hand. The blood drained right out of me. It was the same envelope I'd received the first note in, the one which had told me to go to St. James's Park at midnight.

I snatched it from Eddie's hands and ripped it open, not even caring that every person in the room was watching me do so. Just as before, there was a simple slip of paper and a typed message on one side. Each word inflicted a pain, a fury and a fear deep inside me.

```
I know everything. Just wait and see
what I reveal next.
```

CHAPTER NINETEEN

A THOUSAND TINY CUTS

If Quinn Buckley's words had been brutal before the funeral, their fire only blazed brighter in the days that followed. It was nothing new—just dragging out the old stories and reminding everybody of them, no doubt until something new came up to douse me with.

But now I was certain that Jonathan was on his side. It couldn't even be a question anymore. Quinn's stories had been telling me over and over again that Jonathan was out for revenge. Every secret I'd shared, every moment I still held close despite his betrayal, was woven into these stories, reminding me that the Jonathan I thought I knew must never have existed. Each word I read splintered what love I still harbored deep down for him, and my growing fondness of Grigor allowed me to turn my back on what was left. But no matter how hard I tried to let him go, I couldn't. Not entirely anyway.

The thing that concerned me the most was the note itself. As a family, just like any other, we had secrets. Many of them. They filled up our closets, piling up on top of each other, ready to spill out into the open. But that couldn't happen. Not to us. It threatened everything. So, the question now stood—if Jonathan knew our secrets, what was he going to reveal next?

My final worry was, selfishly, for my own safety. Seeing the envelope in my quarters had sent a chilling fear through me. He'd been here. Or someone had been here. I didn't know how or when or why, but suddenly the only place I felt safe seemed like the place I should now fear. Peter assured me that the CCTV proved nobody had been in my room apart from the maids, one of whom delivered my post—which must have included the letter. The threat over the phone was just that—a threat—another empty attempt to scare me, like the bomb in Westminster Abbey that had never existed in the first place. But the plan had succeeded. Even with two security guards outside my door every night, I couldn't fall asleep in the dark, alone.

"I'm going to take you away." I was shaken out of my bleak thoughts by Grigor, sitting in an armchair in the corner of my living room, lacing his hands together like he did when he was thinking about something. It was a couple of days after the funeral and the start of a new week. The early afternoon sun spilled in through the window, bathing Grigor in gold so he looked like a god who belonged elsewhere, somewhere far away from here.

"Take me away?" I shifted to my side on the sofa where I'd been lying to get a better look at him.

"Yep. Away from all this rubbish. You don't feel safe, so why stay? We could get out of here, go somewhere you could get yourself together, where the cameras aren't watching."

I snorted. "So, what you're trying to say is I'm a broken mess who needs fixing? Noted." He rolled his eyes, slipping down from the chair to sit on the floor beside me in a swift and graceful movement. I rolled onto my back, knowing full well that Grigor could convince me to do anything if I looked at his face for too long.

"Don't you think you deserve to get away from here?"

"I think I deserve someone to reach up into the sky and rearrange the stars so this run of bad luck comes to an end," I said, bringing my hands up to rest behind my head. "I can't just up and leave though. I'm the king. People need me."

Grigor nudged me so I had no choice but to look at him. I tried to focus on the bridge of his nose, the tip of his chin, the crease in between his brows—anywhere but his eyes. I felt exposed when I looked at him for too long, like he was seeing through me, dissecting me from the outside in, undressing my thoughts and observing my fears.

"Just because you're the king doesn't mean you're not allowed a break." He ducked his head to catch my eye, peeking up at me through long lashes. "Let me take you somewhere. We'll do whatever you want to do. I'll even let you beat me at a board game of your choosing...." His brows came together, peaking in the center of his face until he looked like a sad puppy. "At least think about it?"

There was hardly any space between us now. He was so close that it was almost impossible to resist the urge to reach out for him. But then my mind dredged up Jonathan's name and I remembered a moment, not too dissimilar to this one, lying on the sofa together with Jonathan's head resting on my stomach, looking up at me.

"Imagine if we could just get out of here," he'd said. "I'd take you far away. We could just be you and me, no hiding."

"Don't make promises you can't keep," I'd said back, a smile tugging at my lips.

"Who says I won't keep it," Jonathan had said without hesitation, facing the challenge head-on. "I will. One day I'll take you away from here."

We could just be you and me.

Now Grigor was here, offering the same thing. Out of anger and spite, I wanted to act on my urges. I wanted to divert the love I held for Jonathan elsewhere, into someone else who would stand with me against the world. But Jonathan's face blunted those wants. I'd been betrayed once before. I couldn't let it happen again. The grief I harbored over my father, surging in the wake of his funeral, also reminded me of his words about trust. Having Grigor close by made me feel safe. But maybe that was exactly why I should be worried. So I sat up quickly, moving into the corner of the sofa and pulling my legs up to my chest. Grigor took the hint and retreated to the armchair.

"Shouldn't you be with Eddie? I know you don't come all this way just to see me. He's your best friend. He needs you too."

"Is that my order to leave?" he asked evenly, no flicker in his tone to suggest he was stung.

I shrugged. I didn't *want* him to go. I wanted to be able to trust him. But everything that had happened lately reminded me trust needed to be earned. It couldn't just be given out for free, especially in a place like this.

"Eddie probably needs you, that's all."

Grigor sighed. "He's brought the shutters down. He doesn't want to talk about it, almost acting like nothing ever happened. I've tried to break through that wall, but you know how he is. He won't let anybody past arm's length."

"Sounds like my brother," I muttered. "Do me a favor though? Keep trying. Please? He needs somebody, or he'll break. He won't admit that himself, but it's true."

We both knew it'd be a fruitless task, but Grigor nodded anyway and stood up.

"No time like the present, I suppose. You going to be all right in here? I can come back?" There was a hint of hope in his voice, and I could feel the sparks of warmth it gave me. But I ignored them and nodded instead.

"I'll be fine."

Grigor hesitated by the door, like he wanted to say

something. Like he didn't want to go. But, admitting defeat, he turned and left, leaving me alone with my thoughts for company. I stared at the blank space he'd left behind. I'd got what I asked for. He'd gone. So why did I want him to come back?

⟋⟋⟋⟋⟋⟋

The Budd estate was hardly small. It sprawled over a quiet patch of country land in a corner of Surrey, surrounded by rolling hills and thickets of trees. Sheep and cows grazed out in the paddocks; a collection of stables housed a dozen elite racing horses; the waters of a small lake rippled beyond the garden, with a tiny wooden jetty for fishing. The manor had been built in the eighteenth century. Now it was up for sale.

My car slowed down as it glided along the winding driveway later that afternoon, pulling to a stop next to a lorry. The grand oak doors of the manor, with knockers made of solid gold and sculpted into the shape of a lion's head, opened as I stepped out of the car, an immaculately dressed maid waiting to welcome me. She saw my face and immediately folded into a curtsy, a flash of panic crossing her features. The king rarely went anywhere without announcing his arrival first. But I hadn't been given the chance to give advanced warning since Ophelia was avoiding my phone calls.

"Your Royal Highness," the maid said in a tight voice. "I'm sorry, we weren't expecting your arrival. The place is quite a mess. I can only apologize."

I shook my head politely, barely registering the incorrect title, offering her a small smile, which seemed to make her relax. "No bother about the mess at all. I was just hoping to see Ophelia if she's home."

The maid's eyes pinged down to the ground, a blush creeping up her neck. "I'm afraid she isn't home, Your Hi—"

"Who is it, Geraldyne?" the unmistakable voice of Ophelia called from inside the house. I raised an eyebrow. Geraldyne stuttered, the blush now engulfing her face entirely.

"I meant to say, she isn't taking visitors right now, sir."

Geraldyne stepped out onto the stone threshold, closing the door slightly behind her to hide the rest of the house. It was clear Ophelia didn't want to see me. But I hadn't come all this way just to be declined at the front door.

"I know things are tough right now, but I'd really appreciate just a few moments of her time. As king, I only have her best interests at heart. I want to make sure that she's okay." It was bad manners to throw the king card out there so flippantly, but if I had to resort to low tactics in order to finally see Ophelia, then so be it.

"Oh, Y-Your Majesty, I'm so sorry. Of course. Let me see if she's up for visitors." She curtsied again and disappeared into the house.

The door opened again, this time flung wide, as two burly men struggled to maneuver a bronze statue outside into the waiting lorry. I peered around them to get a better look. A ton of antiques, gilded frames and rolled-up tapestries were already loaded inside. A pang of guilt stabbed my chest. The removal lorry wasn't taking those things to a new house. They were taking them to auction to clear a debt.

"Is your name Eddie?" a tiny voice asked. I turned to find Ophelia's sister, Everly, on the doorstep. She was no older than seven, with soft blue eyes, honey-colored hair that fell around her shoulders and a scattering of freckles over her nose and cheeks.

I crouched down to her level. "Eddie is my brother. I'm James. We look alike, right?" I offered the girl a smile, but she tilted her head and looked at me some more, narrowing her eyes like she didn't believe a word I was saying. She opened the door wider and pointed into the next room where a TV was playing the news. It was footage of the funeral, Eddie and I standing next to each other at the palace gates.

"You look like him," she decided.

I laughed. "That's why we never stand next to each other for too long. People would get confused."

"That's enough, Everly." Ophelia appeared, putting a hand on her sister's shoulder and steering her away into the house. "Go and play with your toys."

She waited for Everly to disappear before turning back to me. She was hollow. There was no other way to describe it. It was like looking at a broken doll, one that was empty inside.

"What do you want?" she asked, her words nearly

folding in on themselves. I took a step toward her, but she mirrored it with one of her own, flinching away from me. It punched me in the gut. I didn't know what to say. All I could see was a casualty of my own creation.

"I wanted to check you were okay," I tried.

Ophelia's eyes began to pool, gleaming with tears. "It's not a good idea for you to be here," she murmured.

"Please, Phee. Talk to me."

She teetered on the edge of a decision, thinking so hard that I could almost hear the storm raging within her head. But finally she wilted and stepped aside. Without a word, she led me through the halls into the large, now almost empty living room, switching off the TV. A velvet sofa decorated with gold and red cushions, and a large rug that covered most of the wooden floor, remained. The bricks around the fireplace were blackened by soot. With no obstacles in their way, our voices echoed up into the high ceiling.

Ophelia sat at one end of the sofa while I sat at the other, wondering how I could've let the crown and everything else come between us.

"We missed you at the funeral," I began tentatively.

Ophelia refused to look at me, drawing one leg up underneath her and pulling at the tassels of a cushion. Dark circles haloed her eyes, and her jaw was sharper than it'd been the last time I'd seen her.

"I wanted to be there. I just didn't think it was a good idea after . . . everything."

We both knew what *everything* was. Quinn had made

sure that if we were ever seen together again, even spotted in the same room, it'd unearth the story that had started this whole mess.

"I miss you, Phee. We're still friends, right? I know things are messed up right now, and I know I haven't been there for you—not properly. It's going to take more than an apology, but I want to help."

Ophelia pulled harder on the cushion, a thread coming loose, but she said nothing.

"What Quinn did was awful, and if I had known that it was going to end that way, I would've never let it happen in the first place. But I want to protect you. *We* want to protect you, and make sure that you're okay." I reached out, to let her know I was here and that I meant every word, but she recoiled and jumped up off the sofa.

"I don't want your help. I don't want to be stuck in this spider's web anymore. I've been used as a pawn by your family and I want out. Everything they touch falls into ruins, and yet they'll always carry on unblemished." I stood up too, but she held up her hand to stop me in my tracks. "The crown protects you. It protects all of you. But at whose expense? And at what cost?"

It stung like she'd struck me across the face. But it was true. No matter what, no matter who, the Royal Family came first. We stood on the shoulders of others, atop a fragile pyramid that could come crashing down at any moment. But, until now, we'd always been left unscathed. The same couldn't be said for those we left in our reckless wake.

"You're too late to protect me," Ophelia whispered. "The damage has already been done. Protect yourself instead. It's what you're good at."

Her tears finally broke, falling freely. I took a step with outstretched arms, but she backed away, shaking her head.

"Talk to me, Phee. Let me help."

Another silence lingered. Ophelia looked up into my eyes and I saw a glimpse of her—the friend I'd had before all of this happened. But it was a mere moment, and when she blinked, she disappeared once more.

"I can't." She stood aside and pointed to the door. "Please, James. Just go."

I had no choice. I could see what my family had done to her. What *I'd* done to her. Maybe it was for the best that I left her alone, at least for now, so she might start piecing back together the parts of her we'd broken.

"If you ever need me . . ." I trailed off and bowed my head, making for the door.

"James?" Ophelia called as I stepped outside into the sun. Hope fluttered in my heart and I turned around. She wrapped her arms around herself. "Stay safe." It was final, as if she planned to never see me again. But before I could do a thing about it, she closed the door and disappeared.

I slid into my waiting car, the engine purring to life. As we pulled away, I glanced back at the house. Everly was watching from an upstairs window, her head still tilted to one side. A line of trees slipped between the car and the house. When we'd passed, she'd gone.

CHAPTER TWENTY

To Be Worthy of Love You Must Simply Exist

It's never good news when there's a knock at the door in the middle of the night. Good news can wait. Bad news can't. It can only mean that something terrible has happened.

At first, it sounded like a far-off dream, merging with nightmares of my own where the number of protestors outside tripled and quadrupled, until they were big and strong enough to storm the palace and overthrow our defenses. I was locked in a room, alone and in the dark, as they battered down the door to get at me. And then the knock came again, and it pulled me back into consciousness, the nightmare disintegrating into thin air.

I woke drenched in sweat, my bedsheets sodden, heart pounding. Moonlight filtered into my bedroom through a crack in the curtains, but everything else was drowned in darkness.

Knock! Knock! Knock!

It was becoming more frantic with every beat. I quickly pulled back the covers, wrapping myself in a dressing gown, and slipped out into the living room to open the door. Just before I did, I remembered the last time this had happened, when Gayle had awoken me to tell me of my father's death. I paused with my hand hovering over the handle. What fresh horrors awaited me now? Another knock forced me to square my shoulders and face them head-on.

Gayle stood in the corridor, flanked by the guards who were on duty for the night. The dim lamps mounted high on the walls cast light down upon her, illuminating a face that had been overcome by panic.

"What is it?" I asked immediately. Bad news doesn't require pleasantries.

"It's your mother," Gayle began, and I gripped the door as the floor beneath me swayed. Gayle caught herself and quickly held up her hands. "No, she's fine! It's just... Quinn has published another story." She paused, and in that moment, she looked beyond her years, like she'd lived double her time. "It's bad. It's really bad."

I nodded curtly, stepping out into the corridor, not even bothering to find shoes or socks. I followed Gayle through the palace toward my mother's quarters. The door was already ajar, voices murmuring beyond. I tensed as Gayle hesitated, took a deep breath, and entered.

The sitting area was bathed in gentle lamplight, which pushed the shadows back into the corners of the room. Mum sat on the sofa, silently distraught. She looked like she'd run out of tears to cry and was now still, eyes fixed on something the rest of us couldn't see. Peter was already there, placing a drink of pale gold liquid down on the side table next to a picture of me and Eddie in our school uniforms, arms slung around each other and bright smiles lighting up our faces. My brother now sat upright on the other side of the room, watching, his face smoothed of any emotions. But, even in the soft lamplight, I could see his jaw twitching. He looked up as I walked in, then glanced at the newspaper sitting discarded on the table. I grabbed it, heart in my mouth, and began to read.

A ROYAL AFFAIR KEPT SECRET FOR DECADES

REVEALED: The sordid affair that left a kind king heartbroken

BY QUINN BUCKLEY, *ROYAL REPORTER*

Alexandra Hampton has fought hard to maintain an untainted image, but that reputation today lies shattered as the *Daily Eye* can exclusively reveal that the Queen Mother has been hiding a sordid affair that saw her break the heart of a king who called her the love of his life.

The explosive secret that has been buried in the dark for years today comes to light, revealing

that Alexandra Hampton conducted an affair with an unknown partner in the first years of her relationship with King George. The affair is said to have started when she was still a duchess and continued even after her husband became king.

Our well-placed source, who requested to keep their identity anonymous for fear of repercussions from a ruthless Queen Mother, revealed that the affair broke the heart of the king at the time, although he eventually chose to forgive her and move on under the agreement that the secret never see the light of day. The royal couple went on to have two children together—King James and his twin brother, the heir to the throne, Prince Edward.

Of course, King George had experienced heartbreak before, after the untimely murder of his true love, Catherine St. Paul, only days before their wedding was due to take place. King George always proclaimed that Alexandra was his second chance at happiness after his devastating loss, making the betrayal all the more shocking for its cruelty.

FULL STORY CONTINUES ON PAGES 4 and 5.

The newspaper trembled in my hands. I clutched it so tight that it was on the verge of being ripped apart completely. I wanted to crush the words I was holding, crunch them until they disintegrated like they'd never existed in the first place. The anger I felt about everything, simmering from the day I'd been forced onto the throne, spilled over the edges, thrashing through my body until it filled every space it could reach. I scrunched the newspaper up in my hands and threw it against the wall.

This was it. The next secret that Jonathan somehow knew—one that even I wasn't aware of. He'd been biding his time to enact his revenge on us, and now he'd gone and done it. Had he ever truly cared for me at all? Had his whole plan been to integrate himself into my family and get as close as possible just so he could sit back and watch us implode? Was he one of *them*? One of the people who stood outside, chanting and jeering, protesting to get us off the throne and out of the palace? The last grain of love I felt for him dissolved, replaced by the searing embers of hatred.

"We've contacted our lawyers, of course," Gayle said in a small voice.

"It's too late for that. What good will lawyers do? The damage is already done." My words sounded cold and flat, harsh even to my own ears.

I turned around to face the room, finding my mother on the sofa. She felt my eyes on her and looked up to meet them. Everything I needed to know was there, glinting back at me. But still, I needed to be sure.

"Leave us," I said. There was no movement. "Now."

Gayle and Peter made for the door without question, leaving the three of us alone. Mum didn't take her eyes off me, watching as I sat down next to Eddie. I took a deep breath, trying to soothe my anger, or to at least separate it. I wasn't angry with her. I surprised myself by knowing that to be fact.

"It's true, isn't it?"

Mum didn't blink, nor did she shrink away from my question. She nodded. I sank fully into the armchair, the weight of what was happening hitting me in the center of my chest and leaving me breathless. How had Jonathan known that? How had I not?

"I don't hope for forgiveness, James. I don't ask for anything from you but your understanding." Mum sat up a little straighter, still proud, even when she'd been knocked down. "Whether you hate me, or at least hate what I've done, I need you to hear it from my own mouth. Both of you. I won't let that scumbag talk for me."

"I could never hate you. You're my mother," I said.

"Our mother," Eddie corrected.

Her eyes teared up for a moment as she took us in, but she quickly blinked and composed herself.

"You have to first understand the time that I came into the picture. Your father was greatly loved. He was charismatic and generous, kind and gentle. That was what made me fall in love with him." Mum smiled to herself as if she was watching memories unfold in her mind. It didn't last long. "But those people who loved your father like he was their own also loved Catherine. And I could never have lived up to her."

She got up and walked over to the window, gazing out at the night as she reminisced. "They loved her like she was their own darling princess. They wanted her to be queen more than I'm sure she even wanted to be queen herself. She was a young girl, in love with her prince, and he loved her more than anything. They deserved a happy ending together. I really do believe that.

"But not all love stories end that way. The king and his queen don't always trot off into the sunset together. When that man murdered Catherine in cold blood, he ripped apart the heart of this country. They wept in the streets like she was their own daughter. And they wept for your father too, for he'd been left alone, his true love cruelly taken away from him."

I'd seen the pictures. They were embedded in our history, as much a part of it as I was now. The relationship, the death, the grief—it lived on through the years, through the generations, never forgotten.

"I don't doubt that Catherine was a good person. Your father would never have loved her if she wasn't. But in terms of courting the public, she had one thing on her side that had nothing to do with her grace or her beauty." Mum paused, her shoulders rising and falling evenly. "She was their delicate English rose, with blushing cheeks and these astounding blue eyes that could pierce and break the hearts of armies. She fit the role of the fairy-tale princess perfectly. And when she was gone, they couldn't possibly imagine that someone might one day take the space she'd left behind."

Mum was in a world of her own now, leaving the door open for us to follow her into it. I could imagine it all as she spoke, her words swirling around me so that the memories came alive.

"We met at a party, your father and I. I worked for the

charity that organized the event, but I was never supposed to be anywhere near him when he arrived. He was royalty. I was nobody. It was luck—some fate sketched out for us in the stars—that he stumbled into my path, and once he looked into my eyes, I knew. Or at least I dared to hope."

I instantly thought of Grigor, how when he searched for my eyes, I felt that rush welling up inside me. How I too had dared to hope for...something. I still didn't know what I really wanted, but I couldn't deny that feeling.

"When your father and I first started dating, he wanted to scream about it from the rooftops. He didn't care to hide because we'd found true love together, and that's something that should never have to be hidden away. But I asked him to keep it a secret. I knew, as a Black woman, what waited for us. He said he didn't care what other people thought, but for me it was more than that. I shamefully wanted to wait, so he would know for sure that he loved me as much as I loved him. I doubted his feelings because I felt as if I wasn't worthy of receiving the love and devotion of a king—of anybody, but certainly not him. I didn't come from aristocracy, or any background deemed fit for royalty. And so, I wanted him to *know* that I was what his heart desired, because there wouldn't be a chance to go back once we took that step.

"He knew what was coming. We both did. I never let him forget what lay ahead of us, and I think, in a cruel attempt to hurt myself, I hoped he'd have his doubts and would leave me heartbroken. It would prove what I'd been thinking all along—that I wasn't worthy of his love. But he didn't. Once your father set his mind to something, he was never going to be swayed. Of course, the reaction was terrible. People thought it was too soon after Catherine. And they immediately compared me to her. They found my most unflattering pictures and printed them next to Catherine's in her tiaras and jewels. I was the witch who'd hoodwinked the king, and they weren't going to lay down their pitchforks until he saw the truth."

I could see them together—a couple in love, standing side by side, hand in hand, facing what the world had to throw at them.

"It was worse than even I could've expected. They called me every name you could think of. Whenever we went anywhere, there were fifty protestors all screaming in my face. It had to take its toll. It *had* to. The months rolled on and it didn't stop. We were miserable, and a distance started to force itself between us. And that's when the doubts I'd expected began to creep into the picture. Being the king is about honor and duty. Your father had people in his ear, trying to persuade him that it wasn't too late to get rid of me and save the monarchy from perishing, which it surely would if I was let in."

She was talking faster and faster, the words tumbling out in their urgency to be heard, creating visions before us with their intensity. "He resisted, but those doubts began to fester. If we stayed together, would he be ruining his own family? He wanted to please them, his people and me. But he couldn't do it all."

For the first time since she'd started, Mum turned from the window. She wanted to make sure we heard every word—*felt* every word. She sat down once more, facing us. Facing everything.

"I felt unloved. I felt alone. Every thought I'd had since I was a girl about how I wasn't enough—how I would *never* be enough—threatened to drown me. And so, I fell into the arms of another man. I won't sugarcoat it. I fell in love with him as he did with me. I was a woman hardened by years of being told that I couldn't ever be worthy of love, and when he showed me that he cared, I crumbled. I regret that it hurt your father. I regret that more than anything. But I will never regret falling in love and feeling that love returned. We all deserve to be loved, no matter how much our darkest thoughts might tell us otherwise."

My mother's happiness battled my father's pain in the depths of my chest, conflict pulling me in different directions. But I could understand why my mother had let herself fall. I knew what it was like to crave love—to want to stand with someone so you could dare to face the world together. I knew what it was like to feel that hand slip away, leaving you in darkness. And I also knew how it felt to feel another light creep into the picture, one that might just save you.

"He was a great man. He didn't deserve to be dragged into our mess. And in another lifetime, we might've stayed together and been happy. But the shadow of the throne always hung over us. Despite what those rags say, it lasted a few months before guilt made me come clean. Your father listened and, although it pained him, he understood why. He even tried to shoulder blame, although I wouldn't let him go that far. But we knew we could never reverse what had been done. Even the people who told him it wasn't too late knew that, in truth, we were past ever choosing a different path. We could never part. Tradition wouldn't allow it. We had no choice but to make it work. And we did."

I came back into the room from the past, looking at my mother in a light I'd never seen her in before. The ghost of my father sat with us. It was like I could feel him there, holding my mother's hand as she explained as best she could.

"I want you to know that your father and I loved each other. Every day of our lives, we loved each other. Those moments before you were both born were the hardest, but we fixed what had been broken and came through it together, to live a life I will always cherish. We must live with the regrets of our mistakes and desires, but I choose to liberate myself of mine. I let my heart dare to be loved. I don't think that's such a bad thing."

I surprised myself by realizing that I didn't care what had happened. I only cared about now, when my family were under attack. These stories, these secrets, they were meant to divide us. If the media couldn't get to us, they would make sure that we got to each other and tore ourselves apart. I wouldn't let that happen. I couldn't.

And so I stood and crossed the room, wrapping my

arms around my mother. "Thank you for telling us that," I said quietly as she hugged me fiercely back.

Eddie stood too, and for a moment I thought he'd join us. But then I saw the look on his face, the glint of anger in his eye. He took us both in. Then, with a shake of his head, he walked out, leaving us alone. One arm still around my mother, I felt the hurt deflate her.

"He'll come round," I said. "He just needs time."

The light of a new morning had rebirthed the sky, washing its darkness away. Who knew what world waited for us as it woke? Quinn Buckley's twist on fact would be out there now, waiting to be devoured by those who wished to see our downfall. *Our* downfall, specifically. Cassandra would escape that sword. I had no doubt that she would rejoice when she read the story. The image in my mind of her happiness bred another, darker thought— she would have a lot to gain from something like this.

Mum seemed to have rebuilt herself now that she'd freed her secrets. I'd heard everything there was to know. I understood it all. But I had one more question that I needed to know the answer to.

"What happened to the man you fell in love with?" I asked.

Mum smiled to herself, but sadness crept up into her eyes.

"He let me go," she said simply. "As all good men do—he accepted my decision, and he let me go."

CHAPTER TWENTY-ONE

THE POOL HOUSE

The palace security had never been so intense. As the news began to break alongside the day, the number of people outside the gates only grew. They shouted vicious things at the tops of their lungs, hoping their words and slurs might penetrate the bricks. As a result, the guards around the palace had doubled in number. They swarmed around the entrances and along the fences, patrolling every square inch outside to ward off any danger. But being inside, looking out, still felt unsafe, like a prison from which there was no escape.

"I don't know about you, but I'm not sitting around here all day being miserable," Eddie grumbled, rolling off the sofa and up onto his feet.

It was late morning, the August heat suddenly replaced by a cooler breeze and a steely-grey sky that lingered close to the trees. I'd requested Eddie join me for breakfast, hoping it would penetrate his bad mood, but I was surprised when he arrived at my quarters as if last night had never happened. I chose not to bring up Quinn's story again.

"We can't exactly go waltzing out there, can we?" I muttered, watching the TV on mute. I didn't need to hear what they were saying. I could see it written on the reporters' faces, in the way their mouths twisted into angry words, eyebrows pulling together. Quinn's face had been on and off the news channels all morning, his smug grin now permanently etched into my mind.

"Who said anything about going outside?" Eddie shrugged and started for the door. "I'll be back, and with a plan."

He was met by Gayle and Peter, who looked thrilled to be delivering yet more good news.

"Ah, what delights are you coming to please me with now?" I said with a wry smile. "More death threats, perhaps? How many are we on so far today?"

"Thirty-three at last count, wasn't it?" Eddie quipped, skirting around the pair of them with a smirk. "That's four less than yesterday though, so I'd say that's a success."

"Not funny," Gayle muttered as Eddie and I shared a grin. "I'm dropping by to say the lawyers are working on an injunction to stop any further stories from leaking, and we're preparing a statement to send out imminently."

"Saying what?" I asked.

"That the stories printed are absolutely not true."

I laughed, because at this point, what else was there to do? "More lies. I'm sure that'll help solve matters."

Gayle shook her head. "It's not about lying. It's about playing them at their own game. People like Quinn know exactly what they're doing. He's made the...the transgression—"

"Affair. You can say it. We won't all turn to stone."

Gayle sighed. Peter stared at the floor, as if he'd walked in on something not meant for his ears.

"Quinn has twisted the affair to his advantage, making it sound as sordid and sleazy as possible," Gayle went on. "He knows how people still feel about your father and Catherine, so he's using that as leverage against your mother. Surprisingly, though, he's shown us his hand."

I frowned. "He has?"

Gayle nodded. "He's no longer just targeting you. He clearly thought you were a weak link, that your nerves over becoming king would make you an easy target. Now that he's seen you haven't been shaken, he's poking holes elsewhere to try to bring this family down. Basically, he's proved to us that he's running out of ideas."

As if the devil himself had called upon him, Quinn's arrogant face appeared on the TV screen. "He doesn't look like he's running out of ideas," I mumbled, as he threw his head back to laugh.

"Mark my words, Your Majesty. He's playing games that we've been playing for decades. Let him enjoy his celebrations today. It will always be us who have the last laugh."

I should've felt...relieved? But, instead, I felt sick. This *game* wasn't fun. It would never end well, and the stakes were too high for whoever lost. They might even be too high for whoever won.

But Gayle didn't seem to notice. "Rest assured, sir, I am certain we will emerge from this game victorious."

She marched out of the room, almost jubilant. Peter grimaced. "It's not going to end well, is it?" he said, as if he'd read my mind.

"I doubt it. Even if we make it through this, there'll be something else, and then something else, and then something else. It'll never stop. There will always be another game to play. The only way Quinn will stop is if..." I hesitated, knowing that abdicating the throne wouldn't even release me from these games. I was stuck in the royal cycle, whether I stepped down or not.

My phone buzzed in my pocket. I half hoped it'd be Grigor, but it was Eddie's name that beamed up at me.

> The pool house in an hour. Bring
> your trunks.

I didn't even question what he was up to. I slipped my phone back into my pocket, grateful for the distraction. I was only too happy to try to ignore my problems for an afternoon.

⟨҉⟩

The royal swimming pool sat tucked at the back of Buckingham Palace. The pool stretched from one side of the room to the other, its floor made up of an extravagant mosaic. Double-height windows lined the wall, allowing sunlight to trickle in and dance over the crystal-clear waters while grand columns made up of smooth white stone were positioned at regular intervals along the poolside, creating intricate archways where sun loungers and tables were placed. At the far end, a hot tub was separated from the rest of the pool by a low wall that barely kept the waters apart. It was a peaceful place to be on any normal day of the week, but Eddie had made sure that, today, it was the complete opposite.

Louie, Delphine and as many friends as he could invite had shown up from midday in their fleet of sleek cars, skirting around the back of the palace and into the garden where a set of steps led into the pool house. Security were stationed outside, checking bags filled with swimming costumes and towels before letting anybody through. Peter looked like he was about to have kittens at any moment. I was sure throwing a party hadn't been on his list of appropriate activities for today.

"You really think this was a good idea?" I said to Eddie, sitting on the side of the pool and dangling my legs into the water. He'd been floating along its surface on a giant slice of inflatable pizza for hours, while other guests lounged on the sunbeds or lazily swam about, all of them seemingly without a care in the world. The serene music that usually floated from the speakers had been changed to something more fitting, its bass pumping through the pool house.

"When was the last time we had some *fun?*" he asked, hands behind his head and eyes closed.

"Uh, the party? And that didn't exactly end well, did it?" The chandelier had been fixed and replaced within a day, but the whole thing had still been a disaster. Despite myself, I wondered if everything with Jonathan would've gone the way it did if the party had never happened.

Eddie opened one eye to glance at me, probably to make sure I wasn't about to drown myself and ruin his spontaneous party. "It's all so uptight in here. Everything is doom and gloom. We deserve to kick back and have *one* afternoon where we don't have to think about what's going on."

"You can switch off that easily? You're better than I then," I replied.

Eddie sighed, trying to shift on his pizza slice without falling in. "Look, you better get used to it, okay? You're king. They want to see you prove you've got what it takes—or they want to see you break. And what can you do about that? Absolutely nothing. So, to hell with it. Just relax an—"

He rolled onto his side and fell off the float, disappearing under the surface of the water. I burst out laughing as he reemerged with a splutter. "You know what? I suddenly feel better already." Eddie's glowering face made it even more amusing.

"Your friend's here," he said, nodding behind me and paddling away just as Grigor sat down beside me, dipping his legs into the pool.

"Do you think he minds us talking…?" Grigor wondered aloud, watching Eddie retreat until he'd joined a small gang who were floating in a circle and chatting animatedly.

"He probably thinks it's weird." *It is weird*, I thought to myself. I could feel Grigor's eyes on me but refused to meet them, staring into the depths of the pool instead.

"Is it weird?" he asked in a careful tone.

I didn't know what to say. My gut told me to drop everything and run, to get as far away from what my heart was suggesting that I pursue. My mum's words, said in secret as day began to break, came back to me. I deserved to feel love—to *be* loved. But after everything, it was difficult to convince myself to take the risk. How could I, after recent events? Quinn, Jonathan, those people standing outside with their signs—they all told me that the risk was too big.

Grigor leaned forward, slipping into the pool and circling in front of me. Water droplets dripped from his hair onto his cheeks like tears.

"If you want me to go—if you want me to leave you alone—then I will. I don't want to make things more difficult for you than they already are. But I know what I want." He took a few steps in the water so he was closer to me and reached out to rest his hand on my calf. His touch crumbled the defenses I was trying to rapidly build.

"I want to see you happy, James. I want you to know that you have someone you can trust. But if you want me to leave so you can figure everything out, you only have to say the words."

He looked up into my eyes and I felt myself waver. The slightest breath, one more word, and I'd fall. I'd be helpless to it.

"Just say the words," Grigor repeated softly.

It was enough. Maybe I was a coward. Maybe I didn't deserve to be king because I knew I would never be able to do this alone. I needed someone. And so, I shook my head.

"I don't want you to go," I said, and his smile crushed the final brick in my defense. I found myself smiling back. Had I made the right choice? At that moment, I didn't care. For once, I was doing something for *me*. Not for my country or because of my duty. Just for me.

"Do you mind if I interrupt?"

Ophelia stood behind me, holding her arms around herself and looking like she'd rather be anywhere else but here. After the way we'd left things, my stomach flipped at the sight of her. The dark circles under her eyes had only gotten worse.

"I'll leave you guys to it," Grigor said. He squeezed my knee, then swam away to meet Eddie.

Ophelia sank down next to me, eyes darting over the people in the pool. Cassandra, Delphine and a gaggle of their friends lounging on chairs opposite spotted her and immediately began whispering in voices that weren't trying to be subtle. Ophelia blushed and dropped her head.

"I just wanted to say . . . you know, that I'm sorry about how we left things," she said, her words barely above a breath. "I was stressed about . . . well, everything. There's a lot going on right now."

"It's okay," I said, trying to sound upbeat to counter the misery Ophelia was wallowing in. "All I want is my friend back."

Ophelia sank into herself, as if I'd said something wrong. The breath left her body, leaving her deflated. Before I could say another word, she jumped back up. "That's all I wanted to say. I'm sorry."

"I wonder if they've even got Wi-Fi in that new *terraced* house of theirs," Delphine sniped, raising her voice just enough so we could hear it across the pool. With glassy eyes, Ophelia all but ran, the laughter of Delphine chasing after her.

"Hey, Delphine," I called, standing up. "The palace switchboard has asked me to pass on a message—if you're going to keep calling to try to get Eddie's attention, you might want to make your number anonymous so we don't know it's you."

Delphine's blush was furious, but I didn't stick around to wait for her apology. I'd had enough. Distraction was only a good idea for so long before what you were trying to ignore reared its ugly head again. I made a beeline for Eddie, who now sat in the hot tub, eyes closed and head leaning on the side.

"I'm going to shower off. You good to clear everybody out of here?" He didn't even open his eyes.

"Yes, boss," he murmured sleepily.

I made for the door at the far end of the pool house, but was interrupted before I'd even taken more than a few steps.

"My, my, my, what trouble you've been getting in lately," a smug voice said. Cassandra looked as jubilant as ever, like she'd already claimed victory, or at least smelled it in the air. "It seems you're as good at keeping secrets as your mother."

"Fuck off."

For once I didn't flinch away from my cousin. Maybe I'd been hardened by the endless attacks against me and my family. Maybe I was finally starting to understand, or at least accept, the power of the crown and the position I held. I was the king. For how much longer, I couldn't be sure, but right now was all that mattered.

"You really think my demise will see you wearing the crown?" I spat, rounding on Cassandra. "If I fall, I'm taking this whole place down with me."

I could see a storm swelling behind Cassandra's eyes. She would never back down, but I refused to be moved either. If it was war she wanted, then I would meet her in battle.

"You forget I know you better than you think," she said, a threat lingering behind her words. "Just try to take me down. I dare you."

With one final glare, Cassandra whipped around and headed back toward Delphine. Trying to swallow my fury, I slipped through the changing room door, pushing it closed and leaning my head against it until the raging waters settled within me.

Cassandra had made it clear she wanted the throne. She'd also made it clear that she held allegiance only to herself and would do anything to sit atop the mountain. She wouldn't think twice about tearing me down. There was something about her words though—the confidence they rested on, as if she knew all the secrets in the world. That, plus the fact she'd been sneaking out of the palace, clearly not wanting to be seen. It all came together to create a feeling of fear, because maybe my enemy was closer than I had thought.

The changing room was more of a miniature spa, with massage tables, plush sofas and a giant oval bathtub curving up from the ground. Luscious flowers crept over the walls and ceilings, their drooping leaves and colorful petals offering the feeling of being lost deep in a rain forest. The shower was hidden inside a tiled alcove, the golden head almost bigger than a car tire. I turned it on, switching the dial round until hidden faucets in the walls began releasing jets of steaming hot water too. I closed my eyes and let it rain over and around me, trying to wash my fears away.

Thoughts projected themselves onto the backs of my eyelids, creating visions in the dark. There was Jonathan's face, split wide with a handsome grin as we stood under the shower together after a midnight swim, the fear of being caught momentarily deserting us. But the memory was tarnished now, soured by betrayal. His face morphed into Grigor's, that easy smile lighting up his eyes, which both asked a question and answered it too.

It felt pathetic to be worried about something as inconsequential as boys when Quinn and his dangerous games were only getting worse, attacking us from every angle. But still it played on my mind.

At first, I didn't realize I'd opened my eyes. Everything was as black as if they were still closed. But then I blinked, and blinked again, and realized I'd been plunged into pitch-black darkness. I reached blindly in front of me, finding the shower knobs and turning them until the water stopped. My heart began to pound as I stood still, listening for something. Anything.

Then there was a footstep.

"Hello?"

My voice echoed around me, reverberating off the shower tiles. I felt in danger, but that was impossible. The palace was surrounded by guards. Nobody could get past them. Could they?

There was another footstep in the darkness. Closer than before. Silence ensued, though my thoughts were blaringly loud. I wanted to shout for help, but my throat was closing up. They were getting even closer. Whoever it was. They were coming for me.

The footsteps began to hurry, the sound of them pinging off the walls. Then the sound of the door opening rung out and light poured into the room, darkness quickly following as it closed again.

Shaking, I felt my way along the wall, using touch and memory to guide me toward the door where the light switches were. When I flicked them back on, I found myself quite alone. Except for a forest-green envelope, resting on the counter.

The floor beneath me seemed to warp and tilt. I didn't want to touch the envelope, like it was a bomb that could explode at the slightest wrong movement. But I had no choice. Whoever had left it had been in here with me. I had to know. I swiped it off the side and ripped it open. With trembling hands, I edged the note out of its envelope and read the typed message.

```
I hope you're not tired of our games
just yet, Your Majesty.
The biggest secret is yet to come.
Who do you really trust?
```

I didn't know what it meant, and in that split second, I didn't care. I yanked a towel from the shelf and pulled the door open. But the pool house was now empty. Whoever had been here had gone, and they'd left me a sinister parting gift.

CHAPTER TWENTY-TWO

DON'T LET ME FALL

The car was packed. There wasn't much in my hold-all aside from enough clothes to last a few days, but Gayle had nestled a board game at the very top, with a note that told me she'd handle everything while I was away. I was leaving the palace. I had to.

It was clear now that I was in danger. More danger than we could've guessed. Someone was taunting me, and it was someone who had access to my inner circle. They'd been in the pool house, watching me, waiting for their opportunity, wicked intentions tucked beneath a smile. Even with all the security, they'd somehow gotten in. Every guest was being questioned, but so far there'd been no progress.

There were too many questions to ask, with no sign of an answer to any of them. But my biggest one, the most important one, was how all of this related back to Jonathan. It was impossible that he could've made it into the palace without being seen. So, that meant there was someone else. Or maybe it meant that Jonathan was the distraction while the real person was doing the dirty work under his cover. Had it been someone else all along? I didn't know who to trust. All my instincts said nobody. But I couldn't stick around and try to figure it out. So, I was leaving, but I wasn't going alone.

"Ready?" Grigor watched me coming down the stairs, his eyes carefully roaming over me. He'd been by my side since I'd burst out of the pool house and onto the lawn, shouting for help. He'd refused to leave me, and I was grateful. It was him who reminded me of his suggestion to escape, and Peter had agreed it might be a good idea to get away as quickly as possible. He hadn't been too happy about the idea of heading to Grigor's holiday home on the south coast, but he reluctantly admitted that, after the pool house drama, we'd been compromised from the inside. What if the enemy who stalked me also knew where our usual safe houses would be? We couldn't take that risk. Nobody else could know where we were going.

I gave a small, tight nod, my glance skipping around the Grand Entrance as if the person behind all of this was still hiding in the shadows. Peter stood by the door, restless, his hands bunched into fists by his side. I knew he felt guilty. He was meant to be the one who protected me at all costs, and somehow, someone had managed to slip right past him. I'd told him it wasn't his fault, but even I couldn't deny that I no longer felt safe. If Peter couldn't protect me, who could?

"The decoy cars left ten minutes ago. Walsh says the cameras are on their tail, and the guards report that the protestors have dwindled to a few dozen now they think you've left." Peter's mouth was barely moving. "Our car is ready. Nobody knows the exact location of where we're going apart from you two, me, Hutchins and a small protection unit. Once we're out of London, we should be safe."

"Perfect," I murmured. "I guess we better go then."

We moved for the doors but were stopped by an urgent call. Mum flew down the stairs, Eddie hot on her heels, somehow looking smaller than she'd ever seemed before. She crossed the floor and crashed into me hard, wrapping her arms around me.

"I wanted to say goodbye before you left. Don't worry about anything here. We've got it under control."

She looked over my shoulder, fixing Grigor with a steely eye. She didn't say anything. She didn't have to. Her face said it all. Grigor bowed his head, acknowledging what she was silently telling him. I knew she was curious about him. Wary even. Gayle too. But they saw that I'd put my trust—or at least some of it—in him and so they didn't ask questions. Besides, he was Eddie's best friend. His family was entwined with ours. He was one of us.

Finally, Mum let me go and rested her hand on Peter's arm. "Look after him," she said quietly. Peter nodded tightly.

Eddie stayed by the steps, eyes flitting between me, Grigor and Peter. His face was drawn in on itself. He probably blamed himself for what had happened in the pool house, or maybe he found it weird that it was his best friend who was taking his brother off into the sunset to hide.

"Have fun," he said, then mounted the stairs before his defenses came tumbling down in public.

We stepped out into the afternoon light, around to the back of the palace in the blind spot away from the cameras. Peter held the door of a Range Rover open for me and Grigor, Hutchins already in the driver's seat.

"Afternoon, Your Majesty," he murmured, starting the engine. The words made me feel queasy.

"Please, just call me James. While we're away, I'd like to at least try to forget I'm king."

"You've got it, Your—sorry, James."

Peter jumped up into the passenger seat, wound tighter than a spring. His eyes darted around, checking every inch he could see. "The blanket is right there, James," he murmured. "It's just until we get out of the city."

Grigor grinned as he picked up the blanket between us. "It's no wonder you're called James. This is starting to feel like a 007 mission."

I sank down into the footwell, between the back seat and Peter's, legs drawn up to my chest, arms around my knees.

"I guess I'll see you soon." Grigor lowered his voice. "Don't miss me too much."

He threw the blanket over me, hiding me from sight, an extra precaution behind the tinted windows. I rested my chin on my knees as the car rolled forward. It paused at the security gate, Hutchins waiting for clearance to leave. And then we were off, escaping from the city and, more importantly, away from those who hunted me. But as we drove, I thought back to what my father had said in his letter about trust, and in the back of my mind, I began to wonder. Grigor had replaced Jonathan as the rock I needed. But had I put my trust in him too soon?

⬿〰⬿

The house sat on the south coast, alone behind large gates and a wall of tall shrubs, its tan bricks and white windows soaking up the sinking beachside sun. It belonged to Grigor's family, a holiday home that sat empty for most of the year except for the gardeners who showed up once every few weeks to tend to the immaculate lawn. Flowers grew in a tamed entanglement in the front garden and around the edges of the house. As soon as you stepped from the car, you could hear the waves crashing against the shore, the salt thick in the sea air. It wasn't a palace, but out here, isolated from everything, it felt safer than one.

"Just stay here a minute while I check inside," Peter said, his door already half open.

The idea that any danger could lurk this far from home put me on edge, but stranger things had happened recently. Grigor passed him the keys and we waited a few minutes, until Peter reappeared on the front steps and gave us a satisfied nod. We were safe.

Hutchins helped Grigor with the bags and we mounted the steps together, passing Peter and entering through the solid oak door.

"It's beautiful," I murmured in awe as we stepped through the hallway, past the stairs and into the kitchen. The entire back of the house was made of glass, giving uninterrupted views of the beach that ran on from the end of the garden and into the waves. The sun was just beginning to touch the horizon, bleeding reds and oranges into the waters first, followed by pinks and darkening purples. The colors oozed into one another and seeped closer to the shore as the night swept in.

"You should see the bedroom," Grigor replied. He'd said it casually enough, and his eyes were fixed out on the waters, but it suddenly hit me that I hadn't even thought about where I'd sleep—where *we'd* sleep. There were enough bedrooms for us to take one each, but did I really want that? To sleep alone in a stranger's room?

Grigor gave me the grand tour, while Peter and Hutchins sorted through security measures, briefing the remote teams over the phone while huddled over notepads. Grigor and I climbed the magnificent stairs, my feet sinking into thick cream carpets, eyes sweeping over family pictures that hung on the walls. There was Grigor as a kid, looking deeply suspicious of a parrot on his shoulder. Then again as a young boy blowing out nine birthday candles. There were holiday pictures in far-flung places, Christmases, birthdays and anniversary dinners too.

"You're close with them, right?" I said as Grigor guided me down the hall.

He nodded without hesitation. "They're all I've ever known. As far as parents go, I think I lucked out second time around." He paused outside a bedroom door, eyebrows slightly raised and a smirk pulling his lips up into a disarming smile. "Your room for the stay, Your Majesty," he said, forcing his voice even deeper and stepping aside with flair.

I grinned and followed his gesture, stepping inside the master bedroom. Just like downstairs, the back wall was made up of a floor-to-ceiling window looking out over the ocean. A door to the side led out onto a small terrace, a white wooden fence that matched the windows the only thing between us and the beach.

Another door led into a marble bathroom, the free-standing bathtub curving up into an oval. There were two sinks, a large mirror covering almost an entire wall and a walk-in shower that could easily hold half a dozen people.

"It's not bad, huh?" Grigor said as I came back into the bedroom. He was lying back on the bed, propped up on plush pillows with his arms behind his head, gazing out to the beach beyond.

"Are you kidding? I'd never leave this place." I perched on the bed, watching the darkening waters roll into the sand.

"I thought I'd be a gentleman and offer you the best

bedroom in the house. I suppose I can settle with second best for a couple of nights."

"You mean you're not staying in here to protect me? I thought you were all meant to be keeping me safe...," I said coyly.

"In that case, I'll let Peter and Hutchins know we're all sharing a bed tonight. I think it's big enough." Grigor laughed as I rolled my eyes, getting up from the bed to inspect the view properly. It felt peaceful. More than peaceful. Like an idyllic sanctuary that I'd painted in my head to escape from everything.

"But seriously, if you want me to stay with you, then I will," Grigor said to my back. My heart paused, then started fluttering. I was glad he couldn't see my face.

"I want you to stay," I said quietly.

There was a silence, then the faint rustle of the bedsheets as he got up. I felt my shoulders instinctively tense up, but then his arms slipped around me and my worries began to fall away. He rested his chin on my shoulder, and we watched the last sliver of sun disappear as darkness prepared to steal the light.

"Then I'll stay," Grigor said.

⚬〰〰〰⚬

We passed the night playing games at the large dining table, the windows flung open so the sound of the waves lapping the shore floated in on the summer night air. Even Peter and Hutchins got involved, although only after I ordered them to. As the night rolled on, the sound of laughter wove itself with the waves. I felt my shoulders relax and my jaw unclench. My worries hadn't disappeared completely, but they were now far enough away that I could mostly forget they were there.

"Uno," I said smugly, laying down a card and clamping the other to my chest.

Grigor eyed me suspiciously. I raised my eyebrows in challenge.

"Don't let me down," Grigor said to Peter and Hutchins, slapping down a card with a plus two on it. Hutchins grinned and placed a matching card down. Everybody turned to Peter, who was fumbling with more cards than he could hold.

"Don't forget, I'm technically your boss...," I tried.

Peter peeked over his hand at the table, rolled his eyes and reached for the deck. I hooted as the others groaned, ready to lay my card.

"Oh wait..." Peter grinned, retrieving a card from his hand. He laid it down. It was black, with a plus four winking up at us. Grigor and Hutchins held their stomachs laughing as it dawned on me that I hadn't won.

"You're both fired," I muttered, although I couldn't help but laugh with them as Grigor threw me eight cards from the deck.

"A king doesn't get special privileges in this game," Grigor said smugly. "It's all-out war, Your Majesty."

Grigor ended up winning, of course, and he wore his celebration on his face without even trying to hide it.

"Maybe they do Uno championships or something,"

he said as we escaped upstairs after the dueling and terrible trash-talking was over. His gloating wasn't going to end any time soon.

It was late—way past midnight—and the sea was now invisible as it merged with the black sky above. Peter and Hutchins were doing one last check of the house and its grounds. The remote security team were on watch. But that was the least of my worries right now. All I could think about was Grigor.

He closed the bedroom door so the light from the hallway was snatched away, leaving only a pale puddle of moonlight to illuminate us, and then went over to open the window, allowing the sound of the ocean to find us again. He fell straight into bed, slipping his shirt up over his head. Heart in my mouth, I did the same and slid under the covers.

"It's so peaceful here," I whispered. I couldn't really see his face—just the outline of him, on his side, facing me. In the break between waves, I could hear his slow and even breathing. Without his entrancing gaze on me, I felt like I could almost tell him anything.

"Can I ask you a question?" Grigor said suddenly.

My body instinctively began to tense, but I forced myself not to shy away. If I couldn't be honest with him in the dark, then what chance did I really have with him at all? It scared me to realize that I was hoping he'd stick around when I no longer needed a knight in shining armor. My feelings for him were nowhere near what they'd been for Jonathan, but they were growing all the same.

"Of course," I said.

There was a pause, like he was trying to figure out the right way to ask the question. And then, "Do you want to be king?"

"I don't have a choice," I said automatically. "It's my duty."

"I know you don't have a choice. But do you *want* to be king?"

I thought about it, the darkness pressing in, the breeze and waves tinkling around us. I knew the answer. Or at least I thought I did. But nobody had ever asked me that question before. Did anybody ever want to be king or queen? Was it a responsibility that anybody *really* wanted? That's what made Cassandra so ruthless and terrifying, because for her, the answer was yes.

"No," I said carefully. It scared me that I'd finally admitted that out loud to somebody else. But lost in the darkness, the heat of Grigor's body so close to mine, I let go.

"I never wanted to be king. My dad told me when I was six that I would wear his crown one day, and I spent every moment after that learning how to stand in his shoes. I watched as my dad became one of the greatest kings to ever live, and I knew that I'd never be able to live up to that. That they'd never let me..."

I trailed off for a moment, letting visions of my dad play before me in the dark. The grief I'd tried to bury only resurfaced and I knew now that it always would. I could have days or weeks, maybe even months, of thinking I was okay, but it would always linger just out of sight, ready to catch me at my lowest moment.

I let out a steadying breath. "I don't want to be king."

"Why can't you step down if it's not what you want?"

"Kings and queens can't step down. It destroys the trust we've worked so hard to build. The crown is at its most vulnerable when it changes hands because that's when it asks the public to believe in something new. If I were to give up without even trying, they'd see that as weak. It would leave my family vulnerable, and I can't put them through that." I sighed. "Besides, I doubt Eddie would want that responsibility either, although he'd bear the weight of the crown better than me. Sometimes I wonder if we could switch places without anyone realizing."

I imagined Eddie sitting on the throne instead. Would he cope better? Probably. But would he eventually crumble under the pressure? Would he fade like a shooting star under that ceaseless gaze?

"I don't think that's true," Grigor said. "Eddie's my best friend, but I don't think he'd make a better king. He's like fire, all impulse and chaos. You're the opposite. You're like water. Calm and steady."

It didn't feel that way—at least not to me. But maybe there was a seed of truth there. I'd never looked at it that way before. To be king, you needed to be constant. Would Eddie be that, or would his fire burn out?

"Sometimes I'm scared that I'm not enough. That I'll never be enough. That I'll never be the king people want me to be." Now that I'd started, the shield of darkness protecting me, I couldn't stop. Every thought that I'd kept to myself was knocking on the door, waiting impatiently to get out into the open and breathe.

"I'm scared that I don't know how to be king. That I'll let everybody down. There's a pressure I feel weighing on me, like being the first Black *anything* is too important to mess up. Being king is the top job. It means something. Even if you don't believe in our family or the monarchy, it means something for a Black person to wear this crown. So, I can't mess it up, because if I do, they'll say we should have never been here in the first place. And they already think that."

I took a breath. It had tumbled out of me, and I couldn't take back what I'd said now. But I didn't want to.

"You are more than enough." Grigor reached for me in the dark, his hand grazing my arm and then slipping down to find my hand. He clutched it tightly, and I held him right back. "But you have to believe it for yourself. You can't let them believe it for you, because they won't give you the chance. Just like water, remember? There might be ripples and tides, even waves and storms, but the waters will always still."

The urge to be near Grigor as those words left his mouth eclipsed everything else. I moved closer to his silhouette, until we were lying side by side, my forehead lightly pressing against his chest. Grigor didn't hesitate to fold me into him, pulling me closer still until our bodies were one.

"What scares you the most?" I asked as we lay there in the dark. As king, everything was always about me. I'd spilled my secrets, but I wanted to turn the tables now. I wanted to know more about this mysterious boy who'd appeared when I needed him most.

He didn't hesitate. "Being given up on again. Being left."

His voice maintained the same, even note, but I could feel his body tensing against mine. I let my arms find their way around his back, to hold him, and he eventually softened again.

"By your parents?" I asked.

"My real mum said she'd come back for me. She never did. And my dad left us before I was even born. I've been scared of it happening again ever since."

"Your mum said she'd come back for you?"

Grigor shifted slightly, rolling onto his back, our bodies separating but still scorching from the other's touch. "She left me a letter when I was born, just before she gave me up. She said she did what she had to do for us, and that she'd come back for me when the time was right. But she never did. She died before she got the chance to."

"I'm sorry." It was all I could say to this boy who'd papered over the cracks but still nursed the pain they caused him.

"Don't be. It's other people who should be sorry. The ones who should've protected her. Not you." The darkness seemed lighter now that we'd shared so much. The moon splayed its light over the bed, haloing us together. "I don't tell people my secrets. I'm glad you can't see me right now," Grigor said, breathing a laugh.

"In that case, thank you," I said.

"For what?"

"For trusting me."

Grigor chuckled. "I fear I'd tell you all of my secrets given the chance."

"Then can I ask you something else?"

Grigor rolled over onto his side again, facing me. Now my eyes had adjusted, and with the help of the moon, I could make out his face a little more clearly. He looked back, and even in the dark, it felt like he could see me. *Really* see me.

"Why me? Why now?"

The question scared me. It had from the moment Grigor pulled me aside at the party. Even more so now that my trust was so feeble and broken. But I needed to know. I needed to make sure before I let whatever this was pull me in any further.

Grigor hesitated. In the silence I wanted to take it back, terrified that I'd shattered the fantasy of what I might want this to be. But finally, he spoke.

"I wanted to before. I saw what people like Quinn were saying about you, that maybe you weren't interested in finding a queen at all, and I...I don't know. I guess I hoped it might be true. But I just never found the right time. You were always surrounded by people. You were always..." He faltered. "You were always with him."

Jonathan's name felt forbidden here. It crouched in the darkness like a thief, ready to steal the light I was still trying to find in myself. But I couldn't think of him. Not now, in this moment. Instead, I tried to push him from my mind, suppressing the guilt that followed.

"And then the party presented me with an opportunity, and I knew if I didn't seize the moment then, I'd regret it."

Hope and desire lingered in the dark around us, begging both of us to take the moment in our hands. Grigor didn't flinch.

"I've wanted to do this for a long time," he said.

Any final doubt dissolved when our bodies came together once more. There was a breath between us, and then nothing at all as his lips found mine. It felt like free-falling. I didn't know where I'd land or what awaited me at the end. I didn't know if he'd catch me. But in that moment, it felt euphoric. I felt free.

CHAPTER TWENTY-THREE

THE END OF ALL THAT CAME BEFORE

The sun rose differently here. It crept over the waters, softening the shadows of our room with its glow. The birdsong in the garden and the waves gently lapping the shore woke me early. We hadn't shut the curtains and now the sound of water greeted me where I lay, its tide lazily pulling forward and then backward before unfurling toward the beach once more.

Grigor was still asleep, his face smoothed by his dreams. He looked at peace. I wanted nothing more than to climb back into his arms and to stay there for as long as possible. To hell with the day ahead. But I left him to sleep, slipping out from under the bed covers and padding out onto the terrace. A set of wooden stairs, painted white, led down to a path made up of large, smooth stones, which cut through the grass to a small gate that opened up onto the sand. I followed it out and sank down onto the beach, the faint chill of an early summer's morning teasing my skin as I watched the sunrays glaze the water.

I wanted to stay. London was home, but it was also prison. There, I had to play the role perfectly, never stepping out of line. But here, I felt safe, away from it all. There were no maids and butlers and advisors. There were no eyes watching me, scrutinizing my every step, ready to cast judgment. There were no responsibilities. Here, I wasn't king. I was just another seventeen-year-old boy.

"Can't sleep either, huh?" Peter joined me, sitting down on the sand by my side. I was surprised to see he wasn't wearing his usual suit and tie, the only uniform I'd ever seen him in, even at Christmas. Instead, he wore trousers and a T-shirt, his gold locket glinting around his neck. It sparked a moment of amusement in my head, to see him this relaxed. But then it dawned on me that he didn't have a life of his own either, which was why I never saw him this way. But he genuinely didn't seem to care. All he cared about was doing his job by protecting me.

"Think we can up sticks and move out here permanently?" I said, only half joking. "I think they've probably got it covered back home. We could stay out here on the beach forever."

"I've never really been a fan of the beach, but right now, I'd be inclined to say yes." Peter smirked to himself. "How are you feeling?"

I thought of Grigor, asleep in our room. I thought of last night. "Like a million dollars. I could get used to this *being normal* business."

Peter chuckled, his eyes fixed on the horizon. "Enjoy it. It's not fair that you don't get to be a regular kid growing up and finding your way. Every kid deserves that."

I sighed. "My lot in life is good. I shouldn't complain. Not when there are people far worse off than me."

Peter shrugged. "It does no good to compare our miseries. But I do wish you'd had that chance. Or at least a couple more years to be young and free."

I gave him a gentle nudge and we shared a smile. "You should escape while you still can. There's nothing forcing you to stay here. You could be out there living *your* life."

Peter tilted his head, as if he were contemplating it. But he shook it with a wry smile. "My life is protecting you. I wouldn't have it any other way."

We made our way back to the house, chatting about nothing as if we were any two people in the world, the sand between our toes and the sea breeze chasing our backs. In the house, Hutchins was perched on the edge of a chair in the kitchen, watching the news, a cup of coffee in his hand.

"Morning," he chirped as we came through the back door. "What activities are on the agenda today? Snorkeling? Sandcastle building? Collecting the trails of mermaids?"

"The mermaids only come out at night, I'm afraid," Grigor said, stifling a yawn as he wandered into the

284

kitchen. As he passed, he grazed his hand against my back. It was fleeting, but my whole body reacted as if it'd felt an electric shock jolt through it. He laughed under his breath and flicked on the kettle.

"I was thinking we could travel into the village. It's tiny and there won't be any bother there," Grigor said. Hutchins snorted.

"I think the small matter of *the literal king* being there might cause some bother," he said.

Grigor shook his head. "A cap and some sunglasses and nobody will be able to tell the difference. What would the king be doing here, after all? The only way they'll figure it out is if *you* don't stop looking like a military operation."

Hutchins went to retort, but I cut in. "I like that idea. It's just a village, and I have you both with me. People have no reason to think I've even left the palace. Tell the remote guard to stand by and we'll be fine."

I looked to Peter for support. Really, it was my call. If I made the order, they'd have no choice but to follow it. But I didn't *want* to make orders. So, I tried to widen my eyes and look like rejection would break me into a million pieces. Peter rolled his eyes.

"Your puppy dog eyes need some work, Your Majesty," he muttered, already sliding his phone out of his pocket and dialing a number.

"Did he . . . just call the king a dog?" Grigor grinned. "I wouldn't have that."

"I did. And I'll call you much worse." Peter's call

connected. He wiped the smile from his face and disappeared into another room to make arrangements.

"Ready for your first day pretending to be normal?" Grigor sidled up beside me as Hutchins went to join Peter. "It's easy, really. You just make sure you blink three times a minute, and don't step into direct sunlight in case you burst into flames and reveal your true royal colors."

"Funny," I muttered.

Glancing quickly at the empty doorway, Grigor took a step closer, laying his hands on my waist and pulling me into him. The joke dancing over his features was gone.

"I'm glad we came here together," he said.

I leaned into him, nestling into the hollow of his neck. "Me too," I murmured back.

He held me for a moment less than I wanted him to, before stepping back with a wicked grin.

"Now go and practice your walk. Slouch a bit—that straight and regal back of yours will give us away in no time."

Peter and Hutchins appeared in the doorway. Peter looked slightly on edge, but he nodded. "We leave in ten," he said. "Try to look like you're *not* the king. We'll be waiting in the car." And with that, they both disappeared outside.

⁂

The village was quaint, the kind you'd see on a postcard. To get there from the house, we wound along seafront roads, the windows open and the breeze whipping between us. Peter and Hutchins had dressed down to look less formal, and the remote guards were parked just outside the village. Everything was going to be fine.

When we arrived on the cobbled streets, Grigor jumped from the car and began heading toward the village square, weaving around people who were mostly older and retired, pushing shopping trolleys or linking arms as they shuffled past. I ducked my head instinctively, tilting the cap I was wearing even lower over my face. But nobody batted an eye in our direction. It felt like being invisible. I loved every second of it.

We fell into an old arcade that overlooked the beach, offering no more than a few slot machines, racing car simulators and claw-grabbing challenges. Grigor slipped into one of the driving seats, pretending to buckle up an imaginary seat belt. He gestured to the other cars alongside him.

"Care to lose, Your Majesty?" He raised his eyebrows smugly as he jammed a coin into the machine. I took the seat next to him, laughing to myself at how ludicrous this all was. If this was real life, then I wanted to hold it in my hands forever.

When Peter and Hutchins took seats in cars of their own, I grinned so wide I felt like my face could split in half. They each slipped a coin into the slot and chose their virtual cars, Peter revving his engine as the start screen loaded.

"Hope you're not a sore loser, Peter," I goaded.

"Just don't fire me when you come last," he replied, and shot out into the lead as the game started.

We spent the morning in the arcade, bouncing from one machine to another without a care in the world. It was quiet in there anyway, but nobody paid us the slightest bit of attention. Even when we slipped into the café next door for lunch and I accidentally knocked my hat off my head, nobody seemed to notice it was me. I was at ease, lulled into a fantasy that couldn't last. It wasn't long until the bubble eventually popped.

"In breaking news, the mother of a palace intern has come forward and claimed that her son is missing." All of our heads whipped up to find a solemn news anchor staring down the barrel of a camera on the TV screen above the counter. Behind her, a picture appeared. My world froze. Then it shattered completely.

Jonathan's face stared back at me.

"In an interview with royal reporter Quinn Buckley, the mother of eighteen-year-old Jonathan Kent said that she hadn't heard from her son in almost two weeks. More alarmingly still, she added in an extraordinary accusation that the Royal Family were refusing to help, and might even be hiding information on her son's whereabouts."

"Jesus fucking Christ," Peter whispered.

All of our eyes were glued to the screen as the picture gave way to a video of a Black woman, who I assumed was Jonathan's mum, sitting opposite a man I now knew all too well. Quinn Buckley was trying his hand at acting sympathetic, but that cruel glint still flashed in his eyes as he circled his prey.

"It's so unlike him. He usually calls every few days, or at least sends a text if things get busy. But I haven't heard from him since the king died." She looked distraught. Her voice broke around each word, like she was barely holding it together.

"And have the palace been any help in trying to find him?" Quinn asked gently.

She shook her head quickly, tears escaping from the corners of her eyes. "They won't tell me a thing. They've cut off all contact. They know something about this, I'm sure of it."

Quinn sat up a little straighter, leaning in like they were trading secrets. Except these secrets were being broadcast to the entire country. The entire world.

"You think the Royal Family have something to do with this?"

Jonathan's mum hesitated, eyes flicking past Quinn to look at somebody standing off camera. Then she nodded and lifted her chin.

"I know they've got something to do with this. They're hoping I remain quiet, but they're hiding what's happened to my son. I want to know what's going on. I want to know what they've done."

Quinn paused, letting her words sink in for everybody watching. Jonathan's mum had just accused the palace of being behind her son's disappearance. This was a nightmare.

"What makes you so sure that the palace is responsible?"

Quinn asked carefully, leaning forward, hungry for the final blow. But I already knew what the answer would be, and it was about to ruin us.

"I know the palace are behind my son's disappearance because..." Jonathan's mum looked down at her lap, then stared straight into the camera with a fierce determination. "Because it was Jonathan who was in a relationship with the king."

There was a gasp around the café. I could almost hear the held breath of the country, of my people, as they watched me being taken down. I was sinking, and fast.

I was dragged back into the now, in this quiet seaside café, by Hutchins. "Guy on your two, Pete," he muttered.

Peter quickly ducked his head as if he were reading something on the table. He flicked his eyes in the direction Hutchins had pointed out. I followed his eyeline and saw a man sitting in the corner, newspaper forgotten on the table in front of him. He narrowed his eyes in our direction, not even trying to hide the fact he was staring. He muttered something to the man opposite him, who swung around to get a better look.

"It's obvious, isn't it?" an old white man with no hair in the next booth said as a matter of fact. "Kid got scared his little boyfriend was going to tell the world and offed him before he got the chance. Poor lad's probably buried under Buckingham Palace."

"We need to get you out of here, sir," Peter said tightly. "Hutchins, call backup. Tell them to get the cars ready. We need to get home."

Peter stood up, hiding me from the stares of the men in the corner. But whispers had started to swirl. One head turned, and then another, and another, until every eye in the café was trying to get a glimpse of me. Grigor added himself to the shield, guiding me out into the street. A black Range Rover skidded around the corner ahead, coming to a stop a few meters away, its back door already flung open. Grigor pushed me inside, jumping in after me. The guard didn't wait for the door to close and sped off, talking to Peter through his earpiece.

But I couldn't hear a word he was saying. All I could hear were my own thoughts, erupting one after the other, and then all at once. Jonathan had never been working with Quinn Buckley. He hadn't revealed anything. He wasn't behind this mess.

A sickening guilt overwhelmed me. I'd let my feelings of betrayal distract me from the person I knew. I'd let them cloud my judgment. I'd believed that Jonathan had disappeared to hide himself from us, so he could take us down in revenge.

But Jonathan hadn't disappeared. He was missing.

Part IV

BURIED SECRETS SOON BLOSSOM

CHAPTER TWENTY-FOUR

HOME

The London skyline glinted like a warning as we drove
back into the city. Just as before, I hid under the
blanket, except now I was heading for a war zone instead
of a restful retreat. This whole thing was a nightmare,
one that I couldn't wake up from. Again and again, I'd
been pelted with these stories, yet more of our secrets kept
escaping from their cages. What scared me most of all was
wondering where, and how, it would end.

It was late afternoon, hours after Jonathan's mother
had taken her shot at the palace. We'd packed up immediately and headed straight for London. Just outside the
city, we'd stopped and let Grigor get into a separate car.
We couldn't be seen together. Not now. It would be the
final nail in the coffin if I weren't already buried alive. I
needed to sort this mess out with my family, and quick.

"How bad is it?" I asked from under the blanket, clenching my teeth as we slowed at the gates of the palace. "And don't lie to me."

There wasn't an answer for a few seconds. It was Hutchins who cleared his throat. "It's bad, Your Majesty. Protestors everywhere." I thought I heard Peter tut.

"Just stay down under the blanket until we tell you to get out," he said. "We're almost there now."

I could hear them. It sounded like hundreds of people shouting and jeering. Something hit the car window with a dull thud. I held my legs tighter against my chest. The car hit a bump, then rolled forward some more before coming to a stop. Somebody sighed as they unclipped their seat belt.

"You're safe, sir," Peter said. "The door's already open."

I threw the blanket off me and jumped from the car, dashing inside the palace to find Gayle already waiting. She was paler than I'd ever seen her before. She looked ill. We took each other in, neither knowing what to say first. There was no point in pleasantries, but nobody wanted to shatter the brittle illusion that we'd be okay. Both of us knew that too much had happened. We would never be able to recover from this.

"Conference Room?" I mumbled. Gayle nodded, waiting for me to pass before following in my wake.

Mum and Eddie were already there, sitting in silence like statues. Mum had folded her hands in her lap but leaped up to embrace me as soon as I entered. Eddie sat still in his chair, looking like he wanted to be sick. I sat down at the head of the table, squeezing his shoulder as I went by. Peter and Gayle trailed into the room, closing the door. It was just us—like it had been when this nightmare started. Facing the world together.

"How could this have happened?" It was me who broke the silence, my rage capsized by fear. My words sounded small over the enormous table, but now wasn't the time to act lesser than myself. I was scared, but I wanted answers.

"It doesn't make sense," Gayle said quietly. "We were so certain that Jonathan was behind this. It's impossible that he's not."

"Well, we've clearly been proved wrong," I snapped.

"With all due respect, Your Majesty, I'm not sure that we have." Peter rubbed his hands together, staring down at the table. He was thinking something over, weighing up his words before he spoke them. "There's a possibility that Jonathan isn't behind this. But the details shared with Quinn say otherwise. Who else would know such intimate details about your relationship? We can't ignore the fact that only you and Jonathan knew of them."

I leaned back in my chair, heaving a great sigh. I didn't know anymore. It didn't even feel like the answers were close. We were standing in darkness with no sense of direction.

"Maybe he was forced to tell Quinn Buckley," Eddie muttered. We all looked at him. He shrugged. "If those secrets could've only come from Jonathan, then could it be that he was forced to reveal them?"

"But who would want to do that?" Mum asked. "Who has a big enough motive to abduct Jonathan and force him to talk?"

Eddie snorted and pointed at the window, the patch of blue beginning to darken. "Literally every single person out there would love to get dirt on James. And I can bet there are a bunch of people on this side of the palace gates who feel the same."

I shivered. It could be anybody. Except...

"It can't be just anyone. The letters, remember? Whoever has been leaving me those notes has access not only to this palace, but to me." I thought back to the dark green envelopes I'd received, and the terrors enclosed within. "Whoever's behind this, they're closer than we think."

Peter leaned on the table, focused on me. "The letters. How did you receive them?"

I thought back, picking through the blur in reverse. "The last one was left in the pool house. There were dozens of people there—any of them could've left it. The second letter was delivered to my room during the funeral. And the first..." I trailed off. My heart sank. "Grigor gave it to me," I whispered.

At the mention of his best friend, Eddie bolted upright. "Grigor gave you the envelope himself?" I didn't trust myself to speak. My heart felt the first pangs of betrayal. This couldn't be happening again.

"Let's run with that for a second. Grigor hands you the first envelope. Why?" Peter asked.

I tried to straighten my thoughts, a nearly impossible task. "He said a maid left it," I murmured eventually. I glanced at my brother. "Apparently she didn't want to interrupt my...conversation with Eddie. Grigor took it and handed it to me. And..." I trailed off as another thought occurred, one I hadn't told anybody else out of shame for being so stupid in the first place.

"And...," Peter pressed.

I sagged back into my chair in defeat. "Grigor said he received an envelope too. That's why we met that night in the park. I went because I thought the note was from Jonathan—I thought he wanted to make things right. But when I got there, it was Grigor who showed up." I sighed. "He said he'd received an envelope but had thrown it away before arriving."

I kept my eyes on the table. I couldn't stand the looks I knew would be painted on my family's faces. Out loud, it all sounded so obvious. And hadn't I held those exact same suspicions before I allowed a current of neediness to wash them away? Had I ignored every sign in front of me because I was so desperate to not be alone?

"I'd never seen you talk so much with Grigor before your father passed away, and certainly not alone, and yet it's him who's been there at every turn since," Gayle mused. "He was in the park. He was in the pool house. He's been in your quarters. He has access to you that very few others do." She took a deep breath, weighing up all that'd been said. "Could it be possible that he's used

Jonathan's apparent betrayal to his advantage, to pull you further into his grasp? Has he been playing a game to get you exactly where he wants?"

The silence Gayle left was bloated with evidence I'd refused to see. And yet still, to my shame, I searched frantically for an answer that'd explain it away. In the face of these new possibilities, I couldn't accept that another person I held close was, in fact, a complete stranger to me.

"But *why*?" Mum said, shaking her head. "Grigor and his parents are like family to us. What possible motive could the boy have to exercise deeds so wicked?"

"What if it's not him?!" I blurted. "What if Grigor's just been in the wrong place at the wrong time? What if the real person behind this knows I'd eventually begin to suspect Grigor and is hiding behind that?"

I could hear the desperation in my voice, a plea to excuse him from this. My family glanced pitifully at me or bowed their heads to avoid my eyes altogether.

"What about Cassandra?" I tried, wilder by the second. "Could it not be her?"

Gayle leaned forward, looking nervous. "We had confirmation from security this morning about where Cassandra's been disappearing to, Your Majesty. My apologies—the mess with Jonathan's mother happened right after I found out."

I sat up alertly. Peter did too, leaning toward Gayle like he could pick the words out of her brain before she said them.

"She's been meeting with Quinn Buckley, sir. Private

lunches and dinners. When she's been sneaking out, she's been going to see him."

I could've yelled or cried or fainted on the spot. "She's meeting the man who's out to tear us all down? The man who actually wants her to be queen? She *has* to be behind this!"

Mum grimaced. It wasn't the reaction I'd been hoping for. "I admit, it doesn't look good, but we can't let our dislike of Cassandra cloud our judgment here. We're family. Would she really go so far as to publicly crucify you—us—for her own gain?"

"Yes!" Me and Eddie said together. Mum sat back, mulling it over.

"We must be careful of our next steps. We can't rush headfirst into anything," Peter said firmly. "One wrong move and we'll sink this ship completely. We have to be sure—absolutely *certain*—before we make a decision."

Everybody looked at me. It was my call. My head said one thing, my heart another, and I didn't know which to trust. Jonathan could be in danger. If we didn't act quick, then who knew what could happen. But I couldn't afford to be wrong. I couldn't let my heart lead. Not when it had already been broken and betrayed before.

"Close in on them both," I said. "Use every resource we have. If one of them has Jonathan, or if they're behind this in any way, then we'll know. We work overnight to figure this out. And then by morning, we *must* make a choice. For Jonathan's sake."

Gayle nodded. Mum slowly agreed too. Eddie stood

up, his expression set in stone. Grigor meant something to more than just one person in this room. If he was behind this, Eddie would be heartbroken too.

Everybody began to leave, but another idea was brewing in my mind. I couldn't just sit back and wait. I had to do something. And I needed help.

"Peter? Can I have a word before you go?"

Peter nodded, closing the door after Gayle and turning to face me. I counted to five, to be sure we wouldn't be overheard, then lowered my voice.

"I have an idea. You're not going to like it, but I have to do something."

Peter narrowed his eyes, then closed them completely as I told him, letting his head fall back against the door with a dull thud.

"You realize how badly this could backfire, don't you?" he said.

I nodded stiffly. "I do. But right now, I don't think we have a choice. We have to take a risk."

Peter shook his head, blowing out a breath. "I'll make the arrangements."

He took out his phone and began dialing, talking in hushed whispers once Hutchins picked up the call. I wandered over to the window, looking down at the trees and out at the darkening early evening sky. Danger lurked out there. It watched me wherever I went. If I was wrong about this, then I might've just destroyed my family forever. But if I was right, then we had a very good chance of catching whoever was behind everything.

And that was a gamble I was willing to take.

Peter hung up the phone after a few minutes. He nodded sharply. "We go first thing tomorrow morning. We've set up a place where you won't be seen."

I took a deep breath. It was too late to go back now. But if I had to wait until morning, then there was something else I wanted to do first. Every thought in my head told me no. But I had to do it.

"I need to see Grigor," I said. "Tonight."

Peter hesitated for the briefest moment. "Yes, Your Majesty," he said, and stepped aside.

CHAPTER TWENTY-FIVE

A Secret, a Lie or a Cruel Mix of Both

Grigor's house was nestled in the grounds of Kensington Palace under the shade of a large oak tree. It was only a few miles from Buckingham Palace, so it didn't take long to get there at all, but the last rays of daylight were soon swallowed by the dark as we pulled into the palace grounds.

Peter parked the car in front of the house, the security car gliding into a space next to us. He eyed me in the rearview mirror as he turned off the engine.

"Need me to come in there with you?"

I shook my head quickly. I wanted to do this alone. I had to. I wasn't even sure what I wanted to say yet, or how I was going to find enough evidence to support the fact that it couldn't be him behind this. It was impossible.

"I won't be long. Keep the car running," I said, slipping out and heading for the door.

My mind raced as I got closer. It was all I could do to put one foot in front of the other and keep walking until I was at the door, the light on the front of the house pouring down on me. I gathered myself, taking a deep breath, then knocked.

There was movement from the depths of the house, someone coming down the stairs and along the hall. They fiddled with the lock and then swung the door open, peering out into the evening to see who'd arrived unannounced.

"Oh, Your Highness! I'm so sorry, we weren't expecting you!" Grigor's mum, Mary-Anne, dipped her head and bent her knee swiftly, stepping aside to allow me through.

"It's me, James," I explained, as she shut the door. *Your Highness* was Eddie.

"Oh my gosh, I am SO sorry, Your Majesty!" Mary-Anne dipped into another curtsy, blushing furiously. She was white and middle-aged, with greying hair and puffy cheeks. A smear of red lipstick coated her mouth, matching her blush. She looked nothing like Grigor, of course.

"Grigor's not home, Your Majesty. Although he shouldn't be much longer if you'd like to wait? He didn't tell me where he was going, but he said he'd be back soon." Every one of her sentences flicked up at the end in her singsong voice, as if she were asking me a question.

"I don't mind waiting," I murmured, thankful for

some extra time to think about what I was going to say to Grigor. I wondered where he could be if he wasn't home after our mad dash back to London.

"Well, why don't you go on up and wait in his room. Patrick's through there admiring his new chess set, and he'll only bore you to tears if you stay down here for longer than twenty seconds!" Mary-Anne pointed to the stairs, bordered with a sleek metal banister. "His bedroom's on the second floor, first door on the right. Shout if you need anything!"

I climbed the stairs, taking in the family pictures hanging on the walls that were just like the ones in the beach house. Again, there were no baby pictures—Grigor had been adopted when he was two years old—but every other stage of his life had been documented.

His bedroom was simple and well-kept, a large four-poster bed taking up most of one wall, the crisp white sheets immaculately tucked in. Doors opened onto a Juliet balcony that looked down over luscious gardens where a large fountain tinkled like music. There were pictures and art on the walls, all swooshes of color that bled from one into another. I inspected the signature at the bottom and realized he'd done them himself. It reminded me once more that I didn't know him at all, and that terrified me more than anything.

I looked around the room like it might be hiding secrets. And maybe it was. Would I ever have another opportunity to confirm my fears or prove them wrong? I didn't know what he could be hiding up here, but the urge to snoop was overwhelming. He'd be back soon. That gave me some time—not much, but it was something.

I didn't know what I was looking for. It wasn't like I was going to find Jonathan under the bed. But I needed *something*. If he was behind all of this, and I prayed with every fiber of my body that he wasn't, then there had to be evidence here.

The drawers gave me nothing except clothes and long-forgotten trinkets discarded without care. There were scraps of paper with unfinished sketches, diaries that hadn't been opened much less written in, a box of matches, scattered pens. Nothing. I tried the wardrobe instead. His clothes were hung in an orderly fashion, all freshly cleaned, ironed and categorized. I swept a bunch of them aside and inspected the boxes at the back, but they only seemed to hold old toys and board games.

I pulled one shoebox out and flipped the lid to find unimportant letters and snapshots of school friends standing outside classrooms or on ski trips in their masks and goggles. I sighed. I should've trusted him. There was nothing here that proved anything.

I went to close the lid, but the corner of another picture, facedown in the pile, caught my eye, Grigor's name and a date scrawled on the back. I shuffled the other photos out of the way and scooped it up, turning it over to find a faded snapshot staring back at me. And then there was the unmistakable sound of the front door opening, followed by Grigor's voice calling out to Mary-Anne.

My hands shook, dropping the box and half of its contents on the floor. I swore under my breath and quickly dropped to my knees, stuffing everything back into the box. The picture was the last thing, still in my hands. I placed it back inside just as footsteps on the stairs made my heart race. But nothing could make it beat faster than what my eyes had seen.

It was Grigor as a baby, swaddled in a blanket in his mother's arms as she lay in a hospital bed. I flipped it over to check the name once more and my blood ran cold. The footsteps were halfway up the stairs, but I couldn't move. What I had seen surely couldn't be true. It was impossible.

I slammed the box shut and stuffed it into the back of the wardrobe right as Grigor pushed open his bedroom door, a smile already pulling at the corner of his mouth.

"This is a nice surprise," he said, striding into the room and pulling me into him. I let him. I didn't want him to think anything was wrong. "I wanted to see you, but I didn't think you'd be ready yet."

I needed to get out of here. I needed to get back to Peter.

"It was just a quick visit to say hey, that's all. But I can't stay. Peter's waiting for me outside." I tried to smile, but Grigor frowned in response.

"You've only just got here. You can't stay a little while?"

I shook my head a little too quickly. "Can't. Sorry. They...they need me back at the palace." I was giving myself away. My panic was edging into my words. He knew something was wrong. So I kissed him.

His body was rigid for a moment, but then it melted into mine and he kissed me back, as if he needed it more than air. When I pulled away, he seemed to relax.

"At least let me walk you out then," he said.

I nodded and let him guide me down the stairs as if I couldn't find my own way. At the door, his hand lingered on my waist, not wanting to let me go. But I stepped outside, away from his reach.

"I'll see you soon," I said, and tried my hardest not to run back to the car.

"Everything all right, Your Majesty?" Peter asked warily as I got in and slammed the door shut. I was breathing heavily. Peter began to pull away. Grigor watched us from the door until we were out of sight.

"What's happened?" Peter tried again.

"It's Grigor," I said in disbelief. "It's him."

Peter slammed on the brakes. We were at the gates of Kensington Palace, about to leave. They were open, ready to let us on our way.

"What do you mean, it's him?"

I shook my head, trying to dislodge what I'd seen and make sense of it in some way.

"I found a photo of Grigor when he was a baby. His mum is holding him," I uttered.

Even with my eyes open, I couldn't see anything but that picture. That woman, holding her baby before she gave him up. Before she promised to come back and give him a better life. Before she'd been killed and lost the chance to stay true to her word.

I knew her. Everybody did.

"His mother," I whispered, "is Princess Catherine."

CHAPTER TWENTY-SIX

MOTIVE

Grigor's mother was Princess Catherine. I could think of nothing else. The thoughts tumbled through my mind so fast I could barely hold on to one before it was replaced with another. Despite where the fingers pointed, I'd clung to the idea that it couldn't possibly be Grigor because he didn't have a motive. Now he had one. His mother was irrevocably tied to my family.

From the very beginning, I'd wondered why Grigor had suddenly crept into my orbit, and yet I'd ignored those thoughts, terrified of what insecurities they'd reveal. When I believed it to be Jonathan, the betrayal had made me desperate to be held by someone else. And so I'd fallen into the arms of the first person who happened to be in the right place at the right time. His words from last night came back to me.

You were always surrounded by people.... You were always with him.

Had Grigor been there for me by accident, or had he removed Jonathan from the equation knowing that lonely darkness would push me straight into his trap?

"You're absolutely *sure* it was Princess Catherine in that picture?" Peter asked for the fourth time. We were locked away in my quarters, midnight fast approaching. I didn't know who I could trust, so for now, I wanted to keep it between the two of us.

"She's a part of history. *My* history. I'd know her face anywhere. It was Princess Catherine, holding Grigor as a baby. His name and date of birth were scrawled on the back. There's no doubt in my mind."

I saw the picture when I closed my eyes. I saw it when I opened them. It was branded on my brain and the backs of my eyelids, burning into me so I could never forget it. The only way things could get worse was if Grigor's deception meant we were actually half brothers, but I'd already done the maths and the dates didn't match up. Grigor was two years older than me, born a week before my father returned from his royal tour of Africa, before he'd met Princess Catherine in real life. They'd only been courting through letters until then. At least something was finally in my favor.

"So, let's say Catherine gives Grigor up as a baby. Why?"

It was irritating me that Peter was still speculating over whether I was telling the truth. I knew what I'd seen.

311

"It's obvious, isn't it? She knew the rules." Peter raised a questioning eyebrow. "My father was a prince, looking for a princess to become his future queen. But she had to fit the role. Catherine would've never been considered as an option if it was known she'd given birth to a child from a previous relationship days before meeting my father." I shuddered at the archaic traditions that shrouded my family and the institution we served.

Then something Grigor said under the cover of darkness reappeared in my thoughts.

"She gave him up in the hope that she could give them a better life. That's what he told me. She left him a note and promised to come back for him."

It was like being struck by lightning. I jumped up from my chair and paced to the window and back again, thinking out loud.

"When we were away, Grigor said something else. He said..." I struggled to think, to get it right in my brain. "He said that she was meant to come back for him, but that she didn't have the chance. That the people who were meant to protect her were the ones who should be sorry."

Peter was on his feet now too. "Who was meant to protect her?" he asked, although we both already knew the answer.

"Us. We were meant to protect her." It was piecing together so quickly now that I could barely keep up. "We were supposed to keep her from harm, but she was murdered under our guard. She never had the chance to make things right, and he resents that. But he doesn't blame

Catherine. He blames *us* for not protecting her so that she could come back for him."

I snapped out of the trance my thoughts had encaged me in. Peter's face said everything I needed to know. What I was saying seemed so ridiculous, so far out of the realm of possibility, and yet, it made sense. It all did. I wanted to be wrong so badly it hurt, but the evidence was stacking up and it couldn't be ignored, even if my heart pleaded for ignorance.

"So, you think this is revenge?" Peter asked carefully.

I shrugged. "It's the only thing that makes sense to me right now. Who else would have a motive to take Jonathan and turn him against me and this family? Who else has access to me like he does? We barely used to speak, and then he swooped in at my lowest moment, when my dad's body was still warm. He knew it wouldn't take much to get past my defenses because they'd already been obliterated—first by my father's death, and then by Jonathan's disappearance and supposed betrayal. He knew I'd be weak, that I'd need a rock to hold on to. And he was only too happy to step in, so he could get close to me and take us all down from the inside."

I turned to Peter, shaking.

"It's him," I said. "It has to be him."

Peter tilted his head, grimacing.

"What is it?" I pressed.

He sighed. "I see the way he looks at you, sir. Like his world might stop for a moment if you weren't in it. If he's behind this, then he's fooled all of us. I'd hate for us

313

to make a wrong move now. Not when we're this close to figuring it out. Let's at least look at the other suspects before tomorrow morning comes."

The morning—I'd forgotten all about it. Only now did I remember that Peter and I had concocted a secret plan of our own to help prove once and for all who was trying to tear us down.

"Okay," I breathed, perching on the edge of the armchair and raking my hands over my head, trying to think straight. "So, there's Grigor. And then there's Cassandra."

"Motive?" Peter asked.

"She desperately wants to be queen, and she'd do anything to get on the throne," I answered without pause. "She hates me. Eddie too. And she's been meeting up with Quinn in secret. She's hiding something." Her betrayal would also be the least hurtful, I reasoned to myself, and would therefore be the best outcome.

Peter nodded. "Next."

I sifted through moments over the last days and weeks, trying to pick out who'd been present. "Ophelia?" I tried. "She's been avoiding us like the plague since Jonathan's disappearance, and when she decided to reappear and apologize at the pool, I received one of those envelopes."

Peter weighed this up. "You really think she could have something to do with this?"

I hesitated. "Not really. But we can't trust anybody, right?"

Peter sighed. "Correct. Next."

"Gayle."

314

Peter choked on thin air, coughing and spluttering for a few seconds before he could bring himself under control. "With all due respect, sir, how on earth have you jumped to that conclusion?"

I sat down in the armchair and leaned back, screwing up my face. "She was the one who told Jonathan to leave in the first place, and then she had his room cleaned almost immediately. We don't know what was said, or how it was left. And let's not forget—she left the first note, remember?"

"She already explained why she did that," Peter reminded me.

I shrugged. "Did it sound like a reasonable excuse to you? That she wanted to scare Jonathan into keeping his mouth closed? It sounds to me like she'd go to any lengths to protect the crown."

Peter cleared his throat, obviously thinking carefully about how to word his next thought. "If that's the case, why would she want to take you down?"

I thought about this for a moment, mulling it over. "I've been nothing but trouble to the crown since I started wearing it. Maybe she thinks that the monarchy will be irreparably damaged if I stay on the throne for too long. She might want to get rid of me to protect the institution before I destroy it altogether."

Peter didn't look convinced, but he moved on anyway. "Grigor, Cassandra, Ophelia and Gayle. Those are the only suspects you want to try?"

I let those names sit with me for a moment as my

thoughts turned to everybody else. But it didn't take me long. The only other person was Peter, and if I couldn't trust him, then I may as well implode the monarchy myself.

"There's nobody else," I said, letting that final thought flutter out of my head. I was surprised at the strength of my words. "We move forward with our plan tomorrow morning. Nobody else knows of it and it'll stay that way. Then we follow the clues to the end, and we nail the bastard behind this."

CHAPTER TWENTY-SEVEN

TURNING TABLES

I drummed my fingers on the table I was seated behind, trying to keep my dark thoughts at bay. I didn't need them now. If I listened, I'd stand up and run back to the palace. But it was too late to back out of our plan. We were here now, and we were going to see this through to the end. Whether it was a *good* idea remained to be seen. But we'd soon find out.

Peter and I had snuck out of the palace before seven a.m., greeted by a day that held the promise of rain in clouds that formed a claustrophobic ceiling over us. It was so early that only a few members of staff were awake, and they'd never dream of stopping the king to ask where he was going. When we returned to the palace, though, we had to be ready to answer to Mum and Gayle, even if I technically didn't need their permission.

The restaurant was small and unassuming, just how we wanted our meeting place to be. It was tucked away in the back streets of the city, a CLOSED sign turned out to passersby. We sat in a back corner, alone but for the two waiters behind the counter, who were trained to not see us unless we needed them. They'd been expecting us and knew how to keep a secret. Our family had used this place a million times before, sometimes just to get out of the palace, other times for meetings that could never take place within its walls. This morning, we were here for the latter.

"Last chance to back out," Peter murmured. He hadn't taken his eyes off the street since we sat down. Somewhere around the corner, Hutchins was sitting in the car, ready to jump into action at a moment's notice. But aside from the three of us, nobody else knew what we were doing.

I shook my head. "We're here now. And besides," I said through gritted teeth, "we'd already be too late."

On the tail of my words, the bell above the door tinkled and a tall man wearing an expensive suit strode in. I could smell him before he'd put one foot into the restaurant. He'd doused himself in something lavish, and its potent stench hung in the air. He paused, letting the door close behind him, glinting eyes dashing across the room until they found us sitting in the corner. He smiled and I felt my skin crawl. I unclenched my fists in my lap and clasped my hands together instead. The last thing I needed to do was jump across the table and punch Quinn Buckley in the face. Especially when we needed his help.

"Good morning, Your Majesty," Quinn said, his tone slick with sarcasm.

"Ah, the man behind my demise," I said cheerfully, switching my fear for the confidence of a king. Now wasn't the time to cower away. "Good morning, Quinn."

Quinn threw his head back and laughed, taking a seat opposite me. He sat with the air of a man who dined with kings and queens for fun. He seemed at ease, as if he hadn't been trying to ruin my life at all costs. Up close, his smug smile was even crueler, holding back secrets that were buried just beneath the surface.

"I have to say, I'm somewhat surprised to find myself in such fine company this morning," Quinn quipped. "It's not every day that the king himself invites you for a personal breakfast."

"Breakfast would be going too far, I'm afraid. This meeting must be brief, and, of course, conducted in absolute confidence, so I fear we'll not even have time for coffee."

Quinn grinned, and I admit, my hands twitched in my lap for a split second. Peter seemed to sense it and sat up a little straighter, ready to pounce.

"A man can't deal in secrets without his coffee, Your Majesty. I'm sure you'll beg my pardon." Before I could say another word, Quinn leaned back and snapped his fingers. "A coffee, if you please," he said to nobody in particular. He didn't take his eyes off me. "Black, with an extra shot."

The coffee appeared almost immediately, steaming hot

in front of Quinn. He let it rest in his hands for a brief moment, blowing steam off the surface. When he was satisfied, he threw his head back and swallowed the contents in one gulp. If it seared his throat, he didn't let on.

"Now then, let's not waste time with pleasantries if you're in such a rush. What can I do for you, Your Majesty?" His words were light and shade, cheery on the surface, but with menace swirling beneath them.

I steadied my nerves. This could backfire so terribly that I'd be doing Quinn's job for him. But a risk could harbor great rewards, if only it didn't bear ill will first.

"I think you know what my first question is. I want to know who's been helping you write your stories." One side of Quinn's mouth contorted into a smile through which a cunning retort was ready to escape. I beat him to the punch. "But I'm sure even you don't know who they are. Whoever is helping you wouldn't want to give themselves away, would they?"

Quinn fixed me with cold eyes. "What makes you think I don't know who my source is?"

I laughed myself this time, although I didn't find much funny. But I remembered words Gayle had once said—this was all a game. If I wanted to beat Quinn, then I had to play him better than he could play me.

"If I were to hazard a guess, I'd say you've been receiving anonymous tips. A green envelope, am I right?" Quinn narrowed his eyes but said nothing. "They include stories about me and my family. I bet they come with just enough reassurance that what they're claiming is true—maybe there's some proof included with the note. And you run with it, twisting it into whatever narrative you think will take me down best. Am I close to the mark?"

"Warm," Quinn muttered darkly. Relief distracted me for a moment. It'd been a shot in the dark, but now I knew that I was at least half-right.

"I'm sure you can understand that I can't let this continue. You've caused enough damage to my family, don't you think? It's about time that you fix your mess, Quinn."

I refused to take my eyes off him. I wouldn't blink first.

"And why would I want to help you?" Quinn scoffed.

I shrugged. "Call it a favor. Or call it an order from your king."

For the first time, Quinn backed down, although only slightly. But I'd cracked the door open—I could see it in the way his eyes narrowed, the way his jaw tightened and his shoulders tensed—and I wasn't about to let it slam shut in my face now.

"If you help me, then I'll pardon you in return."

Quinn snorted. "Pardon me? What are you planning? To behead me at dawn?" He laughed, but it was higher now and had lost its sharp edge.

I leaned in closer, lowering my voice and bolstering it with quiet menace. "I know where you live. Where you work. Where you walk your dog in the mornings. I know you go to a gym miles away from your house, not because it has a pool like you told your wife, but because it's closer to Sarah's apartment. Does your wife know that you're having an affair?" Quinn started at that, but I kept going. "I'm not the only one hiding secrets here, Quinn. I'm just the only one who's had the misfortune of their secrets being blasted out into the world. The only one so far, anyway. That can easily change."

I sat back in my chair, hating myself for stooping to Quinn's level but letting my rage from the past few weeks fuel me. Everything was balancing precariously on this threat. I'd never wanted to be a ruthless king, but now I had no choice. I had to play by the rules of my enemies.

Quinn was barely hiding his fury. He'd been playing chess for too long, swiping pawns and pieces for his own. But now he'd made one move too many, and I'd cornered him.

"What do you want?" he asked through gritted teeth.

"I want your help to catch whoever is behind this," I said firmly. "I want it to stop. Now."

"And how do you propose we do that? Do you not think I've been trying to figure out the source for myself?" I swallowed a laugh. Of course he'd been frantically trying to unveil the person behind this—he'd wanted more ammunition to fire at us.

"You didn't have my help before. But I have an idea that'll put an end to all of this." I slowly exhaled, settling my brain. "I've planted stories with those most likely to betray me. Each story is different. And before you think of printing any of them, they're all false."

Grigor had called to make sure I was okay after I'd left his house, and I'd used the opportunity to plant a story that I'd started balding from stress and would be getting a hair transplant next week, something I hoped I hadn't jinxed by speaking it into existence. Then, before dinner, I'd made sure to let Cassandra overhear that I'd seduced the Prince of Spain when he'd visited the palace earlier in the year. To be fair, remembering the eighteen-year-old heir to the Spanish throne made me wish that lie was true. I'd then messaged Ophelia and told her the same thing but instead used the nineteen-year-old Prince of Denmark, a lie I was less impressed about because everybody knew his body odor announced itself before he did. And finally Gayle . . . well, I wasn't proud of this lie, but I'd told her of my concerns that Quinn was going to find out I'd christened the throne with Jonathan in a way I'm sure the monarchy never intended.

No two lies were the same. Now all we had to do was wait.

Quinn shrugged. "And what good will that do?"

"If your source is among them, then one of my lies will reach you. Once you receive it, you call me. And when you've told me which story has landed in your hands, we'll have our culprit."

Quinn chuckled wryly. "You've really thought this through, Your Majesty. I applaud you—really, I do. But may I ask, what do you intend to do if this little game of yours doesn't go to plan? What if none of your suspects take the bait?"

I'd thought of that, and my answer wasn't one I was happy with. The truth was, if this didn't work, then I didn't know what I'd do next. It was the only plan I had. It wasn't foolproof or guaranteed in any way, and I didn't even know if it would work at all. But I had to try.

"The plan will work," I bluffed. "So long as you stick to your side of the bargain, then the person behind the envelopes will be revealed and we can put this mess to bed."

Quinn thought it over, his face remaining impassive but for a twitch in his jaw. After a few seconds, he breathed a humorless laugh and sat back in his chair. "How must it feel to suspect every person around you? To not be able to trust a single soul." He weighed me up, his glance skipping over me. He was trying to regain the upper hand, to leave now with a shred of the confidence he'd walked in with. "What makes you think that outing one traitor will end this? Canaries sing behind those palace walls. You must know that others are biding their time."

"You mean my cousin?" I smiled as fury sketched lines over his face. "You're not the only one who has eyes and ears all over this city. You think I don't know that Cassandra has been sneaking out to meet you? As someone who's become an expert at not being caught doing things they shouldn't, I'm surprised you weren't more careful. Lunches with a princess? You may as well have flown a banner over the palace."

The last of Quinn's composure was dissolving before my eyes. He had nothing left. But as I watched him flounder, a realization began to dawn.

"You know she's not behind this, don't you?" My heart leaped against my chest as I started to connect the dots. "She's been telling you things, but nothing of any merit. Nothing that could destroy us. Just petty stories to get herself good press."

I thought of all the lies that Quinn had printed, and how Cassandra had remained angelic in every article. Now it made sense. She'd been using Quinn for her own gain, trading secrets for favor. If she were behind this, Quinn would forever be in her debt.

"But then those envelopes started arriving on your desk and you thought you'd hit the jackpot," I continued. "You thought it might even be her, but why would she not tell you over lunch? If she knew about Jonathan, she wouldn't write that secret down. How could she cash in on her rewards if you didn't know it was her?"

I saw something in Quinn's eyes, as good as a confession. But instead of relief at eliminating a suspect, I felt the knife twist itself even further. I'd pinned every hope on Cassandra, praying that out of everyone, she was behind this. But my hopes had now disintegrated. I couldn't ignore sense, no matter how much I might want to.

I stood up abruptly, putting an end to our meeting. Quinn looked like a crumpled piece of paper, his body caving into itself now that it didn't have any secrets to hold it up.

"Nobody can know about this meeting. Not a single soul," I said. "Keep an eye out for one of those green envelopes any day now. And be sure to call immediately once you receive it." I turned to leave but paused at the door. "Oh, and, Quinn?"

He turned in his seat, eyes ablaze with resentment.

"Say hi to Sarah for me." I smiled. "And your wife too, of course."

I stepped out into the sun, feeling both lighter and heavier than when we'd arrived. I'd narrowed down my suspects, which meant we were closer than ever to ending this. But the identities of those who remained in the spotlight made my heart sink.

I slid into the back seat of the waiting car, just as my phone buzzed in my pocket. Hutchins revved the engine, waiting for Peter to climb into the passenger seat. "Hope it went well, Your Majesty," he said.

But I didn't reply. I was holding my phone, reading the text, every hope I'd held on to imploding.

"What is it, sir?" Peter asked as he sat down, worry lines appearing around his eyes.

"Get us back to the palace immediately," I whispered. "They've caught her."

Hutchins stepped on the gas and the car shot forward, heading in the direction of home.

Peter frowned. "Cassandra?"

I read the text again. Each word of it twisted my stomach. I shook my head.

"Ophelia."

CHAPTER TWENTY-EIGHT

HIDING IN PLAIN SIGHT

The mood outside the palace had shifted. If clouds had been gathering before, they had now burst and an angry storm was beginning to break. We had tripled the number of guards in anticipation, but even so, they were outnumbered by the protestors gathering beyond our measly shield. They chanted and yelled as my car sped into the grounds, hurling rocks and other debris and thrusting their signs up into the air with a roar.

WHERE'S JONATHAN?

WHAT HAVE YOU DONE?

MURDERERS!

The sound only stopped when the palace door was slammed shut behind me. But although I still heard the yells echoing in my ears, my mind was elsewhere, racing against me as I sprinted through the hallways in pursuit of answers.

Ophelia jumped as I burst into the Drawing Room, breathless and frightened, with Peter a second behind me. She was as pale as moonlight, her body trembling like a petal lost in the winds. She couldn't sit still, her legs fidgeting as if she desired nothing more than to run for her life. But she was flanked by two burly security guards, and faced by Mum and Gayle.

"We found her in your quarters, Your Majesty," Gayle said steadily. "CCTV picked her up in the hallway. We searched her but she has nothing."

"I needed to talk to you," Ophelia said desperately. Her words trembled as if they were terrified of being heard.

There was another roar from the crowd outside. It surely couldn't be long before their cries shattered the glass in the windows or shook the walls until nothing of the palace was left standing. We'd be a smoking ruin by morning.

"Talk to me about what? What were you doing in my quarters, Phee?"

Ophelia shifted nervously under our stares. "It's just...I just..." She tried to take a breath but it only made her stuttering worse. As she went to speak once more, the door opened, sending Ophelia into a panic all over again.

"What's all the fuss abo—" Eddie began as he barged

into the room. The swell of noise outside must've marked his arrival through the palace gates. He stopped in his tracks when he saw Ophelia, his eyes skimming over her tear-stained face and then quickly sweeping over the rest of us. "What's going on?"

"Ophelia has something she wants to say to James," Gayle said as we turned our attention back to her once more.

"Ophelia...," Mum tried gently. But it was no use. Tears glittered in Ophelia's eyes and then fell, streaking her face with sadness.

"Please...," she whispered in my direction, but it was all she could say.

"James?" Peter's voice pulled my eyes away from her. "You need to see this."

Everybody turned to find Peter by the door. He had a bag in his hand, holding it slightly away from himself as if it could explode. "Is this yours?" he asked Ophelia. She said nothing.

"It was in her possession when we caught her," Gayle answered instead. "We've already checked its contents. Why?"

Peter reached into the bag, retrieving something from its depths. A part of me began to break, then shattered completely when I saw it. In Peter's hand was a green envelope.

Ophelia let out a strangled cry, flinching away from it. I took the envelope from Peter, tearing it open in a trance. I looked down at what I held.

```
For all you've done, for all you've
taken from me, I hope this family
suffers.
```

Ophelia had been on my list, but that had been to
avoid blaming Grigor. I didn't *actually* think she could
be behind everything. And yet I now held the evidence
that proved it. She'd been caught red-handed, in the act of
leaving another note that was meant to put the final nails
in my coffin.

I thrust the envelope into my pocket and whirled
around to face Ophelia. One word clawed its way into my
mouth, spewing out into the air before I could stop it.

"Why?"

The word sat broken between us all. Ophelia sniffed
and tried to raise her eyes to meet mine, but she quickly
averted her gaze like she'd looked up into the sun. She was
still trembling, her breathing shallow and fast.

"I trusted you, Phee. I swore to protect you. Why
would you do this to me?" My face felt hot from the tears
I was trying to suppress.

"I'm sorry," she whispered. Each word broke my
heart. It was a confession. No attempt to free herself of
blame. Just reluctant acceptance and a tainted apology.

So, this was it. This was what I'd been desperate to find
out all along. And although there were several pieces of the
puzzle still missing, there was one that trumped them all.

"Where's Jonathan?" I asked bluntly.

Ophelia's mouth opened but nothing came out. She

bit her bottom lip, her gaze flitting around the room until she let her head fall, her shoulders shaking.

"Where's Jonathan?" I repeated, louder.

"I can't tell you," Ophelia whispered.

"WHERE IS HE?" I roared.

Ophelia jumped. I felt my mother's hand rest on my arm, pulling me back down to earth. Rage and desperation wouldn't get me the answers I needed.

"Take her downstairs," I muttered. "I don't want to see her until she's decided to talk."

I gestured to the guards, who stood Ophelia up and marched her out into the corridor. She looked impossibly small between them, her hair covering her face. But for a split second, it parted and revealed her tear-stained cheeks. When the door closed, I turned to Gayle.

"I want answers. We've caught Ophelia, which means she must know where Jonathan is...." I trailed off, took a deep breath, and tried to push forward. "We need to put an end to this, or who knows what will happen."

"I'll talk to her," Mum said, somehow still calm in the face of this nightmare. "Maybe the words of an old queen can coax something out of her."

She and Gayle rushed out after Ophelia and the guards, leaving me to wallow in miserable silence with Peter and Eddie, most of my questions still unanswered.

"James...," Peter tried. But I didn't want to face it. Not now. So, without a word, I ran.

⟨∞⟩

It felt good to stand on the edge of the palace. The roof was three stories aboveground, looming over St. James's Park and the memorial fountain. The first winds of a summer storm whipped around me and I felt myself sway. I could fall over the rail and there'd be nothing but the morning air to catch me.

"I thought I'd find you up here," Eddie said, stepping through the open window that led out to the small platform where the flagpole proudly stood. We used to climb out here when we were younger to look out over the city, still just kids untarnished by this royal circus. The thrill of hiding in plain sight used to make us feel invincible, but we hadn't been up here together in a long time.

I stepped back from the rail, Eddie coming to stand beside me. He placed a comforting arm around my shoulder as we took in the view just like we used to. His breathing was synchronized with mine, our hearts beating as one as if they recognized that we'd come into the world together.

"I can't believe it was her all along," I said, repeating the one looping thought that hadn't left my mind. "I don't understand why she'd want to humiliate me in front of the entire world. I don't get it."

"Money, I guess," Eddie said. "Debts to pay, a reputation to save. People will do almost anything when they're feeling desperate."

I knew that wasn't true—Quinn didn't have a clue who his own source was. But I was tired of thinking it through, of unearthing answers that only revealed more questions.

"But she's my friend."

"*Was* your friend," Eddie corrected. "You can't let her get away with what she's done to you."

Eddie made it sound so simple. I remembered what Grigor said—how Eddie was fire and I was water. His flames were burning hot, like he'd taken the attack against me personally. In a way, I guess he had, just like brothers are meant to.

"I don't know what to do next. How do we even get ourselves out of this mess?" I sighed, peering just far enough over the ledge to see the remaining protestors below.

"By lying," Eddie said, his words blunted. "Just like we always do."

My phone buzzed with a call in my pocket, the vibrations urgent against my body. Peter probably. I ignored it. Whatever it was could wait.

"That's the thing with this place. Nobody ever tells the truth. At least we have each other though. Dad always said we needed someone to trust, and that's what brothers are for, right?" I said, ignoring my phone buzzing once more.

Eddie breathed a laugh. "Is that what Dad told you? He never told me that. He never told me anything. But, of course, our whole family's job was to prepare you to be king one day, so I guess it didn't matter what I knew."

I could feel the argument from before the funeral brewing again. But Eddie's feelings of inferiority were the last thing on my mind right now.

"I don't know what Dad told you, but I'm sure he would've wanted you to know the same thing—that you can trust me with anything. We're family."

"Family," Eddie scoffed. "This place doesn't know the meaning of the word."

I could feel my frustration matching Eddie's. A pity party wasn't helping anything, and I was sick of my brother making it sound as if I'd ever chosen this path in life. But Eddie wasn't about to stop any time soon.

"Did you know I heard you guys talking once? When we were younger, eight or nine maybe. I was behind the door, and I could hear Dad telling you about being king, and you asking why it had to be you and not me, or both of us together. And do you know what he said?"

"Probably that you were the lucky one who wouldn't have to take on this responsibility," I muttered.

"He said it had to be you, not because you were older by eight minutes, but because you'd wear the crown best. That it had to be you because you'd know what to do, and that in time, you'd understand why you'd make a better king." Eddie smirked. "I'll never forget that. You were always the favorite, and the rest of us were expected to live in your shadow. It was never what was best for both of us, or all of us—it was always what was best for James, the future king."

My phone buzzed again, but I barely registered it this

time. I didn't know where this was coming from, and I couldn't even remember the conversation Eddie had apparently recalled from all those years before. Right at that moment, I didn't care either.

"Are you not over this yet? The whining is getting old, even for you," I said, my voice rising with anger from deep in my chest. "Have you not seen my life lately? It's hardly a fucking fairy tale. I can't trust anybody around me, and one of the few people I've ever loved has been taken from me. Yet you want to stand here and moan about the fact you're a fucking prince, as if it's the biggest burden in the world. Well, I'm sorry, Eddie, but I'm all out of pity for you."

My phone buzzed again, and this time I answered it, Eddie falling back as I raised it to my ear. "What?" I snapped.

"Are you alone, Your Majesty?" Peter asked, slightly breathless.

"No. Why?"

Peter sighed. "In that case, don't react to what I'm about to tell you. Pretend it's any other call, all right?"

"Of course," I said, trying to calm my breathing to a normal rate.

"We just got a call from Quinn. He got back to his office to find another envelope delivered this morning." My heart instantly fluttered, then settled into a thunderous pounding. "I asked Quinn to confirm the story, and sure enough, it's the one you told Ophelia about the Prince of Denmark. It all checks out. We already know it's her. She's as good as confessed."

335

"Ah right, got you," I said, just to say something because I didn't have a clue where this was going.

"But I wanted to tie up any loose ends to see if I could get a positive ID on Ophelia, so I called the courier." Peter was talking more and more quickly. "The firm couldn't give out information on who sent it, but they told me the envelope was picked up around eight a.m. and delivered to the *Daily Eye* straight away. I asked if they were sure, and they said there couldn't be any mistake—they log every pickup and delivery time. But that doesn't add up, sir. It's barely nine now. If that envelope was picked up an hour ago, how can Ophelia have sent it when we'd already caught her?"

I clamped the phone to my ear, certain I had misheard.

"Sir, I think Ophelia is in danger. I don't think she's behind any of this. She's nothing more than a chess piece to shift the blame onto. Remember how she said she couldn't tell us where Jonathan is? I don't think it's because she doesn't *want* to tell us. It's that she *can't*. She doesn't know where he's being kept."

My head was pounding. Ophelia being the mastermind hadn't made complete sense to begin with, but although her betrayal had devastated me, I'd been relieved to have finally put an end to everything.

"Okay, is there anything else?" I asked, trying to keep my tone even.

Peter paused. "There's one more thing. Call it another hunch, but I went through the tapes again from the night Jonathan disappeared. I combed through the outdoor

336

cameras a second time and I even called in a favor to get access to the street cameras too. Nothing. There's no sight of him anywhere."

In that moment, I knew what was coming, and my body froze.

"Sir, what if we've been looking in the wrong place? What if we've been looking on the wrong side of the palace gates?" Peter hesitated. "What if Jonathan never left the palace at all?"

I felt the floor sway beneath me. I could hear Peter repeating my name over and over again, but it was getting further away. My hand holding my phone fell limply to my side.

"What's happened?" Eddie said behind me, traces of our argument still in his tone.

I was barely listening. Peter had just flipped everything on its head. All I could think about was Jonathan. If he was still in the palace, and had been this entire time, then...

"What is it?" Eddie asked again.

"It's Jonathan," I said in a trance.

"What about him? Has Ophelia said something?"

I shook my head.

Eddie breathed a laugh. "Of course she hasn't. She wants this family to suffer, she said it herself."

Silence—only broken by the whipping breeze, by the warning call of a bird in a nearby tree—grew between us.

"She said that?" My voice was calm in my ears. Inside, I was imploding.

337

Eddie paused, and my heart did too. "Well, it's obvious that's what she wants, isn't it?"

I could feel the green envelope burning through my trouser pocket where I'd left it.

"Where have you been this morning?"

"Errands," Eddie replied without missing a beat. But the word was weak, throwing everything into a new light. I could suddenly see in perfect clarity.

Who had access to both me and Grigor and would be able to send us each a note to meet in St. James's Park at midnight, setting us up for the waiting photographer? Who could've made sure I received those envelopes, having found one themselves that had apparently been dropped on the floor in my quarters? Who had Ophelia's sister mistaken me for when I visited their house? Who hadn't been home when Ophelia was caught in my quarters, at the exact time the final envelope had been sent to Quinn? And since I was the one who'd opened the green envelope before burying it in my pocket, who could've known that Ophelia had said she wanted my family to suffer in the last note, if they hadn't written it themselves?

Peter's words rang in my ears, presenting me with the final missing piece.

Who could've taken Jonathan and kept him inside the palace without any of us knowing?

The puzzle was complete. I looked at the picture it made for the first time and one face stared back at me.

"It was you," I said, and turned around to face my brother.

Eddie's face was blank, staring back at me. Then it twisted into a grin, one that pinched at my insides and threatened to stop the beating of my heart. He clapped slowly, as if I was stupid not to have figured it out sooner.

"Well done. I thought you'd never get there," he said.

It broke the last part of me. The hope that this could all be resolved disintegrated before my very eyes. And in that hope's place grew a bitter pain, one that was already seeping into my blood and curling around my body until the two had become one. A wound that would never heal.

Eddie took a step toward me. I tried to match him, taking one step back, and then another, until the railing was pushing against my waist—until I stood on the edge of the palace with nowhere to go, trapped on the roof, facing the enemy.

CHAPTER TWENTY-NINE

THIS IS HOW IT ENDS

Eddie stopped a few paces away from me, staring me down. I stared straight back, looking at my twin brother—at myself—straight in the eye because I was damned if I was going to look away now.

"So this is how it ends, is it? On the roof, just me and you?"

Betrayal, grief, sadness, confusion and pure rage competed for my attention, but I wouldn't wilt in front of him now. I wouldn't let him see me weaken.

"You'd go this far to humiliate me? To share my secrets with the world like this? Why?"

Eddie shrugged. "Let's see, shall we? There's the *woe be me, I'm always going to be second best* thing, right? We've already been through all of that. Living in your shadow is meant to be a privilege, something I'm eternally grateful for. Well, I refuse to stand behind you for the rest of my life."

He took another step, but I had nowhere else to go. The railing dug into my back, the only thing between me and the drop. Eddie didn't seem to care. His eyes were lit up with the rage he'd been hiding just beneath the surface.

"That's not it," I said, trying to buy myself more time. It couldn't end this way. Even if I believed my own brother wouldn't go as far as to push me over the edge, I couldn't underestimate him.

"There's more to it than that," I pressed. "There has to be. You didn't go through all of this just so you could... what? Wear the crown? If you'd asked nicely, I would've bought you a plastic one to wear inside the house, seeing as it means that much to you."

Eddie's lip twitched, his smirk slipping. But I had to keep him talking.

"You really want people to duck and cower when you walk past? Will it make you feel like more of a man? Will you feel better if I live in your shadow instead? Is that it? Is that what all of this is for? Can't you hear how pathetic that sounds?"

Eddie advanced on me, so there was now only one step between us. His eyes had hardened, burning with fire. I felt the winds buffeting my back, gravity trying to pull me into its clutches as I leaned away from him, over the railing.

"It'd be so easy," Eddie growled. "One little push and you'd be gone. Don't test me."

"Do it then," I blurted. My knees were ready to give way. "What's stopping you? You're not man enough to face up to your role, and now you're not man enough to do something about it? Which is it, Eddie? You'll do anything to get hold of the crown, but the blood of your brother on your hands is a step too far? Is that it? You've taken everything else from me. Why stop there?"

I was shouting now, every seed of anger and rage inside me unfurling. Eddie's own fury matched mine, placing an unfamiliar mask over a familiar face, turning him into a stranger.

"I guess I should have expected that you wouldn't be able to finish the job with Ophelia not here to do the dirty work for you. Tell me, how did you turn one of my own friends against me?"

"You did that all by yourself. You dragged her into your mess and then you dropped her like she meant nothing. It didn't take much to make her see that you were only out for yourself while the rest of us were left to face the consequences of your actions."

His words winded me. I remembered the missed text messages before the funeral. She'd tried to reach me, but I'd been too wrapped up in my own world to care. I'd left her to fend for herself.

"I only needed her so you'd never suspect me. The bomb threat at the funeral was far-fetched, but I knew if Ophelia made the call, then it would never be traced back to me. I wanted to see you suffer. I wanted to see the fear in you, knowing you couldn't do anything to fight back." Eddie paused in his gloating, happy with himself. "Ophelia had her uses. She told me what you said about the Prince of Denmark. I knew that was a lie. Then I overheard you talking in earshot of Cassandra about the Prince of *Spain*, and I worked out exactly what you were doing. You were planting stories, waiting to see which one would reach Quinn."

Eddie scoffed as my face fell. I'd thought my plan had been almost foolproof, but I hadn't once considered that I'd need to protect the secrets from my own brother.

"Ophelia told me she was going to come clean, so I passed the little lie you gave her to Quinn and slipped the envelope in her bag while you were all watching that performance she just gave. Honestly, if she wasn't going to take the fall for this, she might have had a future as an actress." Eddie shrugged and glanced past my shoulder at the drop behind me. "That just about covers everything, so I think we're done talking now, don't you?"

In that moment, I saw why it had to end like this. He couldn't let me escape. The only way he'd get away with this was if he could frame Ophelia, and if I wasn't here to tell the truth.

"I still deserve to know why." I straightened up, refusing to wither before my brother, even though fear threatened to buckle my knees. "You owe me that much at the very least."

"You still don't get it, do you?" Eddie was on the edge,

verging on hysterical. "But I guess it shouldn't come as a surprise that you can't see the answer right in front of you when everything in this world has been handed to you on a silver platter. All while the rest of us are starved but for the scraps you leave behind. You just take and take and take. Have you ever once stopped to consider what it's like to have everything you hold dear taken away from you, so you're left with nothing?"

His words broke around his last question, his front cracking for a split second. My fear wasn't gone but it was masked by confusion.

"What have I ever taken from you?"

But Eddie just shook his head. "You're out of questions, I'm afraid."

He raised his hands. I watched them as they moved toward me, time slowing down, while my heart pounded in my ears. This was it. This was how my story would end. I'd never have all the answers. I'd never know why.

"Stop right there."

A tense voice punched the silence, shattering the moment into a million pieces. I clenched my phone in my hand, breathing a sigh of relief that Eddie hadn't realized that I'd never ended the call. Peter stood behind him, gun raised. Eddie hesitated, his hands still in the air between us, now as if in surrender. But then something flashed in his eyes— -a last flicker of desperation. I realized it then too. The only way he could get out of this was to become king and absolve himself of his crimes. But for that to happen, he'd need me out of the way.

He moved suddenly, thrusting his hands into my chest just as Peter barreled into him, knocking him to the ground. I fell backward, the railing bending my body in half. My phone slipped out of my hand, falling to the ground down below. My other hand grabbed the railing as I began to fall after it. I grasped the bars harder, trying to stop the momentum, but I was slipping.

Peter leaped up, flinging his upper body over the railings to grab me by the arms. Someone below screamed, followed by a chorus of yells and shrieks.

"I've got you," Peter said through gritted teeth.

He began to pull me back up over the railing, away from the screams below, although I could still hear them when my body cleared the bars and was back on solid ground. I fell to the floor, almost hugging it with relief, my legs no longer able to keep me upright. I breathed heavily, but air still refused to fill my lungs.

Peter stood over Eddie, radioing for backup, his eyes never leaving my brother. But Eddie just sat motionless with his back against the wall, face blank, eyes vacant, as if he were somewhere else. The unknown still lingered over us, leaving me directionless and without answers. But all I could focus on was a new grief, its pain sitting deep within my chest, blooming outward like seeping blood. It threatened to consume me completely. Now, beside the brother who'd betrayed me, I let it.

CHAPTER THIRTY

A CRUEL TRUTH

Nobody ever came to this side of the palace. It was made up of a bunch of unused rooms, below-ground, tucked in a long-forgotten part of our home. Now it was the most guarded place in Buckingham Palace.

Eddie had been brought down here, mostly because we didn't know what to do next. There were questions that needed answering, but there were also moves that needed calculating. What were we going to do now that we'd figured out one of our own was the culprit we'd been desperately searching for? That it was my own twin brother who'd betrayed us? It wasn't like you could send the heir to the throne to prison, nor could we keep him locked up in the palace forever.

Under Peter's direction, a squad of carefully picked guards had been drafted in to secure a room that housed old artifacts and paintings we no longer had use for, as well as those surrounding it, so nobody could get anywhere close to us or to Eddie. The last thing we needed were details leaking to the public before we'd decided our next move. I could only imagine the chaos that would unfold if the truth took a single step outside the palace gates.

Eddie had retreated into himself, barely acknowledging our presence. The only other people in the room were me, Mum and Peter. Outside, five armed guards made sure we were alone.

"What have you done, Eddie?" Mum said, her voice breathy and lost. Her face was contorted with a grief I'd only ever seen when Dad died. It was as if she'd lost a son now too.

Eddie didn't move, sat in an old armchair, his eyes fixed on his lap. I looked right at him, at this person I'd come into the world with, who'd been by my side my entire life. He was me and I was him, and yet now I was facing somebody who I no longer knew, the last traces of our brotherhood fading into nothing.

"What have *I* done?" Eddie finally said. He sounded tired, defeated. He chuckled without humor. "What have we all done—that's the question, isn't it?"

My own fury had melted away into a greater pool of anxiety. Something was still hiding in the shadows of my brother, waiting to reveal itself.

"You want to be king that bad? So bad that you'd try to tear me down in front of the world and then nearly *kill* me?"

Eddie shook his head, laughing to himself. It sent a stab of fear straight through me. It was the laugh of someone who knew more than everybody else in the room did.

"You think this is still about that crown, don't you?" He laughed once more, dropping his head into his hands in disbelief. "It was *never* about the crown," he spat. "It was about revenge."

"Revenge for *what*?!" I cried. "For being second best? If it's an apology that you want—if it's more of the spotlight that you want—then you can have it! I don't care! Take my place, take the crown, take every little thing that I have left. You've already done your worst, so what difference will it make? But don't tell me that this is all about revenge when your excuse for ruining your family's life is nothing more than feeling ignored. We're not kids anymore!"

Eddie shot up out of his chair, trembling with rage. Mum and Peter moved at the same time to stand between us, but I stepped past them before they could and met my brother's glare head-on.

"Go on," I said, my voice getting louder and louder. "For someone who's been doing so much behind my back all this time, you've certainly gone quiet. What's the problem? You can't face the truth now?"

Eddie cleared the space between us, so we were standing face-to-face. "You took everything from me." His whispers were fraught with broken rage. "*Everything*. First Dad—while he was teaching you to be king, what time did he have for me? I could never compare when you were

348

the one destined to wear the crown. And Mum's always protected you with her life, because you're the king, but have you ever seen her do the same for me? Taking my parents away from me wasn't enough for you, though, was it? You had to take my best friend too."

My heart sank as I thought of Grigor. It was true. How could I deny it?

"I saw you that night at the party, in the corner with my best friend. You already had everybody, but you still weren't satisfied. Mum, Dad, Jonathan, Grigor, Gayle, Ophelia, the whole fucking world—you had them all. You didn't leave me with a single person."

His pain matched mine. I could feel it, our bond as twins connecting our hearts too. His burden was now my torture, tearing at me from the inside.

"I needed you to feel what it was like to be left alone. When I saw you with Grigor that night, I knew I had to do something, because you'd already taken someone else from me too."

Time stopped still. Someone *else*?

"Confused?" Eddie glanced over my shoulder. "Just ask her."

Mum fell back, mouth slightly open.

"Me?" she whispered.

I turned to face my mother, the fight quickly dissolving within me. She looked confused, eyes wide, her head shaking from side to side. "I don't know what you mean," she uttered.

"Fine. If you won't tell him, I will." Eddie turned his

349

eyes back to me, and now they were alive with flames. "The morning Dad died, we were locked in that room, wondering what we were going to do next. I left, hoping to find comfort from our loving mother. The one who'd always favored you. I get to her quarters and I can hear her talking. Quietly, like she doesn't want to be heard. She wants to make sure that you're kept safe because you're going to need it more than anyone."

Mum was welling up, the deep brown of her irises sparkling like stars under the tears. She looked resigned to something I didn't know yet.

"She was making sure you'd be protected over anybody else. Including me." Eddie's words were laced with hurt, but he wouldn't stop now. "I wanted this family to feel an *ounce* of what I felt when those whispers pierced my heart. Telling Quinn about the affair was the tip of the iceberg...because it wasn't just an affair, was it, Mum?"

"Eddie, please," Mum whispered.

But Eddie laughed at her plea. "Spare you some mercy? Like you've spared us the truth? Not a chance in hell." He turned to me. I felt like I was no longer standing in the room. My body was empty. I'd left it behind.

"Have you not pieced it together yet, Your Majesty?" Eddie said with cruel delight. "The answer's been standing right behind you this entire time. Isn't that right, *Dad*?"

There was a small gasp, but I couldn't tell where it came from. All I could see was the gleeful face of Eddie swimming before me. He'd finally revealed his hand.

Every part of me felt weak, but with the last of my wilting strength, I turned around to face my mother. She silently wept, her tears streaming down her face. But she wouldn't look away. She only had eyes for me in that moment as the truth began to dawn in my mind.

Peter stood loyally beside her, as he'd stood beside me for so many years. He'd sworn to protect me with his life, a sacrifice that I'd never understood—until now. In that moment, I remembered a conversation, a lifetime ago, about the locket he wore around his neck. Inside were two pictures of his son. Except now I realized they weren't the same child. They were twins, from a previous life, before a lie had been carved for us to live in.

My dad, the king, was dead.

But my father stood opposite me now, very much alive.

"Tell me it's not true."

I heard myself speak as if I were removed from my own body. My mother and Peter—my parents—looked back in defeat. Peter bowed his head. Mum blinked away her tears, trying to collect the remnants of herself that'd been cruelly scattered with Eddie's words. She nodded.

"I'm so sorry," she said, and those words broke the last part of me. "Everything I told you before was true, about what happened between me and your father. We said we'd make it work and when I told him the truth—the whole truth—he didn't flinch. He promised to be a father, not only because there was no other way, but because he loved me, and he loved you too, before you were even born. Blood never stopped him from being your dad."

I couldn't comprehend what I was hearing. Eddie looked grimly satisfied, watching on as the world around us tumbled down at his hand. I felt sick. The lies were embedded so deep within me that we could never be parted from each other.

"I agreed to it too," Peter said quietly, carefully. "I understood what was on the line, and I understood the predicament we'd gotten ourselves into. A better man would've left the palace and let you live a life that had no knowledge of me in it. But I...I couldn't."

His words were brittle, wrapped up in more than seventeen years of lies, secrecy and torture.

"I could never be your father. I accepted that. But, whether right or wrong, I couldn't leave. For that, blame me. I demanded to stay, to see you grow into boys and then men—into princes and then kings. I was a weak man for not leaving and allowing you to move on without me. I'm sorry."

Eddie snorted. "Spare us the sob story." He focused his attention back on me. "Do you see it now? How you took not only my father, my mother, and my best friend, but my *real* dad too? You had everything and he still chose to protect you over me, because, of course, you're more important. Of course, he'd favor you, just like everybody else has. And what has that left me with? Nothing."

He laughed to himself, breaking away and starting to pace, talking to us all and yet none of us at the same time. "I had to do this. All the secrets, the lies, the greed. I needed to hurt you the way you've hurt me. It was the only way to make you see what you've done. The only way to make you *feel* it."

He'd succeeded. Now I could see it, feel it twisting my gut. To get back at me, my brother had taken what I loved most—Jonathan—so I'd feel what he'd endured. He'd exposed my secrets so I'd feel the worthless shame he'd been drowning in. And to get back at our family, our parents and every secret they'd kept, he'd exposed the truth, because only that could hurt as much as a lie.

Eddie stopped his pacing and held me in his gaze once more. The stranger who stood before me stepped aside for a moment, revealing the brother I thought I'd known all my life. "I needed to save you," he whispered. "I needed to make you see what these royal games have done to us— how they've torn us apart. How the secrets and lies will never stop so long as we're a part of it. I needed to end it all." He swallowed, eyes tearing up. "I needed my brother back."

"Oh, and I suppose trying to push me off the roof in an attempt to literally kill me was supposed to help you achieve that?"

Mum started, a gasp escaping her lips. Clearly Peter hadn't wanted to scare her with the details. Eddie didn't flinch. The mask that had been hiding my brother returned. When he spoke, his voice was cutting, severing the last fraying threads between us.

"If that's what it took. I'd rather have the memory of who my brother used to be than live with the stranger you've become."

I met his stare head on. "My thoughts exactly."

Beneath my exterior, the pain of Eddie's final admission seared through me, torturing every thought and feeling that rotted my core. It pulled me deeper into a sea of despair, the clutches of its current refusing to let me go. But despite everything, a final thought rose from the ashes, burning brighter with every second. Eddie wanted to end it all, but had he already made his final move? Were we too late?

"Have you told him? Have you told Quinn?"

Eddie's face contorted, taking me in with disdain. "Even now, after I've told you everything, that's your first question?" He smirked as something else occurred to him. "Could it be that you've realized what all of this means? That you were never meant to be king in the first place?"

It was true. My claim to the throne now rested on a lie. Now we all knew that the true heir was Cassandra.

I'd never wanted to be king. I'd never wanted to wear the crown a day in my life. But it wasn't relief I felt. It was ice-cold fear. We were now left in an impossible position. If we continued this lie, then we'd be walking into uncertainty, not knowing whether our days were numbered. How much longer could we keep this secret? Another year? Ten?

But if we blinked, if we let *them* know, there would be no escaping what we'd done. And with Cassandra at the helm, finally sitting on the throne herself as the true heir, who knew what punishments we could expect? We could be stripped of our titles, banished from the palace and cast out into the world to fend for ourselves. With our secrets and lies laid bare for the world to see, we'd be at the mercy of their anger without protection or safety.

I couldn't let that happen.

"Does Quinn know?" I repeated.

Eddie weighed up my question. He shrugged. "Not yet. But he will. No matter what you do to me, the whole world will know one day. Secrets never stay secret for long."

Finally, something was in my favor, and yet I still felt no better. I sighed. I'd made up my mind. I couldn't look at Eddie as my brother anymore. It was impossible now.

"I won't let you ruin us," I said. "I'm sorry. I really am. But if you're intent on destroying this family, then you're with those people outside the gates." Eddie's eyes narrowed, not moving from my face. "If you're with them, then you become our enemy. And you'll be treated like one."

I walked out of the room before he could say another word. Mum and Peter followed.

"You can't keep this secret forever, James," Eddie called after me. "You can't keep lying."

I slammed the door, cutting off his words. My body folded in half as I grabbed my knees, breathing hard. Mum's comforting hand found me, rubbing small circles into my back. She murmured something I couldn't hear

355

to Peter, and after a moment, he left. When I straightened up once more, the ground I stood on still uncertain, my mother was there. She cupped my face with her hands.

"I'm so sorry, James. I won't ask for your forgiveness, and I understand if this changes our relationship forever, but I want you to know that I love you with every part of my heart. When you're ready, I'll be here to talk."

She withdrew her hand regretfully. I had a thousand questions that needed answering, but the one thing I didn't need to confirm was that, despite everything, I still loved my mother. That was never going to change.

"Your Majesty!" I flinched at the title as Gayle hurried round the corner, breathless. She stopped a few steps away, collecting herself. And then came the words I'd prayed for. "We've found Jonathan."

A small light, the flicker of a flame in a pitch-black room, burst into life. "I have to see him," I said immediately, my heart pounding.

Gayle grimaced. "I don't know if that's a good idea, sir."

"What do you mean, not a good idea? What's happened to him? I *need* to see him." Panic began to swell as I imagined what hell he must've endured.

"He's okay, sir. No serious harm—it's mostly just shock. He'll be fine." Gayle hesitated. "But as the person who's been holding him captive this whole time is your clone, I don't think seeing him in this state is the best idea. For his sake."

That cruel detail dawned on me. We were nothing

alike—Eddie had proved as much. Fire and water. But to the eye, we were the same. There was no way to escape that fact.

"Will you let him know that, when he's ready, I'd like to see him?"

Gayle nodded. "Of course, sir," she said, and disappeared back into the palace.

CHAPTER THIRTY-ONE

THE KING IS ALIVE

The sun was setting on another day, wrapping the palace in a golden haze that covered the sins hidden behind the gates. Nothing was solved yet. How could it be? A week had passed and Eddie was still down in those abandoned rooms, guarded day and night. The rest of the palace continued as normal, unaware of the secrets some of us were burying just out of sight.

Jonathan had spoken at length with Gayle and had decided not to say anything about what had happened. I wouldn't have let him lie—he deserved justice for what he'd been through, but he'd simply told Gayle that he wished to forget the whole ordeal. He insisted that he wouldn't continue working at the palace, but he didn't want to see it brought down to its knees either. Jonathan knew what was at stake. And so, even though he wouldn't see me—couldn't see me—he told a lie to save us. To save me.

We'd spread a cover story within the palace that Eddie was sick and had been taken away to a retreat until he was well enough to resume public life again. Of course, it crawled out to the press, although Quinn Buckley was notably absent from the speculation. I hoped our last meeting had gifted him some caution when it came to writing stories about my family. I prayed that he wasn't just biding his time in the dark, that our secret wouldn't find its way into his hands.

Cassandra was suspicious. She knew we were hiding something and no doubt she'd make it her mission to find out what. But Mum had made sure to let her know that we were aware of her affiliation with Quinn, and the fear that she would be stripped of her royal title before she could get anywhere near the throne was enough to keep her at bay. At least for now. I feared what the future held where my cousin was concerned. Only time would tell what devious plans she might concoct to get what she wanted.

Peter had been relieved of his role as my protection officer, at least while we figured out this new normal. He'd given me space to think, to grieve what I'd known and then to begin letting it go. My dad, the king, would always be my father—there was no taking that away from him, and I would always love him as such. But with the promise that Peter would be ready to speak when I was, a faint glimmer of hope sparked on the horizon. Who knew what waited in store for us? I'd given up trying to guess. All I'd ask for, when it came down to it, was the truth. We'd all had more than our fair share of lies to last us a lifetime.

Now, as the sun sank in the sky, melting the first day of September away, Grigor and I sat in silence, staring at the empty space between us. He was on one side of the sofa, me on the other. I don't think either of us enjoyed seeing that void. It reminded us of what we'd once shared, and what we'd now lost. The ticking of a clock on the mantelpiece timed our silence, counting down until it was broken.

"I shouldn't say it. I know I shouldn't. But I miss you," Grigor said. I couldn't look into his eyes, couldn't bear to see what I'd find there. But I owed him that much, so I forced myself to look up. "I miss us."

"I've missed you too," I murmured. "It's just... things are different now."

"Is the way you feel any different? About me? Because if it is, say the words, and I'll let this go. I'll stand up and walk out of here so you can get on with your life." Grigor looked like he'd rather do anything else, but I knew he'd be a man of his word.

"You know that's not what I want," I said, struggling to find the words to say everything I felt in that moment. I didn't want him to go. No matter what had happened, I couldn't ignore the fact that my feelings for him had grown—that they would've inevitably continued to grow if things hadn't changed.

"Do you love him?" Grigor asked, and I could tell it

hurt him to even ask. I could tell that he already knew the answer too.

"Yes," I said without pause. "That doesn't mean that I don't love you in some way too. But..."

"But this has to end," Grigor finished. I sighed, then nodded. He sank into the sofa a little. His mouth twitched, like he wanted to say more. But after a moment, he nodded too.

Another silence drifted between us, neither of us wanting to break it because then surely the line would be drawn, every moment we'd shared left behind it. We would move on, and then who knew what the future held?

"You never told me about your mum," I said quietly. "You never told me it was Catherine."

Grigor sighed, leaning back into the sofa and closing his eyes for a moment. When he opened them again, he looked different, like for once he didn't know all the right words to say.

"I know I should've told you. But I didn't want to ruin a good thing by blurting it out any old way." He stretched his arm across the back of the sofa and that familiar spark ran through me at the possibility of his touch.

"Did you always know?"

Grigor nodded somberly. "It was part of the deal after she died, that I be told on my eighteenth birthday. What a cause for celebration that was," he joked. "So, yes, I knew. And I'm sorry I didn't tell you. If I'd known that would've eliminated me from the suspects, I would've admitted it straight away." He grinned as I threw a cushion at him.

There was a knock at the door, and his smile faded.

"Come in," I called.

It was Gayle. She saw Grigor and immediately blushed, lowering her eyes for a moment. When she glanced back up at me, she looked incredibly awkward.

"Someone wants to see you, Your Majesty," she murmured. With one last remorseful look at us both, she stepped aside, and Jonathan appeared in the doorway.

It felt like I'd been dropped from a great height, that uncomfortable feeling in the depths of my gut settling inside me. I still hadn't seen him. Now he stood in my doorway like a dream that'd materialized into real life.

"I'll leave you to talk," Grigor said in a measured tone. It was slightly strained, like he'd struggled to get the words out. But, with a nod to us all, he jumped up from the sofa and walked away. Gayle lingered a moment longer, then followed suit.

I stood up as time slowed and stilled around us, just like it used to when the secret was only ours. I still knew every line and angle of his face by heart, every glint in his eye, every curve of his mouth. Seeing them all again made me dizzy.

"Let's take a walk?" he asked gently, stepping aside and gesturing toward the door.

The space between us crackled with sparks as we made our way through the palace and out onto the back lawn. The gardens of Buckingham Palace looked as immaculate as ever, beckoning us into their grasp. The sun was slanting through the trees, its light rippling off the leaves. The last warmth of summer clung to us as we began to walk.

We'd been wandering for a few minutes, the silence gnawing at us both. I couldn't bear it, so I cracked first.

"I'm sorry. I'll never be able to say sorry enough," I said, desperate for him to know how much I meant it.

Jonathan shook his head. "I would never hold you accountable for what your brother did." His voice was as soft as I remembered, like a familiar lullaby.

"I'm not just sorry for that," I said, desperate to get everything off my chest and to begin mending the things I had let break in my hands. "I mean for everything. The whole time we were together, I barely asked you anything at all. Your dad. Your sister. I knew nothing of them, and that's because every moment we shared was about me. It always has been. I've been selfish. I've been everything Eddie said I was. I..."

Jonathan stopped and faced me as the apologies died on my lips. My breath hitched in my throat, unsure of what he would say next. Eventually, he slowly shook his head.

"I don't blame you for that." He sighed, letting his thoughts unravel carefully before he spoke them. "I always knew that if we met in another time, another place, things would be different. You were grieving. You needed space and I just wanted to be there for you. You told me you loved me and that was enough. In my heart, I knew that in time we would find ourselves in a place outside of this royal circus. *Then* we could start building something."

It was the Jonathan I knew, still selfless and generous. Still a good and kind person. I was surprised an angry bitterness hadn't taken that away from him after all he'd been through. But somehow, the Jonathan I knew had survived.

We began to walk once more. Out of the corner of my eye, I glanced at him. I wondered what had happened in the twelve days that Eddie had kept him hostage. Those nightmares kept me up at night. I'd never be able to forgive myself for what he'd been through. He didn't seem different to look at, maybe a touch slimmer than I remembered, but there was something unfamiliar about him that I couldn't quite put my finger on. Maybe it was the way he made sure to keep three paces between us, leaning his body away from mine as we walked. Or maybe it was the eyes, darting into the trees and all around us.

"I don't want to talk about it," he said, sensing my thoughts. "Not yet. I'm not sure if I ever will. I just want to forget that it happened and get on with my life."

"Of course," I said immediately. "As long as I know that you're okay."

Jonathan swept the question away with a hand. "I do have one thing to say. It'll only play on my mind if I don't voice it." He paused to take a breath, his gaze wandering back to the palace. "I never wanted to tell Eddie any of our secrets. It hurt me more than anything. But he said he knew where my mum and sister lived, and that was enough for me. I couldn't put them in danger. I didn't have a choice."

I shook my head like I was trying to dislodge something inside it. "I would *never* blame you. Ever. What happened will never be your fault."

"And you shouldn't blame Ophelia either," Jonathan murmured, taking me by surprise. She'd gone back home after we'd caught Eddie. We knew he'd been behind the whole thing and that she was just an unwilling accomplice. I doubted if we'd ever see her again after what my brother had put her through. After what we'd all put her through.

"Eddie was threatening her too," Jonathan said quietly. "She has a sister, right? I heard him talking about her. He was using that as leverage to get her to do his dirty work for him."

I fought to keep my shudder hidden. Even now, I couldn't quite believe what my brother had done.

"I'll never blame anybody but him," I said firmly, and we lapsed into silence once more.

The birds tweeted their evening call, their sounds ricocheting around us. The trickle of a fountain by the lake rode the early evening breeze. Another summer day was coming to an end.

"I never stopped loving you, you know," Jonathan said suddenly. My heart fluttered. "I couldn't, even if I tried. I know you must've hated me for what you thought I was doing, but even when things were at their darkest, I knew I still loved you."

I didn't trust myself to speak, but I needed to.

"Do you still love me?" he asked.

"Of course I do," I said.

"And do you love Grigor?"

I hesitated. I couldn't hurt Jonathan any more than he'd already been hurt. But I couldn't lie to him either. So, I didn't.

"No. Not like I love you."

Jonathan nodded to himself. I wished in that moment I could open his mind and read his thoughts, fish them out and hold them in my hands. But he surprised me even more when I realized he was smiling to himself.

"What?" I asked.

He finally looked at me, the way he used to, before any of this had happened. It was then that I knew we might still have some hope left. We might still have a shot.

"Nothing," he said, chuckling to himself. "It's just, I wouldn't blame you if you did. He's handsome, isn't he?"

We both laughed and it felt like home. That one moment broke down the first of the bricks in the wall between us. It'd take some work—hell, it'd take a lot of work—but maybe one day we'd get there. Maybe one day, being together would be as easy as it'd been before. Just like breathing. Just like he'd never left.

We paused at the far edge of the lawn, looking back toward the palace, part of it still bathed in sunlight. The flag flew high on its pole, rippling lazily in the breeze. Inside, they'd be preparing dinner, plumping cushions in drawing rooms, organizing plans for the impending coronation. My coronation. I'd been king for twenty days and so much had changed already. If I took that oath, I'd be letting the throne hold on to me for the rest of my life. I didn't know what I'd say when the time came. I didn't want to think about it, and for now, I wouldn't. I'd take it one step at a time. I'd learned that was the only way.

The king had died for my story to begin. But a new king had taken his place on the throne. Here I stood, tall and strong, in the dying light of a dipping sun. King James was alive.

ARE YOU WILLING?

I stand alone. The pews of Westminster Abbey are empty for now, but they'll be filled with thousands come tomorrow. Millions more will watch around the world as I sit on the throne and take my oath. My coronation is almost upon me, and I have a choice to make.

The final stragglers from the rehearsal leave through the Great West Door, the sunlight, almost autumnal, bathing them as they go. But one man appears in their wake, watching me from afar for a moment as if he's fearful to take a step. Finally, he sighs and starts toward me. My breath catches in my throat, but I stand tall, facing him. I've been scared enough for a lifetime lately. I don't want to be scared anymore.

When Peter reaches me, he pauses, unsure of himself. But I don't let the moment sour. I cross the space and hug him. His embrace softens around me as his shoulders begin to shake, and when we finally pull away, we're both in tears.

"I didn't know if you'd want to see me yet," Peter says as we take a seat in the first pew.

"I wasn't sure I'd be ready," I admit. "But I'm glad you're here. Really, I am."

I can see the relief escaping him. He looks around the cavernous abbey, taking it all in. His eyes finally land on the throne that sits before us, waiting to claim me. "Have you made up your mind yet?"

I shake my head. It's all I've thought about for days, and I'm still no closer to making a decision. Duty battles with freedom in my mind, neither one willing to let the other win.

"I guess we'll see how I feel on the day. It's not like it's the biggest decision of my life or anything."

We laugh and it puts me at ease, my mind allowing itself to wander away from tomorrow and enjoy today instead. We talk. Not about what happened or about any of the big things. We'll get to those in time, when we're ready. For now, I'm just happy he's here.

When he stands to leave, I feel lighter. Hopeful, even. As he readjusts his shirt, I catch a glimpse of the locket around his neck.

"I'll be watching," he says before he goes. "And I'll be proud, whatever you decide."

Then he leaves, and I'm alone once more.

Ignoring my urge to run from it, I take the few steps

to the front and perch on the edge of the throne. I take a deep breath, freeing my mind of all the dread and worry I've allowed to grow there, and I sit back in its grasp.

In my mind, I hear the question that will be asked of me tomorrow.

"Will you, James Hampton, take this oath to be king?"

I raise my head, the walls of Westminster Abbey my only witness, and I give my answer.

ACKNOWLEDGMENTS

Writing acknowledgments is always one of the best parts of finishing a book because not only does it mean I actually did it (honestly, this would bamboozle teenage Ben, who could never write more than three chapters of a story), but it also means that I get to thank the people who made it all happen.

First of all, this book wouldn't exist without my agent, Chloe, who didn't complain when I came charging into her emails with an idea for a YA royal mystery, even though I was already behind on my middle-grade deadline. Thank you so much for all the encouragement, I really couldn't do this without you.

I don't think I can muster a thank-you big enough to my wonderful UK editor, Amina, who somehow manages to keep me on track even when I'm asking for the hundredth time if I should rewrite everything. Your edits are thoughtful and thorough, and this story wouldn't be even half of what it is now without your guidance.

To the incredible team at Little, Brown and, more specifically, my US editor Erika, who gave this book a chance to spread its wings across the pond. Thank you for the enthusiasm, final edits, and for giving my stories and my voice a second home. I appreciate you so much.

To Ellen, Jack, Matthew, Ellie and Gena—you guys are all right, I guess! Kidding, I love you all endlessly and I hope I remind you of that enough. (I know for a fact I do not because I'm a heartless so-and-so, but, hey, I wrote it in a book so it's immortalized forever!)

My ladies who lunch, although we really need to change that to "who karaoke" because when have we ever done lunch please? Josh, Phil, Kris and Vitor, you guys are absolute lights in my life. Here's to many more hours choosing songs outside of our vocal range.

My Goslings clique, whom I'm going to name so you stop thinking I keep you all at arm's length (I'm sorry, I'm not letting it go): Alan, Luke, Tom, Des, Anthony, Michael, Tim, Dean, Nick, Liam R, Liam D, and all the rest—you make my week, every week. Oh, and an EXTRA SPECIAL shout out to Owen Thomas, who did *not* buy me fish and chips just so he could have this moment. A three-course meal for a character next time?

To my home squad, who drag me away from my desk and make sure I actually leave the flat sometimes—a special shout out to Fred and Becca. I love the rest of you too, but I'm running out of words! And to Sam, Richard and Andy! I'm so glad I found you guys. You make this job less lonely.

To all the booksellers, teachers, bloggers, reviewers and readers—your support is forever appreciated. I hope to meet many more of you so I can say thank you in person.

As always, to my gran and my sister—I love you both to the moon and back. And finally, of course, to my mum. Who would've ever thought you'd have three books dedicated to you now? Here's to many, many more. I hope you're proud. I love you to infinity and beyond.

BENJAMIN DEAN

Benjamin Dean is a London-based author and pop culture writer. He is a former entertainment reporter who has interviewed a host of glitzy celebrities and broke the news that Rihanna can't wink. (She blinks, in case you were wondering.) Benjamin can be found on Twitter as @notagainben tweeting about pop and LGBTQ+ culture to his fourteen thousand plus followers. *The King Is Dead* is his YA debut.